Clive WILKINS

THE MOUSTACHIO QUARTET~ *Xavier MANNIKIN*

The MOUSTACHIO Quartet~ Xavier Mannikin

The writer Clive WILKINS, born in England in 1954, is also well known as a fine art painter. He has exhibited widely throughout the UK, including at The National Portrait Gallery, The Royal Academy and in Cork Street, London where he had a one-man show in 2007. His work is to be found in public and private collections. He has produced portraits of Sir Howard Hodgkin and Sir Peter Blake amongst others and has been presented publicly to HRH the Princess Royal.

His written work has appeared in print on numerous occasions, most notably in his published work 'The Creatures in the Night', a story written and lavishly illustrated by Wilkins in 2008.

He is currently Artist in Residence at the Dept. of Psychology, University of Cambridge, where he is co-founder of an arts/science collaboration entitled 'The Captured Thought', which explores the subjective experience of thinking and the nature of creativity. He lectures to university audiences in the UK, Europe, Asia and in the U.S.A. Key extracts from the Moustachio books are featured in 'The Captured Thought' lecture series.

Clive lives in the heart of England. In addition to writing, he continues to be a painter, teacher, performer, flautist, tango dancer and practitioner of origami.

The

M *OUSTACHI* **O**

Quartet~

Xavier Mannikin

Clive WILKINS

The Moustachio Quartet~
Xavier Mannikin

First Edition published
24th December 2014

ISBN 978-0-9930029-2-2

Published by Wind on the Wire Press

Wind on the Wire

Typeset in Bell MT 9/10pt
[Second Revised Edition 16th March 2018]

The Moustachio Quartet~
is dedicated to
Jean Scott Thomson
~the fixed star in my firmament

Also by the author

The Creatures in the Night

[Dingley Press 2008]

ISBN13 978-0-9547083-3-7

The Moustachio Quartet~ Caruso Maelstrom

[Wind on the Wire Press 2014]

ISBN 978-0-9930029-0-8

The Moustachio Quartet~ Count Zapik

[Wind on the Wire Press 2014]

ISBN 978-0-9930029-1-5

The Moustachio Quartet~ Eissenstrom

[Wind on the Wire Press 2016]

ISBN 978-0-9930029-3-9

THE MOUSTACHIO QUARTET~ *Xavier MANNIKIN*

Foreword

The series of books comprising **The Moustachio Quartet** happened by accident.

They should never have appeared, since the author is, by trade and training, a fine art painter. This may explain the visual nature of the writing and the apparent attention to small detail in the narrative. The notion that a lifetime of ideas in one medium could be transferred into another, and the accompanying conjecture of what the effect might be, is an interesting one.

Writing, like music and dance, unfolds in time, *and through space~* ideas are encouraged to move and develop layers in a way that painting or sculpture is rarely perceived to do. This is the distinct advantage of the form, and why one painter needed to change horses mid-race.

The scene setting can be precise in a visual image or object. It speaks of a fixed time and place, and is resonant by demanding the viewer sees the complexity and power in that one moment~ *the subsequent analysis of detail can be in depth, such worlds existing as a kind of phenomenology~* but such intensity is invariably too great, maybe too much. How long do most people look at a static artwork before moving on? The initial wonder, for many viewers, quickly alters and progresses to conjecture what went before, or what might be coming next. It too often becomes the internalising of an external experience within the existing canon of the spectator's personal history, becoming read as part of an unfolding story that needs to be recognised as having continuity and fixed logic. It becomes altered to no longer be what it is, but instead says more of what we programme ourselves to willingly see, both individually and collectively. It's what we naturally do as part of living, and is how our cognitive processes respond. Much of our success on the planet, *to date*, has been afforded by virtue of our ability to engage in such mental time travel and the holistic analysis of changing perspectives, but always on our own terms, a gift that appears to be virtually unique to our species. Indeed it has been said~ imagination is the door to identity.

Imagine paintings that move, where symbols, metaphors and ideas slide, morph and change form during the course of the narrative, with the aim of questioning how we think, with the intention of revealing the unseen.

The psychological questioning of realities and consciousness, amidst the 'miasma of being' and the questioning of the 'subjective experience of thinking', brought this work to the attention of the Dept. of Psychology at Cambridge University, and Prof. Nicky Clayton in particular. This resulted in key sections from the books being used in university lectures in the United Kingdom, in Europe and in America, as part of an arts/science collaboration, entitled 'The Captured Thought'.

The themes are multifarious and could be discussed endlessly, but not by the author, at least not outside of a lecture environment, since, in truth, the document that is The Moustachio Quartet should be testament enough to the ideas it conceals~ *this is to become its measure for success*. Each book works individually and is a world unto itself, although the true measure of what is being explored and investigated, in Warcapest *and beyond*, is only fully revealed when the action and incidents across the entire series is collated.

Clive WILKINS
16th March 2014
Department of Psychology
University of Cambridge

The

M *O U S T A C H I* **O**

Quartet~

Xavier Mannikin

★ ★ ☆ ★

It couldn't be seen~ although its proximity was palpable.
He was about to be engulfed by Nature beyond his comprehension.

★ ★ ☆ ★

45.

The lights of Warcapest, when viewed at night from on high, shimmer and glow~ like candles on a festive tree celebrating an event, or are they signposts along a journey or windows leading to other places or…

There are patterns that might penetrate the very fibre of the universe, appearing at irregular intervals as harbingers~ augers~ pointers~ signs leading towards an understanding of the thing to which everything is a part. Seeing them becomes the quest, the endeavour, in order to become sensitised to a bigger, all-encompassing meaning. This is both easy and hard, since the best questions have no answer. The days of so many lives, *each one so long,* become confused and infested with diversions until the overarching goal is lost. Each person will need at least one sign in order to stay nourished and alive to the penetrating moment~ to continue proceeding onward in the right direction. Choosing a sign is of paramount importance. Finding even a little sign to follow is imperative. This is the continuing story of one perceived sign~ all recognise its presence and will call it by a name~ should they ever find one that fits. Is it a symbol, is it an event or is it a person? Can it be any or all of these?

Sound is carried, as on a wind, into the sleeping heart of all phenomena, punctuating the moment and calling the/this world into further and continuing action. A bell sounds; it resonates in the empty air. A siren in a far off street at some distance whines and echoes. All lifts into consciousness, becomes alive for us. An instinctive awareness demands a response. A rhythmic pulsation is felt. Something from within moves to meet it. The night sky slowly sweeps backwards; the distant daylight is preparing to return. The text on an advert, engraved on glass, reads in reverse in the streetlight. A kind of tide somewhere is turning, moving in the opposite direction to its purpose. Soon, the light from starry constellations will be lost to the reflections of all the windows in buildings across the distant city. It will become impossible to observe the illusion of seeing the stars from both sides once more.

The new day, still barely visible, not delivered, hardly born, is ready to emerge, but slowly. It is carefully metering out its time.
'Not yet,' it whispers, 'it is too soon.' There is time enough to lie in wait, to luxuriate in the remote observation of a new world hatching~ like an invisible, mighty phoenix rising from the embers of its history. As yet, the deep, heavy slumbers of night persist, undisturbed, blithely unaware of intrusion/of the new birth. Darkness remains glued and is sticking to every part of everything. Time has become suspended, is interrupted temporarily, paused or slowed, just long enough for all to be seen within a differing perspective. A petrified stillness fills the space, existing in the lap of

a nothing, a space in the centre of a naught; a no place for the soulless. Such gorgeous stillness allows the briefly remembered past to creep in, distantly recalling itself, half remembered at best. Simultaneously, 'almost' futures begin to build themselves. They infiltrate, from out of corners that exist nowhere. They materialise like impossibly weightless, golden feathers, each desperately hoping to be pressed and moulded into dull, grey, thinking clay, the matter out of which 'thinks' are made real~ all this within a fog in time. This benign, low-lying cloud of beautiful, myth-making imagination pushes hard to overwhelm. It offers unfulfillable promises of where it will take everything and everyone within its inescapable grasp.
'But not yet!'
Such intense quietude makes a stone of every building. The silence makes a dead beast of every sleeping machine. The empty city and its suburbs appear briefly abandoned, derelict and forgotten. The creatures here are away, dreaming of those imaginary places marginally less real than their understanding of the worlds they inhabit. Memory is more disparate amongst them than they care to acknowledge, their awareness of reality, fickle and misplaced.

Everything is turned off, waiting to be turned on, waiting to return. Were we real at all, we could imagine ourselves drifting towards all this effortlessly, as if with some intent, as if a thing was about to begin, about to be enacted~ a curious story might be about to embark.

We navigate by, past, through, as if 'everywhere', amidst what appears to be a vast ocean of huge but gently flowing waves, viewing everything within this moment, this unfathomable present. Humanity is the boat that appears on the brief page~ its sail filled by one of the passing zephyrs within time. The direction of the little prow may be informative. The gathering storm and tide around the vessel are already determining the key elements for an irrepressible and turbulent future. Night watchmen, sleepy lookouts all, scour the horizon for events~ might they first glimpse the gargantuan entropy that is to subsequently overflow and swamp the interstices of all matter.

The shadows are beckoning, making an eye to see with intensity, to view what is within, concealed. There are invisible breezes and winds everywhere. They cannot be heard whistling remotely on the wires, nor can they be seen to pulse within them~ although they do. Neither can one be seen by the other, nor are they easily understood, as if two worlds were forever able to avoid collision, the one oblivious of its counterpart. However, both, in this moment, lay remotely within our grasp.

The city & all within it, unknowingly, await the mourning. Empty spaces begin to grieve for the lost aspirations & past lives of absent others, as if the secret eyes of sympathetic travellers were here observing & imagining.

★ ★ ☆ ★

Within the nocturnal and sleeping city of Warcapest, everything is a monument to the resolve of ingenious human endeavour; the spirit and activity that made everything in these parts is intrinsic within every one of its possible and conceivable artefacts. Everything records itself within the fabric of time. No conscious patterns seem to be missing; every unconscious pattern is here too, but invisibly so, awaiting discovery. Nothing can be lost if time is seen and understood. Everything is a commentary on what has happened and what will happen~ and can insinuate further what is yet to happen within this entire realm of things. It is not necessarily so elsewhere, or everywhere. Here, in Warcapest, ancient activities continue until such times as new ones supplant those that came before. Everything is built on the developing wishes and needs of a complex and aspiring species, which remain fundamentally unchanged over millennia.

There is a paradox that ought to be alarming. Might the progress of these people develop beyond their capacity and ability to embrace the very changes they invoke and manufacture? As the rate at which they organise and develop themselves increases, so does the opportunity for mayhem and conflict. It has become a dangerous and frequent occurrence within their continuing existence and consciousness, *a state of affairs and ongoing reality not known to those ancient Venetians who once lived undisturbed by change for a period of*

300 years, during their fortunate history. Innovation and change however, is the stuff out of which many of Warcapest's most beautiful contradictions are made. Notwithstanding, the passing of time fortunately remains a very stately affair here. The old world and its traditions are often revitalised, sometimes in bizarre ways, as time moves forward, embracing, as it does, new thinking and technologies, allowing the world to capture the imaginations of those who are still newly young, who are ambitious and progressive. Such continuity, allied to change, is inspirational, a driving force for the ensuing modern age. In Warcapest, the past is only ever, by degrees, allowed to glide away from the present. It slips away virtually undetected. It becomes imperceptibly left behind to die in isolation~ outdated and anachronistic through neglect, the glorious and half-remembered ghost of earlier ages.

However, there are surprisingly peculiar and immovable ancient ways that are belligerent and insistent. They thrive and persist alongside innovation in all epochs; such is the incongruity of existence here. These primordial anomalies remain into the present age and are set to survive in future ones, lovingly serviced by those yet living, for longer than one might expect, by virtue of blind observance and faith in long forgotten allegiances. In memoriam, such traditions can be adored for their historical significance, for what they continue to say. Such phenomena are believed to be timeless. They speak of who this people think they are, describing their ancient ways and unspeakable truths; traits, that it has been subconsciously agreed, will never be lost~ despite no one living having a vocabulary to describe what they are *anymore~* nor have they the ability to understand these things, as they once did. There are unmentionable and indescribable customs, details and ways of implementing procedures that are of indisputable importance to the reality of these temporal, but spiritual beings. Such indefatigable concerns, in the modern age, are becoming translated and redirected to take the now vacant places of once imagined gods. To the chagrin of this people, there is still no proof of their importance or place in the indecipherable universe. Where and when will that verification come? There is, without doubt, a colossal need in them. Without a tangible validation, they have acquired a desperation and imagination enough to have to invent one at last. In consequence, there is a newly popular mammon daring to replace blind faith. They have instead, assumed a self-interest and belief in the technology and processes over which they have a perception of control. They newly pride themselves on the exercise of political and bureaucratic power and recent innovations in science, engineering and industry. There is a quest for progress, aligned to an irrational belief in the supremacy of that 'self-imposed self' that can gain sway and govern, enslave and shackle those weaker 'others' in their midst. This is further supported by a misguided and mistaken belief in their potential to harness that same Nature that has dared to ignore them for so long. The city has become proof to some that they have become god-like in their century of industrial and technological revolution although, rather than embrace anything of Nature at all, let alone understand it, they have fooled themselves instead~ by shutting doors and by building walls against the very thing that they are.

There is an interesting exploration, a journey even, which might be undertaken here. Are there any heroes amongst this mayhem? Can we find one as we search?

See, as we see, spirit-like~ moving towards the heart of Warcapest, floating, like some kind of majesty, into the view of and over the top of an industrial, tall, shot tower. The furnace below is brought up to temperature in anticipation of the new day's toil. The night shift workers prepare, whilst simultaneously cleaning the large, copper sieve. They appear like little moving markers of organised activity in the orange glow. The lofty edifice resembles an enormous clock tower, constructed from brick with flattened pilasters, mapping the many landing stages of its external, metal stairway. The roof crane is lifting lead to the uppermost point, from where, in molten state, it will be released. Each solidifying mass of liquid metal, bead-like, will trace its own line as it is dropped, as alike a world in miniature as one might care to imagine, every little individual point briefly tracing its own indivisible, invisible line as it falls. The buildings throughout the site are blackened and soiled with the residues of oxidized lead from past decades.

This industrial edge, just outside of Warcapest, lies next to the swifter of the two rivers that flow through the heart of the city. The area is populated with a multitude of heavy, concrete buildings, like bunkers, built in a time when it was thought they should be made to last forever, in the belief that the utility of 'once new' industrial complexes and the mechanisms they house should be perpetual, and inexhaustible. Each colossus of technology and engineering, each process by which energy is harnessed, stands proud, defiant, indomitable, dwarfed under a vast impassive sky that glides disinterestedly, nonchalantly above. Monstrous constructions sprawl across the landscape, each isolated within a wilderness, surrounded by unkempt, opportunistic foliage and expedient, mongrel growth.

The metal-framed building immediately below, with a myriad of filthy glass panes clad across its surfaces, is the coal breakers' yard. Each building on this site is dirty, black, dust-ridden and smeared with anthracite particles, denying the interior light it was once intended to see. Only where the glass is broken or fallen out, can shafts of dynamic daylight invade the gloomy interior of a heartless building. Throughout the site, conveyor belts enter and exit buildings at will, at varying heights and angles, intent on delivering coal to the next crushing house. Young trees; thin, green, rampant rogues, break the monotony of a colourless site, right up to the buildings themselves and across the high roofs~ their once fresh foliage prematurely darkened and crisp in the dusty air that stunts their natural growth and splendour. Even in daylight, light is restricted to their leaves.

Adjacent is a power station built in 1902, virtually obsolete and ready to be taken out of commission, noble~ but in its dotage, loyal to its cause~ but worn out and superseded by improved technologies recently built next to it, on neighbouring land. The familiar signature of its wild, gliding, electric hum and intermittent thunder-cracks fill the distant air all around, sounding out into the night like sparks on an enormous flywheel. At the far end of the site, power lines escape and move 'en masse' in the direction of central Warcapest; they hum and resonate in high voltage and full-blown electrical thrall. The building has cement facings of splendid columns and mouldings, gratuitously and anachronistically modelled on the architecture of the Greeks, adding a universal and worldly grandeur. In places, large parts of these glorious details have fallen off over subsequent decades. The dense volumes of concrete, out of which the building and turbine halls are constructed, are at last decomposing and disintegrating. Coarse concrete has broken through and begins to assert itself as the ruinous look of the once magnificent building. Here too, the rude surface is flaked, is broken, visibly bows, burgeoning out of line where the unremitting action of torrential storm rain, over decades, has breached and rusted internal caged metal that was once intended to strengthen the form. In consequence, heavy blocks of broken concrete hang precariously from ceilings suspended on the bent, rusting, wire cages that once lay deep within their construction. *That 'deposition', intrinsic within the fabric of time, exerts itself.* Walls and roofs sporadically seep water and create lime deposits. Water and weathering have penetrated outer skins right through to inner surfaces where stalactites, no less substantial than any imagined elsewhere, have formed as they would in any subterranean cave.

Robust structures within the building's interior, made of iron girders, support the vast platforms onto which are secured enormous castings. These are the powerful turbines~ mechanical life on an epic scale, engines that dwarf the men who service their needs and utility. In the main shed, the turbine is massive, its moving parts a prescription for precision engineering, although external casings have become woefully blistered due to indiscriminate and repeated overheating. Painted surfaces have been persistently scorched and lay peeling, as though infected with some inglorious, indescribable pox. Such superficial damage has been made good or ignominiously retrieved through alternative paint layers of not quite the right hue, or partial undercoats that have failed to cover efficiently. The body of this languishing beast has been overly greased where it can be maintained and allowed to rust where it cannot. The noise is unremitting and overwhelming~ a persistent, never-ending scream of determined intensity.

A soundproofed control room overlooks the area, serviced in a half-light, a subdued and dismal artificial light, by two flat-footed, over-weight operatives, discernable only as shadows on the night shift.

Insulated double doors, designed to keep the internal environment free of dust, ensure that industrial clamour and roar can only invade as a distant dream. The semi-circular interior of the narrow room with brown, tinted windows displays a complex control panel of crazed, Bakelite levers and polished brass fittings. There are profuse buttons and dials, a multitude of illuminated pressure gauges, meters, measuring instruments and displays. The walking and pacing undertaken by a succession of controllers, *over decades,* is apparent in the linoleum tiles across the front of the panel; a path worn down to the concrete has become unmistakable. Everywhere there are signs of dilapidation. All that is missing is the final neglect that is soon to become manifest, *when the facility finally closes,* namely, the rich patina of abandon furnished by human disinterest and entropy, by dirt and dust~ to be followed by the concluding anarchy afforded by rapacious asset stripping and vandalism. At this point, the remaining contents of cupboards and storage spaces will be strewn over floors and surfaces. Features will then have been stripped of their integrity and cannibalised for the meagre pickings obtained by recycling their parts as scrap.

Upstream, there are coal silos and enormous water storage tanks to services the generators of the new gas power station that lays further inland. Cooling towers are in process of being built, with the intention of recycling huge quantities of water. The replacement utility has a larger turbine hall than its predecessor. The generators are the most advanced in the world; their hum is streamlined and harmonious. These objects are redolent of the sculpture of twentieth century abstract artists. Obtuse forms and cylindrical pipework confuse and beautifully confound the sensibilities of the uninitiated. The gigantic hall is reminiscent of a city railway terminus, incorporating an economical cross-barrel vault~ designed with a mathematician's skill to determine complex tolerances, facilitating the impressive use of thin, reinforced metal with the greatest of structural sophistication.

A heavy steelworks behind, on the far horizon, marks its geographical position by sending excess, raw, spent energy into the atmosphere. Billowing steam and smoke is exiting the electric furnaces and the tall chimneys of sinter plants. Chemical emissions rise into the air from venting devices and exhaust systems. Waste discharges variously from diverse complexes and disparate buildings, and can be seen passing through the roofs of the rolling mills, soaking pits and from coking ovens. Steam locomotives cross the site, transporting molten ingots encased in moulds twice the height of a man~ the heat scorching the faces of workers as they pass. There are tall structures reaching high into the air, intermittently scattered. Metal chimneys burn off raw gases, sending plumes of yellow and blue fire and bright flame into the sky. These things glow, like enormous candles, illuminating the underside of clouds in the firmament above. The din of blast furnaces, rolling mills, huge compressor rooms and gas pumping stations fills the atmosphere. The complex sound and acrid smell of infernal industry is carried away in an opposite direction on the prevailing wind, far out across the vast vista, until such effect becomes dampened and is dispersed across open acreages and large distances.

From the centre of Warcapest, none of this can be heard or seen at all. It might as well be a lost world or a distant reality~ the work of an imperceptible magician behind his screen or gods lost in a heavenly cloud, or the secret power of a non-apparent hero hidden within their cloak of invisibility.

In Warcapest now, the streets are empty. The quiet is intense and tangible. Everything appears static and immovable. However, *look closely*~ steely reality has imperceptibly become twisted and ever so slightly undone. It unwittingly shimmers, secretly desirous to bend, willing to become changed or to be usurped.

The parks are closed. Buildings shut. Industry is at rest. The offices and factories are empty. There are few night shifts here to deny workers repose and slumber. Light machinery will stand idle until such time as the dawn arrives and the day officially begins. The metro and transport systems have closed down in response to the hours of darkness. Even municipal fountains are turned off during this time. Throughout the city, switches, levers, plugs and ignition keys will only be once again 'on' when the waking hour arrives.

The factories, department stores and offices in the centre, sleep. In these places, night watchmen are the lone/ lonely secret individuals who can see and explore this uncommon and generally unknown reality~ they wander amidst the heart of things that constitute what human beings have become. In these quiet moments, lurking secrets have space in which to be exposed. They can breathe easily and are to be glimpsed amongst the monumentality of machines, the acres of office space, amongst the workshops, in the garages, on the shop floors, amongst the factory assembly lines. Within all this, there is a hidden symbology, a latent energy that describes humanity and a veiled universe beyond. It lies, hardly concealed at all, within the trappings of the commonplace.

Like a pendulum, reality oscillates between one point and another. Cups may be half full or half empty. One may be in front of, or behind, a line. Patterns so often counter themselves and imperceptibly move backwards or in reverse of the direction they appear to be going, enacting an illusion, like the mime artist who only appears to be walking contrary to the expected line of travel. A head may have two faces, one on each side, the second mysterious, hidden in the dark hood of night that covers the place where a back to the head should be~ like some secret, screaming horror. So shadows shift and slide, glide over and past one another. In the nightmare half-light of night, the alternatives are so much nearer. There, imaginings gather form. The absurdity of fantastical notions suggest ideas beyond themselves that resonate in secret places, seldom yet visited or seen, where light is yet to reach~ or alternatively will never reach. Might blood move around a body in reverse, the pencil grow longer as it writes, its lead renewing itself with inspiration? An inkbottle, likewise, might overflow with the enormity of ideas its contents are about to express. A wine glass might miraculously begin to fill. Is there a being whose great age is contradicted by the youthfulness of their inner self? The cornucopia may have a source or purpose other than to create abundance. Can an eye see the invisible or experience a thing only remotely felt? Is there an impossibility that can be harnessed or utilised? Is there a usefulness we might affect, greater than the sum total of our small, insignificant parts? Can a brain deconstruct/reconstruct, at will, all that it becomes aware of?

So, dawn is on the horizon and just beginning to unfold. Soon~ maybe within the hour, light will begin to invade the world again. Where is the vantage point from which we might see all this? Is there yet a sign that we might be looking for?

46.

Once again a siren is heard, piercing the night with its serial pulse. A deadened crash from the direction of the slower of Warcapest's two rivers sends out a valedictory reverberation and recoil, in response. One might imagine a muffled canon being fired. A traffic light nearby ends its cycle of mechanical clicks and proceeds to alter priorities at the junction, accompanied by a familiar, resonant tone that informs the pedestrian of their right to pass. There is no citizen visible to take advantage of all the opportunities in this captured moment.

A slight breeze proceeds along and through the street, moving minute particles suspended in the air before it, travelling with relaxed intent, forward, towards the far side of the wide plaza, over the black, white, black, white, black, white, zebra stripes of the crossing, and onward in the direction of a magnificent four-storey building that lies further ahead. The building is architecturally impressive in the Viennese Secession style and interestingly utilitarian. The travelling zephyr, like a breath, begins to blow harder, picking up speed and intention~ its thrust is suddenly rapid as it slams into the front of the building, intent on breaching the external walls. An alarming and curious entry is afforded. The presence within this unseen cloak passes silently through the large, double-fronted doors at the top of steps. Within its fabric every detail of the doors is experienced as a reality. Beneath the painted white surface and the gold embossed leaves around the striated central panels, lies a grey oak, part of a once magnificent tree, which now rests, fulfilling its most recent incarnation.

We too are become part of all of this, moving effortlessly within these folds, passing through and over the threshold. In so doing, our position is changed to immediately see the door from behind, the view and vantage point turning about face as though having moved over a line~ it cannot be let go of. Having crossed a portal it usurps attention, demands our gaze; there is surprise in the absolute belief at what has just occurred. The main doorway diminishes in size as we pass, as a corridor stretches out in front of it. Openings into reception areas come into view. An escalator and winding stairway leading to other floors is passed. Numerous, evenly spaced doorways flash by. The gloss of parquet is bleached brighter in the lamplight that pours through the latticed window above the entrance doorway. The luminescence changes as the perspective lowers, the floor finally turning white, saturated with light~ before turning back to black, the view impeded by a night watchman's bulk ambling down the corridor. The man has been passed through without knowing. The employee stops in his stride to question the strangeness of the moment that just occurred outside of his knowledge or supervision.

He stands, scratching his head beneath a flat cap. The blue of his boiler suit appears darker in the gloom. An assortment of cheap, chrome pens catch the light in his top pocket. Keys and a second flashlight are attached to a heavy leather belt around the man's waist; and then there is the bucket placed over his arm. The fellow is unaware that he is newly accompanied and turns to continue his night's chores. Turning a handle, opening a door, he enters a darkened office space. The clock on the wall appears strangely illuminated. The night watchman walks forward, intent on placing the pail to catch dripping water under a rain-sodden lintel, in spite of it being some days since the deluge that rained over the city. The worker rearranges paper in danger of becoming spoilt. The clock ticks loudly as he works, parodying the sound of dripping.

Once stationery and printed matter are neatly re-positioned and safe from the wet, the man walks back a step or two into shadow, assessing his handiwork before leaving. At the door, the threshold between two places, he turns and, at a stroke, banishes the bucket from his sight, proceeding back into the path of the corridor.

The nightshift operative makes his way to the reception where he stops to consult a list taken from a pocket. Time is frozen as the man checks the tasks requiring his attention. His shadowy form stands in the meagre, but available light. A clock chimes out the half hour. The silhouetted figure turns to traverse the open space, walking past display cabinets in the foyer and further onward through the building, into a new corridor running laterally to the main hallway.

The man pads down the centre of the passageway, veering to the right in order to arrive at double doors. The cold, brass handle is turned, facilitating entry into a room used for the cataloguing of orders and other administrative duties necessary to the running of the enterprise, *to which the entire building is dedicated.* It is convenient to use the space, with access doors at each end, as a thoroughfare and shortcut. During the day, such lazy opportunism would not be allowed. On arrival at the next corridor, the perambulating operative crosses over and moves into an open area set aside for the temporary rest and occasional recreation of a large body of employees. Here, there are doors leading to cloak rooms, powder rooms, medical rooms and rest rooms, as well as a small café. At the further end, a prominent decorative wall of glass panelling runs from floor to ceiling in the Secession style, proclaiming the importance of the space beyond. The hall accommodates the typing pool, and beyond, are extensive filing systems storing acres of correspondence for the firm, *whose premises on this night have become haunted.* The night watchman walks past isles of desks, row upon row, each concealing under its lid the Super Sterling typewriter made by Smith Corona. The watchman's torch illuminates the sidewall as he walks revealing, in the light, a series of large painted frescoes, each situated between decorative, wall-mounted lamps. They feature nymphs, gods, goddesses and angels engaged in or observing myriad activities associated with playing cards. The frescoes would best be seen in daylight. In the current half-light, large angular shadows cast by the office furniture flash across their surfaces. The night watchman changes direction and walks down an aisle amongst this sea of desks towards a frescoed wall, from where he collects a ladder that leans against it. A light bulb had recently been changed in the lamp half way up the wall. He begins the task of returning the ladder to the storage area.

The caretaker, on exiting the typing hall, proceeds down the long corridor in the opposite direction to the main entrance, moving towards a service area where maintenance equipment is housed.

Such scenes might seem dull and uninteresting, for time is passing as it does in real measure. There is no hook to hold attention or interest to carry a narrative forward. There is no delight to be had in the glory of a light bulb being changed. But there it is, this is how time passes. This is the real manner in which time passes. But next, there is an intrusion. Imagine or rather picture and hear phones ringing out from within this void, bringing the world to life.

Ring-ring–ring! The sound resounds throughout the length of the hallway. Ring-ring-ring!

The night telephones have all become active across the building, two on each floor and each one at opposite ends of the long corridors; they are calling for, and demanding attention. The ringing seems amplified to the point where it deafens in the quietude of the building. Every phone's ring is endorsed by its brothers and sisters throughout the premises~ the sound of each an echo behind the ringing of the one in front. The man emits a deep, inarticulate grumble as he straightaway moves to answer the nearest ringing conduit to an outside world. The night watchman deposits the ladder length-wise against a wall and begrudgingly begins a flat-footed, slow, hangdog, demoralised walk back along the corridor he had just come down.

Ring-ring-ring!

He turns off his torch and places it into his pocket.

Ring-ring-ring!

His footfall passes over wooden flooring that has worn smooth over many years.

Ring-ring-ring!

The intrusion into his solitude has spoilt the harmony of his shift.

Change in his pocket jingles quietly and remotely against the metal of the torch. His loose internal organs gloop~ little electrical impulses pass through his brain, a sweat breaks out over his brow, an odour rises from his armpits. His brilliantined hair is smoothed flat to his head; he is aware of how stiff it feels. Walking back into the typing pool, moving through the hall, past desks, the worker travels to the far end of the room. Here, a narrow staircase leads to a platformed, glass-fronted office overlooking the typist's area.

Stepping up to the doorway, on opening the door, the man is greeted by the full roar of the phone from within. BRING! -BRING! -BRING! The extensively shelved office of the typing pool manageress contains a comprehensive collection of box files, manila folders and other evidence of stout efficiency. Turning a switch to light the room causes the window view to vanish from the front glass. It is replaced by a reflected view of the interior of the office. The man stands in front of his mirrored image to answer the call, pleased at last to bring the incessant ringing to a stop. With a breathless wheeze in his voice he says.
'Ya who is dis pleeze?'
The night watchman makes a note of the time as it appears on the reverse image of the clock before him. Life and action begins.

How often the ringing of bells~ alongside distant bangs and the sound of crashes~ punctuates existence and in so doing, partitions time.

A brief conversation ensues. Someone wants to gain entry to the building at this unearthly hour and, was it not for their prominence and position in the company, would not be allowed in at all without prior consultation with the appropriate personnel. However, the night watchman is all civility, politeness and compliance. He recognises the cadence and is bending over backwards to accommodate the request, and ensure the needs of the voice are met~ in every regard. The night watchman is asked if he can be at the front door in half an hour to unlock it and let the gentleman in as soon as the doorbell rings.

'Ya, young master. Dis is what I will do. Thank you sir,' he says.

★ ★ ☆ ★

47.

Xavier Mannikin is walking through the centre of Warcapest. It is so late as to be early morning and he knows that soon, the night will be all but exhausted. The evening suited gentleman checks his watch~ it appears to be 3.40am, but he is not entirely sure. Such nocturnal escapades are his forte. Xavier is aware that he does this sort of thing too often, denying himself a night's rest in order to be awake and moving whilst the world around sleeps~ such acts had become something of a rite of passage and resonated deep in his psyche. There is an impenetrable enchantment enacted by remaining conscious whilst the world is dreaming~ even his tired self recognised this. The end game however, *which he liked least about such exploits,* was dawning; the return of daylight was beginning to loom. It dampened the mystique and would soon cause the spell to become broken. Only at that point would his beleaguered constitution give in to feeling tired and fatigued, having significantly overstretched its natural sensibilities. Then, his body will slump and finally crave sleep. As he walks, he randomly picks up a stone; the smooth rounded form attracts his attention. Against his better judgment, Xavier throws it into the air, high into the pitch-black canopy above, with force. He listens for it in the silence; in that instant hearing and quantifying the quietude of the night all around, imagining the emptiness of existence, the miles of untrammelled universe, attempting in that moment to feel the experiences that he has never had~ the things that might be important to his consciousness about which he knows nothing~ they are all out there, somewhere beyond his grasp. A couple of beats of anticipation precede a dull thud in the road ahead as the stone lands on the tarmac, bringing him back to the present. His eyes glint in the dark. It was a crazy thing to do. Even at this late hour someone may have been hurt or he might have damaged a car, or broken a window. It had worked out though and Xavier is glad he took the risk, and pleased it came down. He wasn't always sure that things did what were most expected of them.

The city opera comes into view to the right of him. He notes this most resplendent of buildings from afar and decides to make a detour in order to walk through the main portico. It was used in a former epoch as the horse carriage entrance; it remains cobbled in hardwood blocks used to deaden the 'once' sound of horses hooves. Sepia images stored in his mind's-eye flash up before him, remembered details of a world he knows and shares remotely.

The young man does not look out of place as he approaches the building. Indeed, he might have come from the opera that very night, dressed as he is in white tie and tails. However, Xavier had not been here at all; he had been walking for the last hour, since emerging from the metro, having spent his time since midnight at a milonga on the banks of the main river. During the summer, when the weather was fine, people danced tango under the stars. Tonight there had been some tension. His sartorial raiment and the inappropriateness of his penguin suit had annoyed the tangueros.

Mannikin had started out his night's odyssey~ it seemed such a long time ago~ at the Hotel de l'Empereur. The venue had hosted the annual dinner of the Mannikin Playing Card Co. This was the enterprise for which, without any sense of pride or particular enthusiasm, Xavier was the Marketing Manager. His role in the company, the duties, labels, accolades or whatever they might be, in truth, held little interest for him. Only in the last couple of years had he succumbed to pressure to join the firm because he had exhausted attempts to do other things. Nothing he tried seemed to ever suit him. His father owned the concern and was keen that the business should be passed on to his son.

At that dull dinner, the main attraction, the thing that remained in his memory, was the performance of mystifying and baffling conjuring by Count Zapik, the magician. Mannikin, a natural skeptic, had nevertheless been enthralled and drawn into the charade. The confusion created by the illusions paralleled his questioning of everyday reality. All he saw, undertaken in the name of art, had hurt or confused him at some deep, subliminal level. Xavier knew Count Zapik a little and was strangely drawn to the man for reasons he could not explain. At the after show party, the Count had specifically asked that Mannikin escort his assistant, the beautiful Nadja, back to her room before leaving. She was beguiling, enchanting, so attractive and graceful. She had asked to take his arm for support as they walked. She was electric to the touch~ like Sara Phielnx. They had talked and discussed things at some length on the way back to the hotel room but, try as he might, he could not remember what had been said.

The fresh-faced, young executive had done his duty during the evening, had let the dull formality of the event take its pound of flesh, enjoyed it where possible and then, when he could, escaped. Xavier had launched himself before midnight into the darkened city to follow his idiosyncratic and nocturnal inclinations, to take note of the confusing world he found himself in, and to wonder. In the gloom, he had followed the lines of the streets with his thoughts and had eventually found himself at the tango by the river. The dancing was glorious and he had lost himself to moments that opened for him. The release, as ever, had been joyous; he felt he was outside of time. The spirit of the experience flashes before him; he observes it, remotely quantifying the sensations, checking and wondering if his observations still matched his earlier recollection. Even in this short time, Xavier recognised that his sense of recall, his remembrance and his emotional responses had become altered in some way beyond his control. What had been missed or forgotten? What had altered?

Xavier freezes his bodily actions, intent on remembering, trying to piece things together, no longer part of his surroundings~ a cut-out from the page that he has been printed on, like a deer caught in the headlights of its own experiences~ detached, like a perforated stamp finding itself removed from the book of stamps to which it once belonged~ in a state of thrall, hardly contained in the unfolding moment, held in place by the thinnest of invisible threads. The recent events play yet again. The man searches them some more, anxious that something relevant is hiding from him.

Mannikin recollects removing his tie at the bank of the river~ watching himself as an out of body experience. The tie has returned and nonchalantly hangs around his neck once more, although he cannot remember how it got there. Ordinarily, he wore a loose suit for such events, one that was seated and comfortable to dance in. He had looked far too auspicious for the bohemian tango set tonight. It became apparent that other tangueros thought him inappropriately dressed. Do penguins generally dance tango? Perhaps he looked too well off, like some upper-class usurper of the pleasures of the working masses. Evidently he wasn't sending out the signals to say he lived their life and experiences or that he understood their deprivations and realities, or the honest joy of the struggling proletariat~ they were probably right. However Xavier had, nevertheless, been graciously accepted because the regulars knew and liked him, had taken him under their wing, were prepared to make allowance for his apparent eccentricity on this occasion, and in any event he could dance the tango well enough. There was always a need to ensure equal numbers of leaders and followers so that everyone could keep 'dancing, dancing, dancing'. Young Mannikin was particularly pleased that he had, over time, been allowed to infiltrate and belong to the tango tribe~ but tonight, only by the 'skin of his teeth'. They were rarified cognoscenti in their own right. They, like him, were in search of more, something else; they often seemed to sense that which was missing. This particular point was a crucial part of all their assumed identities and the bond that made the group vibrant. Their edginess made him feel alive.

Such dilettante musings and inner thoughts are moving 'panther like' through his mind, spreading, defining themselves, looking to trigger a response or simply find a place to rest. Around him, in real time, Mannikin is passing the grand entrance to the opera house. He casually glances sideways, catching his reflection in the glass doors and windows as he moves. He stops and sees himself looking at the image appearing back; it too has stopped, strangely muted as if seen through a dark, obsidian glass. The man observes by necessity, moving his consciousness from memory into the present. His breast pocket is bulging slightly, the small camera that he carries within it spoiling the elegant line of his tailcoat. Xavier checks it with a simple tap of his pocket using the tips of his fingers. Furthermore, the black material is creased. He sees and remembers that he had rapidly removed the coat at the river~ making light of the garment, for effect, to telegraph the impression he held it in low esteem. It had been unceremoniously hidden out of embarrassment, out of sight, amongst the other coats and bags haphazardly placed in the centre of the dance floor. The compromised garment reflects back in the opera house window. Xavier is surprised at the ignominious and undignified creases that have remained in the cloth, and how dusty the left shoulder has become. He had not been aware of such changes being inflicted on the jacket at the time or the history that was inadvertently being built into its current appearance; he had been too busy dealing with other issues that obstructed his full awareness of what was happening. Mannikin feels the difficulty of seeing 'everything' most acutely and in this moment, winces.

He dusts his shoulder as he watches his reflection closely and wonders. Which one is the real him~ the one he feels himself to be within his core or the one that can be seen from the outside in the glass, providing proof of his presence and identity? For Mannikin, this is a particularly interesting question. The 'I' he feels himself to 'be' is in this moment the real 'he'; the one in the mirror might not be him at all, it could even be a usurper of his position in the universe. He is unsure, but rather than blame or be offended by the beautiful reflection, he has a strange sympathy for it and is prepared to tolerate its existence. He doesn't know who it is. Was it the person at the formal dinner early the previous evening or the man later that he remembers walking the streets? Surely it is the weightless man who had such fun dancing tango after that or perhaps he is only the person he sees in this moment of self-reflection. He tries to anticipate what he will think next. Where is he going with all this? As he looks, he is confused, hardly realising the extent to which he is staring with an intense, penetrating scrutiny. The time passing is an eternity, for all he knows. The intoxicating concentration fractures and begins to splinter as he becomes distractedly aware of other figures. Two strangers come

into his newly refocusing and expanding consciousness, appearing at the edges of his deteriorating fixed gaze. They are the reflection of a couple passing on the far side of the street behind him. They are wearing light coloured outfits that show noticeably in the mirrored glass. The young men are wearing pointed hats. They walk arm in arm, leaning in towards each other. They appear to be moving anonymously along the street; maybe they are tired, sluggish and like him, intent on returning home after their night's revelry.
'This world has me in it, with these people also, and the reflection has this other me in it~ with these people reflected too, or are they different? My reflection is easy to imagine as another me, one I don't fully recognise and whose presence I keep questioning, yet the reflection of the couple behind me, I imagine being the same people, but merely repeated in the window. How can my observation of self more easily confuse me than my observation of other persons? It is as if my life exists on a stage, like the one in this opera house perhaps; as if my life can be viewed from a seat in the splendid auditorium, simultaneously.'

The Warcapest night is humid and unusually hot~ even for summer. There are little beads of moisture on Mannikin's forehead. The temperature in this late part of the night is oppressive, despite the daylight hours being long gone. Recent weather had been bizarre and mystifying~ as if the universe had opened up to let in a new mystery. Hot days had given rise to electric storms during the night. Impressive lightning had zigzagged across the blackened, weather-filled sky like a dramatic orchestral overture and rain had penetrated, and drenched the city deeply~ with its warm tears.

Xavier's refusal to give in to tiredness and exhaustion is causing his mind to compensate by free flowing in a hyperactive, befuddled manner. Thoughts have become inclined to degenerate into a mindless rant, an internal dialogue of endless, seemingly inane notes or conversations to self; exploring patterns, half ideas, hoped for routes to alternative ways of thinking and new potential directions; attempting to break out of closed loops that run repetitively, incestuously, restrictively through the chemistry and circuitry within his poor brain. There is an underlying hope of a longed-for escape, a breakthrough~ the discovery of a previously undetected pattern that might become available, one that could form the route to a desperately needed new place in his psyche. His mind has become too bright; it is burning, convulsing, hyperventilating, despite its tiredness. It flits too rapidly, fluttering like an epileptic eyelid, rushing through half-opened notions, dwelling on nothings in particular, moving, passing through, passing into, passing the same words and thoughts more than once, passing without recognising the repetition, discovering half remembered visions and spaces wherein once an idea or thought may have been previously caught and may be opportunistically captured again. The man meets them all, or lets them meet him, within the plethora of escaping imaginings that freefall and scatter aimlessly ...

A part of him that deals with self-preservation recognises, with an increasing ferocity, that his delicate constitution needs to find a bed soon. He has become weary and his feet are sore. Such good sense is quickly overruled by Xavier's indomitable spirit, with the suggestion of another option~ that yet more life be lived before the night is over.

Mannikin stops for no reason that he is aware. A breaker in his circuitry has demanded that he slows down. His attention, in consequence, moves out of himself and is drawn to a large plinth supporting an edifice. His head falls to one side, seeking his shoulder as a pillow. Sleepily, drowsily, he considers the large statue, conspicuous in its position, next to the opera. An ancient man sits magnificently, noble in an immense chair, his comfort secured as he looks out from within the gloom of the secluded park area into the night. His gaze is in the direction of a standing sculpture of Schiller, atop its own plinth, across the street at some distance opposite. The bulk of the seated bronze body is in shadow and the head alone catches light enough for the line of the face and jaw to be seen; it is distinctive in its classic majesty. Mannikin peers into the work with intent and wonders where he will be when he looks as old. The young man reacquaints himself with the descriptive plaque on the plinth and muses on the fact that he knows the name, has the briefest of knowledge, although no real idea who Goethe is at all.

Somewhere far off across the city a siren sounds yet again, a plaintive oboe piercing the night with its shrill cry. A crash from the direction of what must be the second of the city's two rivers sends out a resounding boom, reminiscent of canon fire. Coincidentally, a large bell tolls once~ one might imagine that it acknowledges some epic, mythic event happening in a far off place within the firmament. An alarm rings. Amidst this unexpected, nocturnal cacophony, Xavier wonders if the statue might feel as misplaced, odd, as ill at ease in the world as he knows himself to be.

Lack of sleep is taking its toll. Mannikin is agitated and elated at the same time, a curious state akin to 'dissatisfied rapture' or 'ill-tempered euphoria'. He smiles at the ridiculous portmanteaux that have unwittingly unrolled~ inwardly picturing himself walking over them as if they were carpet.

Then at last he recalls the illusive event, which occurred at the milonga, the one his mind had seemed reticent to yield up. Xavier attempts to relive the moment, hoping to get back to the source beyond the mystery, beyond the memory. There was something that had escaped his attention that needed further scrutiny. It wasn't the fracas about his clothes at all~ it was this other thing. How could it have been forgotten until now? Mannikin had used the 'look', the tango 'cabaceo', to invite a young woman to dance; she had come breathlessly, demurely, beautifully into his arms.
'I am so sorry, I cannot dance very well.'

'Pretend we are drowning,' he had said. 'Listen to the music as it breaks over us like a storm in an intoxicating deluge.'
It became the *tanda* of the evening, the most bewitching and electrifying dance possible, made tragic when they at last parted, without words, knowing that they might never meet again.

The tanguero in him remembers this as he checks his watch~ it is 3.38am, earlier than the last time he looked!

Xavier continues, walking past a row of shops. Without warning, a mannequin dummy falls forward onto a window. The true strangeness is that he does not seem to be particularly surprised or bothered. It falls further, passing inexplicably through the glass and into the street. It falls completely, smashing head first onto the pavement, into pieces, each smashed fragment turning unaccountably into a little flash of golden light, flickering and filling the immediate area. As the man walks into and amidst the splendour of this lost moment, the whole scene bewilderingly resets itself and everything returns to how it was formerly. The afterglow however, continues to fill and illuminate his eyes, making them even brighter than before. The event occurs before it happened, disappearing so quickly as to be unobserved or to have never existed. A momentary figment perhaps, a waking dream possibly, taking place within an overly stretched and tired imagination~ a further indicator that his night's excursion needs to come to an end.

The dark figure proceeds, travelling through the cultural and administrative quarter, passing the finest buildings in the city, the National Galleries and Parliament and then further on, out towards the Ringstrasse, to acquire some destination. Xavier is formulating his actions. He could allow himself to finish up in one of a number of places, due to being so centrally positioned; his father's house perhaps or his own apartment, either is within easy reach and both could provide sanctuary at the end of his nocturnal adventure. However, recognising there is still time to be had, Mannikin decides instead to gain entry to the Mannikin building, the administrative head office for the playing card company.

In the distance, against the glow of the streetlights, the silhouette of a policeman leans over a car, an inebriated motorist is reprimanded for colliding with a kerb~ their remote and diminished voices roll, echoing along the street towards him. Mannikin observes the scene with wistful disinterest before stopping opportunistically to enter a telephone kiosk.

Collecting change from his pocket, the man lifts the receiver and dials; he has a need to speak to the nightshift caretaker in the Mannikin building. Xavier's prominence in the company enables him to waive protocol and have free access to the building at all times~ and right now he wants to use the photographic darkroom in the design department. He rubs his fingers over the jacket breast pocket, feeling for the Paxette Range Finder that lies there. The camera contains images captured during the evening, some at the milonga and others taken furtively at the magic performance. Xavier intends to develop the film before morning. Soon a short, but polite telephone conversation takes place.

At last, he is too tired to persevere with any more thinking and continues walking, mindlessly plodding the paving with heavy footfall. His ears are buzzing and ringing~ making a peculiar whoosh he has heard before; he feels his heart pounding. A bell sounds, this time slowly and mournfully on the air at some distance, heralding the fresh light that is now just beginning to pour into the new day. Outside of his knowledge there is a man in a dark, full-length raincoat following him.

48.

The doorbell rings. There is a quick response from the expectant and waiting night watchman, briefly glimpsed, peering though the aperture in the heavy, Jugendstil double door. With fleet efficiency, the caretaker opens a chink in one half of the door and beckons the visitor to gain entrance in a manner suggestive of some secretive or covert manoeuvre.
'It is you, sir; did you knock about five minutes ago? I thought I heard and saw you then, but when I opened the door you were gone or had not arrived, I was confused.'
Mannikin shakes his head and informs the man he has only just arrived, as far as he is aware. In this way, the quiet nocturnal sanctuary of the Mannikin Playing Card Company head office is breached at an unearthly hour, unusually early, scarcely before the day has begun. Once inside, formal greetings and thanks are exchanged. The younger man is appreciative of the unscheduled effort of the older stalwart, recognising the potential for the man's resentment at having to break his comfortable, bleak routine. Mannikin slumps and seems, without doubt, very fatigued from his night's excursion. He is beginning to feel cold, is tired, his face is drained, although he demonstrates pleasure and is pleased to be over the threshold. Once inside the vestibule, he looks immediately up into the gloom of the high, domed ceiling~ exquisite mythical figures, painted by no lesser an artist than Gustav Klimt, observe

the decorum of all that passes beneath. Xavier uses the ceiling as an animal might use the sky to orientate on returning to a familiar territory or reality. The high centre point is a silver, gilded, crescent moon that shines.

Turning to the night porter/caretaker, Mannikin explains that he wishes to gain entry to the design department and the photography darkroom in particular. The man informs him that the studio rooms are locked, but will be opened forthwith at his express wish. Both men set off, walking through the gloom filled corridor to the far end of the building. The footsteps of the younger man sound and echo across the marble floor into the voluminous space as they follow the silent, flat-footed walk of the lugubrious and dour watchman.

They pass through the reception area, negotiating the cluttered floor plan of comfortable seating, coffee tables laid with magazines and a series of tall, freestanding, glass display cabinets laid out in rows. The foyer is patterned and camouflaged by early morning shadows, and weak shafts of light that begin to enter the space through high windows. The antiquated wooden cabinets contain playing cards and designs associated with the Mannikin brand~ many of them distinguished historical packs from times past. The largest of the cabinets leans against a back wall. It is dedicated to photographs in sepia and black and white of previous owners, visiting dignitaries, and includes historic views of the shop floor. The images document the growth and development of the old factory building. Cheerful employees from previous epochs wear clothes from a bygone era. They pose, ensnared in time, engaged in the manufacture of playing cards, their brief lives caught, trapped and displayed. Leopold Mannikin, the present owner, features in his prime, with his son beside him in short trousers. The young Xavier peers out into the lens of the camera, inquisitive, shocked and disorientated. The history and pride of this large manufacturing enterprise is apparent.

It is not easy to see the exhibits or view the history on show. The light passing over, onto and into the glass cabinets from external windows at this time of the morning has become problematic, obscuring the contents. The reality within has to fight for survival. The glaring light ricochets into and off the glass. A layer of dust compounds the problem, trapping light within surfaces it might otherwise pass through with immunity. Reflected images on the outside of cabinets illuminate the case behind and the one behind that, forming a confusion of diverse refraction and light effects which bounce off surfaces in a display of glorious and confusing prismatic splendour~ a miniature cosmic 'game' within a structure whose purpose has been lost within a larger complexity. The rebounding, redirected, leaping light vies for supremacy and attention. There are more things occurring than one might be supposed or expected to notice. It becomes possible, in this fleeting moment, to imagine the substance of the universe, more so than the human reality depicted in the cases. The physical properties of light have become stronger and more pressing, more pleasing in the imagination than the humdrum objects that the cabinets attempt to bring glory to, as alike attending a theatrical performance, an opera, even, in which the ancillary setting and architecture, the darkened auditorium, the chirping noises of the audience, the interest the people have in themselves, outshines and outweighs the wonder and visual delight of the spectacle~ for which all are assembled. The performance and colourful light on the stage has less appeal than the reality that surrounds it. The very thing supposed to be the reason for being, is secretly, silently eclipsed by events that happen in a manner that none notice. Where is the truly critical and impartial eye? Mannikin walks through the building. The fresh-faced executive does not even notice the cabinets as he travels through the space, nor the images of his young self; they are history to him, an experience unlikely to enthral. His consciousness has visited them in the past, there is no point revisiting them again, maybe ever. Xavier had, in addition, also missed the light show today; it never entered his consciousness.

From the far end of the main gallery, two men appear. These figures turn a corner and enter into the long corridor. That is how they arrive there. Each end sees the other end. They walk through the space in time, diminishing in size and increasing in size simultaneously; a line moving in contradiction to itself when viewed from both ends in the same instant.

Soon the design department is reached; the night watchman unlocks the facility, turns on the lights and immediately asks if there is anymore he can do. With a friendly wave and smile the man is dismissed. Mannikin listens to the soft footfall receding back down the long corridor as the room closes in around him. He rubs his face in a manner that suggests he would, if he could, rub it right off~ as if it might be a temporary mask. Xavier, at last, needs to relinquish the role he has been living and has decided it is time to step out of character, for a short period at least.

In a sleepy trance, he wanders through to the darkroom to begin developing the film, moving automatically with economy of effort. Despite his fatigue, he is intent on discovering the latent images that lay secretly within the film's emulsion, as if a secret can be buried deep. The photographer collects his thoughts, reviewing the required and various procedures in his mind's eye, anticipating what needs to be done and for how long, in order to achieve his goal. Mannikin is predicting how to use time and how best to marshal specific skills in order to be successful. He sets to work, first loading the film in the dark onto a spiral for processing~ the procedure is made more difficult by virtue of his left-handedness. Next, the film is placed in the developing tank. Within twenty minutes, requisite chemical processes are complete and after the briefest of washes, the film is 'squeegeed' and the negatives allowed to harden in the drying cabinet. The red safe-light goes on and at the point where Xavier is ready to begin printing, he decides he is, in fact, too tired to accomplish more, despite the desire to do so. Rather than starting to print the negatives, he lays them out on a light-box and begins to check them manually to see what has been captured. They are held against the light in a bid to bend and reverse the images~ to make them fleetingly positive, as he views them with the aid of a x10 eye magnifier. The negatives are clean, the detail and focus is good. The magic performance from the night before presents itself in crisp black and white. The 'aide memoire' is perfect; his mind reruns the event in his imagination~ reliving the experience. The general views are as he remembers, although where the stunning levitation begins, the negatives become foggy and black~ intense light had bleached the action that was occurring. No such light had been apparent in the room as he watched. Xavier is disappointed. A glow from within the audience had also 'fogged' parts of other images and eliminated detail that might have been caught. He is shocked at these unforeseen impediments that have spoilt the negatives. The light might have been poor, it was true, and Mannikin had not been expecting great pictures; his shutter speeds were, by necessity, slow and his apertures large. The photographer in him is nevertheless confused by the dismal results. Rather than print the negatives himself, he decides to call on the skills of an experienced technician to salvage the disappointing film. Curiously, the photo of the woman at the milonga is fine; it is a good picture, although she is too far away and not discernable as the person remembered. The negatives are placed back into the drying cabinet to finish hardening. The man, feeling dreary, lets out a deeply held breath and shrugs.

Collecting an Ilford HP4 400 ASA film from the refrigerator, Mannikin begins to load the new cassette into the camera; the higher rating suits his need for shots that capture brief moments on the hoof. The ability to document a significant fleeting moment and then, at a later time, reconsider its importance or detail, is indispensible to him. Moving into the studio area he haphazardly flops into an ancient leather sofa, causing it to roll a short distance on its castors into the wall behind.

Xavier lies back~ closes his eyes. Before long, he is napping and soon falls deeply asleep. His body is insistent and demands it be allowed to implement its quotidian routine at last. As the world around him begins a new day, Xavier can do little more than withdraw within himself to create fantastical revelries, compilations of strange images and disturbed, fragmented dreaming. He sees Count Zapik from the night before, dark, deeply mysterious, but translated into some kind of a gatekeeper/ caretaker/ ferryman. The magician is opening a large, ornamental gate assisted by an unfortunately paralysed and disabled young girl; Mannikin wonders if it is the beautiful Nadja, curiously transformed. His imagination quickly turns her into a sphinx and then she reverts to the image of the palsied, trembling girl again. Her broken, bent form beckons, urging him forward, gesticulating, gesturing, giving him a special invitation into some new space, her smile crooked, but genuine… the man enters in and then begins to dream of cawing birds, mewing cats and an impenetrable night with glistening stars and, at its centre, a space that he recognises.

49.

Mannikin later walked back to his apartment through the city's early morning congestion and cacophony, making a stop 'en route' to buy provisions. The poor, sleep-deprived man placed groceries into the robust paper sack from the store; repetition had taught him how best to organise the items. Xavier enjoyed feeling the familiar goods within his grip as he walked. He held the parcel using it as an anchor and solace against the buzzing metropolis that briefly invaded and swept past his physical self and consciousness. Despite his dull, impoverished separation from his immediate surroundings, there remained a satisfaction and detached interest in the new day~ he savoured experiences from a safe and remote distance as the world mysteriously unfolded. Regardless of his pressing fatigue, he recognised, *as always, as was his wont,* that none of this was going to last.

On nearing his destination, Xavier began to leave the stuccoed and classically grand part of the city behind~ *breathing and luxuriating in the gorgeously faded splendour of these districts.* The grey man proceeded through a wide and open arch in the side of a large apartment block only recently completed in the Modernist style. It performed the function of a city wall or perimeter to the adjoining residential estate. In this way, entrance was gained into the contemporary quarter, recently redeveloped and completed after

having been laid bare for years past after heavy bombing during the last war. There was no need for anyone to move into this newly defined space unless they had business in the vicinity, were resident or were perhaps following him. Once through the arch, the late-night insomniac had stopped at a corner to see if a half-discerned, half-glimpsed, shady character, whom he suspected of tailing him, was about to materialise. The shadow did not appear, no head tentatively showed itself around a corner, no one entered into the elite suburban space immediately after him, at least not whilst he stood watching. Mannikin had done this the day before too~ had stood anticipant, gazing at nothing, for longer than made sense, causing his heart to beat faster. He often felt under scrutiny or watched and had learned to assume this was due to his naturally delicate nature, or an attendant part of his frail constitution. No one knew more than he, his tendency, *especially when tired or vulnerable*, to exhibit signs of persecution, causing him to become detached and remote. Mannikin decided not to move on until the second hand of the clock above the inner wall of the minimalist modern archway, had circumnavigated the face. He did not need to do this, but it was a comforter. He watched clocks when he felt anxious.
'Oh dear, these are very bad signs,' he said, monitoring his actions. 'I must make sure I don't give myself away~ it's time to begin working harder again. I must make sure I continue to appear normal.'

The residential district beyond the archway in this newly acclaimed, prestigiously designed and expensive district of Warcapest was stylishly strewn with architectural high-rise buildings of various sizes and heights, the tallest of which, *constructed out of metal and glass,* had picture views looking out across the city. This was the splendidly featured building in which Mannikin lived. The area was full of geometric forms, monochrome surfaces, a plethora of rectangles, simple contained shapes and a distinct lack of clutter or decoration anywhere~ the modern world as envisaged by the designers of the thirties, the Bauhaus dream made International. Xavier loved the severity and cleanliness of the area and its determination to simplify, making life *seem* devoid of passion. Such clarity made it easier to measure one's reactions to the world. The absence of fervour in the visual landscape enabled him to hear his own inner emotion screaming with greater intensity. Somehow this was good. Here, he could feel remote, disconnected, anonymous, displaced, indistinct, ambivalent, lost~ although possibly, followed.

Mannikin approached the main entrance and quickly bundled himself into the beautifully austere and immaculate De Stijl building; his apartment was high on an upper floor. He called for the elevator and waited patiently, watching his tired reflection and the space it occupied in the mirrored doors. A discarded mop leant against a wall in the lobby. He observed the passing time, the elevator numerals lighting up in descending order as the lift moved closer, the second hand navigating the face of his wrist-watch~ although the concierge's wall clock refused to move at all, *no matter how often it was looked at in the mirror.*

When the elevator arrived, the spent nocturnal voyager willingly consented to its invitation, allowing it to swallow him up whole. Mannikin leant his poor crumpled self in a far corner of the rectangular box, whimsically, at an extreme angle, *like the mop*, aware of contradictory sensations and gravitational forces as the extensively mirrored interior began to travel vertically upwards. The man deliberately avoided the never-ending repetition of his reflection that was occurring and reoccurring all around him, preferring instead to close his eyes. Eventually the lift came to a halt and the doors glided open. Mannikin made his exit, looking down~ notwithstanding that other part of him that would ordinarily wish to see and glory in a glimpse of his repeated form, endlessly reflected, ever diminishing, moving away in incremental perspectives as he left the space. The lift doors closed behind him and he turned to proceed~ a well-dressed zombie in black, moving along the corridor the short distance to his flat.

50.

Mannikin pushes and twists the key into the door lock and for good measure, presses the bell to the apartment as he crosses the threshold, *although he knows he is not at home.* Xavier pictures himself, to see how he might be once inside~ he is both desperate and grateful to be back.

The nocturnal reveller remains befuddled and confused. What should have only been a quick nap earlier at the photographic studio had become a deep slumber. He had nodded off. Was he in fact still in the Mannikin building? He closes his eyes briefly in the moment and considers that he has not yet left, perhaps only imagining that he has arrived home. Xavier groans inwardly at the audacity of the intruding thought.
'Please let him tell himself he is home,' he hears an inner voice say.

A studio technician, arriving early for work, had woken him. The fresh lovely, clean-shaven, sweet-smelling man was surprised to discover a limp, dour Mannequin~ inert and unconscious, looking for all the world like some fallen shop dummy, all dressed up, although crumpled, overused and wasted~ shattered indeed.

Since that rude awakening, Xavier had progressively noticed the effects of losing a night's sleep. He felt dull, dreary and irritable. His body had distanced itself from reality and consciousness and was travelling through a fog of his own making. Sound seemed deadened, as though it had passed through cotton wool before arriving in his ears. Little flicks of golden light, like short bursts of lightning, intermittently pushed in at the corners of his eyes. It seemed that their tiny rays were entering into his world from another dimension, violating his present semi-consciousness. His normal resistance to invasion was weak and lowered.

He re-runs the present just to make sure it is real~ ensuring that it is here. *He unlocks the door; for good measure he rings the doorbell to the flat as he passes over the threshold, knowing that he is not at home. He lets himself into his apartment, already imagining himself in the space, re-familiarising himself with who he is likely to find when inside~ his inventory of past experiences flashes by; he is not anticipating any major changes to occur. He is pleased at the prospect of being in a space he can predict.*

He carefully shuts the door, exercising a specific shove, a knack like no other, one that is associated with the workings of the doorway in recognition of the slight catch on the bottom trim and a modicum of resistance in the doorjamb. Pinching on the lower runner causes the upper edge to bow and bend inwards as the door pushes tight against the frame. Sure enough, this is his door~ the signature is unmistakable. Xavier looks into the hall mirror whilst placing the groceries on the small table beneath. The wallpaper behind is a bleached, harlequin design. The watchful mirror sees.

'The only living and enlightened 'knowing' thing in the empty flat,' he murmurs to himself. The person looking back is right-handed. The eyes glint in the reflection; they are on fire, *still.* His hair is flat to his head; the face appears greasy. The thing grimaces horribly or perhaps humorously in the half-light of the hallway, like a vaudeville comedian intent on spoiling the picture, or a clown~ *like 'Joey' Grimaldi.* The eyes are looking hard, intent on seeing the image of the man in the mirror. Xavier makes a move towards it, checking the surface, investigating the dust layer, wondering if the print of a nose once put there was still visible. It was, it is. New dust had not yet accumulated enough to hide the unique impression; not enough time had passed for that. The residue of a sneeze is visible; it glistens in a half-light, a proof that his body is where he thinks it is and has arrived~ survived even. One might easily conclude that he sees the man who suffers with nerves as clearly as others see him, that creature who is, without doubt, anxious. The image in the glass is real; it is he, notwithstanding the reversal or unwitting references to clowns. He sees himself as he imagines himself to be, recognising the absurdity here. He has always been more familiar with how his reflection looks than how he actually appears. This may be, or must it be, the same for everyone~ he ponders the point. He needs to get the jaded tailcoat to the dry-cleaners.

Xavier moves into the lounge, almost losing balance and colliding with the door as he enters, before crashing into the gramophone cabinet. Without apparent thought, performing the actions of a necessary but unconscious habit, he picks up and swings the arm on the record player, placing the stylus with practiced certainty onto the dusty record that lies on the turntable. There is an initial, sweet trumpet fanfare, before the dulcet strains of *Io de' sospiri te ne rimanno tanti* (the beginning of Act 3 of Puccini's *Tosca*) glides out across the room. He speaks out loud to himself.

'Ah! The sound floats like delicate, exotic petals carried on the freshest of gentle breezes.'

He breathes a sigh of relief; his facial muscles relax, the music immediately signals a soothing change in his attitude, as the vast canopy of sky over some mythic Rome materialises~ *from out of nowhere~* in his imagination. The music sits within this unfolding mental landscape as the remote and innocent sound of a distant shepherd boy singing echoes far away. The peal of matins bells within the city walls rings out. Xavier places himself, stands in front of the apartment's large picture window ready to embrace the sky, his arms outstretched to receive it, glancing to the horizon and then into the cityscape, making a mental inventory of landmarks, subtly orientating himself, looking for proof that he is indeed where he thinks he is and that all is as it should be. Mannikin stands motionless for a period of time. His head falls to one side as he listens, a quizzical, questioning look slowly emerging on his face. He looks around, surprised, aware that he can no longer hear the glorious, entrancing stimulus. Without his realising, the record player had turned itself off. When had that happened? Did he put the record on, or only imagine that he had? Retracing his steps to the turntable he checks and then emphatically repeats the manoeuvres required to prime the disc to play. The record begins again, this time he listens very carefully to ensure it continues, no longer simply hearing, but determined now that the sound should not stop. Mannikin stands with his hand held against his chin, the other cups his ear. Is Xavier in danger of no longer hearing the composition he wishes to luxuriate in, due to the dull imposition of having to doubt the integrity of the machine playing it, or even himself? The music at last continues, this time from the following track, *Mario Caravadossi? A voi.* A larger bell is heard; he listens, simultaneously remembering the manner in which the pealing of bells is interspersed with detonating cannon in the earlier finale to Act 1, sung by Scarpia. In listening to one imagined place, he has spring boarded and transported himself into another remembered one, choosing not to acknowledge that what he imagines and sees is at any level fictitious. Xavier is merely skimming the surface of ideas that he desperately needs in this moment in order to find a sanctuary. The poor soul has transported himself to an alternative place from where he can hide, feel safe and be invulnerable. The man moves nearer to the window, next to a low table, automatically~ not thinking.

His hand passes across his chest with intent, taking the Paxette camera from the tailcoat breast pocket, laying the device onto the glass coffee table. Mannikin extracts a Weston light meter from an inner pocket and places this carefully alongside the camera. Both are set down with care, consciously absolving a responsibility by parting himself from the items~ not allowing them to be physically attached to him anymore is a form of release. He removes his shoes, allowing each to fall to the floor, anticipating their dull thud as they land. Other items are taken from pockets and placed on the table~ his wallet, a silk handkerchief, loose change, the watch from his right wrist, a cloak ticket from the previous night's dinner and performance. Only now does he remember that he did indeed have a cloak and had left it at the hotel. The man concentrates, looking away from the ticket and directly at the watch before him, letting out a low groan. The curled ticket, held delicately at his fingertips, escapes his pincer grip and falls. Xavier watches as it travels away from him. It descends, in slow motion~ sinking~ sailing incrementally towards the floor; he is frozen in time, unable to move. Only as it lands on the hardwood surface is he released from the spell and able to retrieve the ticket. Xavier lets out an anxiously held breath and on returning to an upright position, begins to scrutinise the orange, manila ticket. With renewed interest, keen to diminish the previous moment's anxiety, he registers the number~ CZ129. It might be the number of a Zeppelin. Glancing again at his watch, he observes the second hand petrified in the moment, pulsating, quivering as if reluctantly attempting to circumnavigate the face. He stands motionless, perhaps gazing, dormant~ vacant. The recording reaches the part where *E lucevan le stelle* begins. The bel canto tenor's voice swells with epic emotion, tragically bemoaning the beauty of a world he is in fear of losing. Xavier follows the magnificent rising cadence in his mind, attempting to ignore the scratches on the disc's surface. In his mind's eye, he fantasises and conceives the torpedo shape of a huge airship exploding in an expansive, star-filled sky, the intense orange heat and fiery glow eating fiercely into the side of his burning face.

The moment passes and his consciousness returns to the immediacy of his surroundings. Recollecting the task in hand, he continues to empty pockets of items accumulated and acquired incidentally, idiosyncratically, perhaps by misadventure: a small foreign coin dispensed in change from a vending machine, the foil and wrapper from a chocolate bar, a champagne cork, the formal invitation to the previous night's dinner~ it reads, 'Master Xavier Mannikin', a paper serviette embossed with the Hotel de l'Empereur's moustachioed crest, the redundant place setting for 'Nadja~ Star of Mystery', a party streamer, a clipped metro ticket, a toy model of a snow leopard from a cracker, the stone previously thrown into the night, a plastic cocktail stick shaped like a sword, some fluff from the bottom of a pocket, and a small piece of folded paper.

Xavier sets off towards the bedroom with these items, accompanied by the sound of tolling bells and detonating cannons, not from the vinyl record this time~ that has become drowned out and distantly lost to him amidst the overwhelming cacophony of his being. He is unaware that his ears have stopped listening, despite such things continuing to echo within the beat and pulse of his heart. He moves, in stockinged feet, the short distance down the inky, narrow corridor, his steps punctuated and reinforced by the rhythm of his triggering synapses. The wallpaper patterns of the enclosed corridor are lost in shadow but pulsate invisibly to different decorations from within his being. He is a walking rhythm machine, full of exploding shapes and ornaments, many of which only appear to be half-formed and confusing. The man is intent on placing the collected contents of his pockets into the top drawer of a tallboy~ an habitual practice that has resulted in the accumulation of miscellaneous, diverse and apparently useless pieces of ephemera, paper and other tiny objects, all of which are regarded as indispensable. He will check and sift through them at some point in an indeterminable, 'sometime soon' future~ in the hope of discovering whether the initial obsession or fascination to collect his chosen detritus revealed a hidden imperative, compulsion, or pattern of which he was unaware. In this way, he tricked himself into finding out who he was. He often felt that an inner music or voice, like some strange hypnotic incantation, had enchanted him, overwhelming his consciousness, like a drug~ perhaps he is the drug. Xavier has become momentously and irretrievably lost in a brief passing splendour. On arrival in the room, *finding the curtains closed*, he opens the top drawer of the tallboy with his free hand to discover that what he was about to do, he had already done. He looks down at the new items already lying amidst the confusion of many previous pockets' contents. Being so tired is allowing more tricks than usual to be played upon his naturally delicate sensibilities. He looks at the hand, which is suddenly inexplicably empty and wonders if he has been here already or whether he had just placed the objects in the drawer, but could not remember. He was not unused to any of this. These were things that he could accommodate and easily deal with. Such apparent time and spatial anomalies were not unknown to him and sometimes were more frequent than he was prepared to allow other people to know. He closes the drawer and walks back along the corridor...

In the dark interior of that tallboy lay an exquisite collection of items, the flotsam and jetsam of his life's pockets, objects whose original uses have become superfluous, but are retained nonetheless as markers of things they represent. They help label the experiences Xavier has had and assist in making sense of thoughts he cannot define or explain.

This is the man who cultivates and charts an ever-present awareness of 'self' existing in a subjective sea of time, always in transition from what was once the future and was now rapidly becoming the past. Far from being fixed in the present, he feels he floats helplessly backwards and forwards in a space he does not understand.

Before allowing himself to finally give up and give in to sleep, which he needs to do more than anything else, Mannikin instigates a manic and pressing need to seek out a large book from amongst others stored vertically on the floor in the corner of his main apartment room. With careless effort, a hefty tome is retrieved, causing the stack of which it is part to crash haphazardly across the floor. Paying little attention to the library that lays strewn, he begins to check the index of the book in his hands, searching specifically for methods describing theatrical stage levitations in a volume on the tricks and methods employed by magicians. Unfortunately, nothing the book contains comes close to explaining the phenomenon seen the night before. He had found himself totally believing in the uncanny levitation of a magician's assistant some three metres in the air. The effect worried him, but strangely also provided comfort, the proof needed to help explain the curious things he too experienced. The kind of anomalies Xavier saw every day within his own sense of reality were there, on show for all to see. He reflects back, thinking deeply about the recent event and the levitation itself~ annoyed that he had not seen or remembered more. If only the photographs had been better, they might have revealed something of the true nature of the effect~ perhaps, in truth, they had! The thought strikes him acutely. The telephone begins to ring. A siren in the street joins in and car doors slam one after another, echoing with the intensity of a dull detonation. He hears all of it. The siren in the street below subsides and the sound slowly fades away. Only the frantic telephone continues to ring, but Xavier makes no attempt to answer. Indeed he looks away. There is no need for anyone to know where he is.

With the book in hand, wedged open between his fingers, he distractedly seats himself and sinks back into a leather swivel chair in front of the expansive window, casually observing the panoramic view out across the city~ hardly conscious, abstractly taking in the rooftops and spires, the ancient sites and the modern constructions, becoming increasingly lost in ambiguous thought. A Zeppelin CZ129 sails into view across the front of his window, filling the vista. His mind flinches at the possibility of it exploding in his fantastical imagination as before, but it is soon gone~ *perhaps before it even had a chance to pass.* The phone rings again, but louder by virtue of its increased proximity; he ignores it still and continues to not answer. Mannikin conjectures that the first time it rang might be repeating itself in his memory. He wonders why the book remains in his hand. In his peripheral vision, he sees a glass vase of lilies that had been thrown out a week earlier. They were weeks old then and were faded and had long dropped their petals. He looks again, recognising how wrong his last memory had been. The fresh blooms that greet him are abundant in their splendour. How could this have happened? Maybe his fiancée had been in and changed them. He is momentarily confused, but quickly moves on. It did not matter that he failed to fully recognise or understand everything he saw. His memories of events were often independent of time, but not without logic. Xavier knew, was aware of, and had come to accept the permutations he had to accommodate and compensate for. He also recognised that he was outside the 'normal' compass of others around him, an enigma, as far as he could tell.

When, eventually, Mannikin managed to lure himself into his bedroom to sleep at last, after having stepped out of his clothes, *which lay strewn on the floor,* he could do little more than throw himself towards the bed in a hapless heap. In the act of landing, he found himself already unconscious, lying without moving, a clock ticking somewhere remotely beyond him. The telephone rang a third time. The room and the worlds he had passed through flip-flopped in his imagination, reversing him as they would if viewed through a mirror and then back again. Xavier Mannikin knew both versions unequivocally.

For every living creature time is fixed, so it seems. Commonly, all sentient beings living within its sway are dragged and carried along by its directional tide over a constantly moving ocean. Time metes out the waves, in which existence can occur, forever attempting to keep moments apart from the next in a firm and consistent manner. For every crest there is a trough. Xavier has the misfortune to find his exposure to time to be curious, irrational and ruthless, as though he were experiencing it within a tempestuous and unpredictable storm~ one which is able to alter time's route and speed at will. By necessity, he has learned to see and manage idiosyncratic anomalies. It is what he has been forced to do as part of living. It has become the constantly annoying itch that he must keep scratching. He is simultaneously aware of how time changes for others, despite such discrepancies generally going unnoticed by them. He is the true aficionado of how time can be erratic and contrary to expectation. For Xavier, the tempo of time is experienced differently. Exceptions to the rule are 'de rigueur'. His 'time' is like getting ketchup out of the sauce bottle~ there is no way of knowing the amount he will get next, at least not for sure. It moves in space and at a pace outside of him, outside of his control and for him alone, in unquantifiable ways. He cannot assume he will be consistently subjected to proper time~ he has experience of it stopping abruptly or missing a beat, or taking him to a new place without his realising, or slowing to allow him to see the world in miniscule detail, as though he were a high-speed camera able to view an exotic humming bird in flight, every moment caught in immaculate brilliance for his gaze only. Yet, when he least expects, absent-mindedly, he misses so much of it.

This dysfunctional aberration can cause him to appear remote, solemn and solitary. Establishing relationships, finding friends becomes complex, almost impossible. His functionality is, on too many occasions, made to appear disturbed; his behaviours can seem indecipherable to others and sometimes, *when his consciousness cannot keep up with unfolding events around him*, to himself also. He is unable to see himself properly or define his identity conclusively within the context of time, or even in relationship to others, whose lives move so differently and conventionally compared to his own. If he cannot fit in or find ways in which to equate with others, how can he properly know who he is, or ever know where he belongs? How can a definition for himself of his perceived place in the scheme of things be made? He cannot accurately regulate the effect his presence is having on a moment or how he can be seen within it. In order to make sense of the confusion and the angst caused by not knowing who he is, the poor man must compensate~ hence his incessant need to remain conscious to every passing moment, wherever possible, to constantly monitor and check for the perceived aberrations and rents in the fabric of time, only able to guess that they exist for him alone by seeing that they do not affect the consciousness of others in the same way. Such monitoring routinely uses up his social functionality, causes others to infer he suffers from an uncommon paranoia or neurosis. Frequently, he sits and stares at the world, testing it, watching it and quantifying each moment. He appears somewhat aloof, but not necessarily more so than many 'odd' others who, in their turn, have their own reasons.

How specifically is it for him? Unlike any lazy, damaged or imperfect brain which does not grieve for information it does not know or is unaware of missing, or has, without realising, lost, he has a sense of remorse and angst that fills every moment of his living existence. Xavier often passes time in contemplation~ independently, in solitude, engaging in reflection~ attempting to endlessly appease or make light of the confusion within his spirit and in his soul. In consequence, he has a propensity to hide in the shadows of his secret places, away from the sun, looking out into the light, communing within the quiet of an empty room, lost in still moments, trapped within the route of the strange line he follows that buzzes and pulsates independently of expectation, and with a curious pattern of which he is not familiar.

His sleep intensifies. He is falling in slow motion into a deep, grey pit, ever floating downward. Some indescribable, invisible wind is rising with the precise intensity needed to break his fall and control his meticulous descent. Xavier's sleep is soft and welcoming; it beckons him to return to a place where his comfort is assured.

Could it be the padded wall of a soft womb where sound is beautifully muted? Does he distantly feel warm juices delicately enriching his skin, as they invisibly reach out to seek and touch his soul with tendrils that caress? They explore his intuitions and dreaming notions, reliving with him his recent past actions. He reveals everything to them, of how his time during the previous night had passed whilst he travelled, enthralled, towards morning. Here it becomes increasingly possible to enter more of his world... it dawns and will increasingly transpire, beyond the shadow of a doubt, that he is a man outside of his own time.

51.

He is too deeply asleep to be woken by the sound of Alyesha Oezza letting herself into his flat. She has a duplicate key by virtue of being his fiancée. She calls out… not expecting an answer.

Beautiful, petite and well groomed, she moves through the flat with deliciously studied, self-conscious ease. Exquisitely delicate, feminine, curvaceous, full bosomed, her movements are cute and full of irresistible romance. She is in her prime. She looks to find signs of her boy, her Mannikin, to establish if he might be in residence or whether he had recently been here~ her eyes are wide with the expectation of what they might discover. She comes across the dust-matted stylus circumnavigating the record; the turntable continuing its rotation, as a little crackle and persistently audible click reveals an inability to turn itself off. A stack of books lay strewn across the oak wood floor. In the kitchen, steam rises from the kettle. Evidence establishes the man's recent occupancy. In silence, she gently, carefully walks through the apartment as far as the bedroom in search of the object of her desire, wondering why he is always so difficult to pin down. Why could she never predict what time he might be anywhere?

She discovers her lost hero sleeping~ picks up the clothes of a fallen warrior and folds them neatly over the chair. Without expression she retraces her steps, imagining herself waiting for him for as long as is necessary, in the main room. She decides to go to the bathroom with her handbag to refresh her face and make-up in the mirror. Carefully rearranging her exquisite underwear, she beautifies herself. Alyesha Oezza cups her full breasts and tweaks her nipples through her blouse as she pretties herself in preparation for time in Mannikin's company.

In a similar but different way, the drawers of Mannikin's tallboy, just next door, have pert protuberances too, proud standing forms, each coincidentally about as far apart as Ayesha's tweaked and erect nipples. Each pair repeats down the front of the furniture to the floor, like milky teats on a muddied sow's underbelly. The quiet, inert furniture stands in the gloom, like some strange alien life, unaware of the purpose it houses or the existence to which it remains unknowing.

After her beautifying, Aylesha Oezza returns to the living room to lie in wait for her cavalier. She sits on the white, soft sofa, cat-like and gorgeous, idly looking out of the window across the grey expanse of what is Warcapest, lost in empty-headed thought.... The day had arrived; she could see it before her with the heat slowly rising. She had thought she might look for an electric fan in the apartment, but quickly gave up the idea, deciding instead to carefully paint her nails in the world's brightest red. She wondered if he would ever wake in time to see her before she had to leave to be at the hairdresser. She felt moist and desperate.

★ ★ ☆ ★

The summer in a city like Warcapest is always a transient affair. It arrives~ and from the very first moment, as soon as the fragrance of the new season ripens, everyone knows it needs to be adored and lived with a passion, recognising that too soon it will be gone. Summers are fleeting. Furthermore, they bubble over too easily into an excess of sultry heat and summer storms, of balmy nights where sleep becomes broken and perspiration and wakefulness turn to melancholia of the soul, tearful nostalgia or morbid anxiety. The ambition of the spirit within every living thing, is to open itself to all of 'it' and be part of 'everything', to live everywhere within these moments. The noises in the city are interesting; they punctuate and illuminate activities that most often cannot be seen. Sounds are carried in strange ways on the air. The heat or implication of the season seems to make the vibrations travel further, farther than they ought or should, enabling sound to become confused as it overlaps and is jumbled alongside other sounds. The dissonance and disparate medley of conflicting wavelengths rises amongst the collective consciousness. It might seem easier to hear, but perception is made chaotic by everything going on at the same time, as ever more presents itself to be experienced. There is an over-abundance of human plenty to assimilate. Passions, desires, thoughts, ideas, cascade indiscriminately across one another in tumult. The impossibility of being aware of all this or understanding any of it, produces a sense of benign hopelessness, one that is as debilitating as heatstroke or summer lethargy itself.

The disparate, nonsensical nature within everything makes it impossible to find a rationale or definition for whatever it is that is in the midst of all. There is no human attempt that has ever yet explained any of it. Such a cause was lost so far back as to no longer be remembered, leaving the flow of humanity to follow its own reasoning, the most naturally occurring patterns prevailing beyond, and without the need for, conscious thought. Questions about the nature of existence are easily avoided. Live life, love life, embrace the sadness of passion and the joys of despair~ is there a need anywhere for more? Living is hard enough without having to accommodate the complexity of a non-apparent madness.

52.

The noise and hubbub of the city extant can be heard beyond an unexpected bank of moving, hissing fog, voluminously releasing itself onto the sidewalk. It obscures the view from the pedestrian pathway on this side of the road, alarming all the traffic that travels towards it. The rich cacophony of beeping horns, sound of brakes and shouting cabbies, demanding that timid drivers just drive through and not hold up the flow, is creating consternation. Visibility has been severely curtailed. A compressed steam outlet has burst and discharges pent up and pressurised gas from overworked and compromised machinery underground~ deep within the metro system. The billowing fog escapes from a street level conduit and fills the morning air. Through the cloak of pure white brilliance, made incandescent in the fresh, sun-filled light, a pale silhouette begins to appear and materialises, becoming increasingly prominent and large as it walks through the blanket of cloud. Shadows dance in profusion and confusion in the water particles, distorting the shape of the figure as it moves, marionette-like through the thick, dense mist. The figure begins to clarify and define itself. And soon Mannikin appears, having traversed a familiar space in very unfamiliar circumstances, this being one of his prime routes to work. He has never known these conditions before, and is interested and fascinated.

The man is again in/on the streets of Warcapest, a traveller fabricating a unique pattern, making an imprint over/across the city. His transient presence is exotic, quickly turning invisible *as he passes* and is a type of unseen mark making. The line he constructs forms itself inconspicuously, imperceptibly, imaginatively in a variety of ways~ like the single strand of a complex web, stranger than any a spider might weave. Mannikin explores and expands his knowledge and perceptions of the daily journey as he travels; he has choices, which he examines and reconnoitres. Recently, he has been contemplating the manner in which each invisible route/mark/line across Warcapest might be seen as map making, a kind of cartography. He imagines himself to be the filament or thread and wonders how best to view his presence drawn over the beautiful city. Perhaps it should be described in sound, a long, convoluted, stretched utterance punctuated by the breaths of other passing travellers. Alternatively, might it be a dance made audible by the clatter of bipedal motion and shoes on pavements, or is it simply a long sentence that travels with curious punctuation as it meanders throughout the city~ saying whatever it can, in order to be in tune with the circumstances it meets? It draws itself, graffiti-like, across the face and body of Warcapest~ his is one of many lines criss-crossing the contours of the city, like temporary pressure marks on a skin that has been wearing rubber bands or tight clothes, or more permanently like tattoos on a circus performer. What is the effect of so many lines/routes being drawn at the same time, so many diverse marks materialising simultaneously across the giant body of the metropolis? What is the best way to view these things and what might they mean, in ways not previously considered? The city, like Gulliver, is tied down with strings drawn tightly across it, over it and through its clothing by harmless Lilliputians.

He casts a glance at his watch as he walks, his mind roaming in its own sweet mercurial way. How many watches had he owned during his lifetime? It was hard to recall. A watch might be owned, but time never could be. He had owned more watches than most people; his invariably kept breaking or stopping, if only to reinforce the notion that time was not designed for him. Perhaps there was a time before time. Perhaps he had things in common with all the people who had lived before the concept of time was invented? He was perhaps before his time. How long ago would that have been? Has there, in truth, ever been such a thing as a time before time? He had no concepts that might allow him to stretch reality that far. His father taught him to tell the time and understand the clock face; indeed it was he who had bought his seven-year-old son a watch from the best jeweller in Warcapest. That remembered day, walking through the city with his father, was momentous~ seminal. The watch on his wrist was a right of passage into a grown-up world. Unfortunately, not one he might easily take advantage of. He was aware of peculiarities and anomalies that beset his shifting sense of time and reality even then, but it was not until he began to wear a watch for himself that he was able to quantify, record and build an understanding of the precise ways that time appeared to pass for him. He remembers those first experiences, the second hand attempting to sweep along its ordained route, following the circumference of the face~ its progression oddly jagged and uneven~ the hands stopping or dropping out of existence~ returning to parts they had missed~ or replaying the same moment, as if stuck, causing the world around him to halt~ before slipping back into the present.

As he walks, a reflection in a shop window comes towards him, causing momentary confusion.
'My father is walking alone, without little Xavier. I had not finished remembering.'
The man he sees is shy and somewhat vulnerable. He stops, looking back at himself, waiting for an opportunity to become reacquainted with his current incarnation of self.

In due course, Mannikin sits down on a bench to catch his breath and, more specifically, to take a photograph of a municipal worker cleaning an empty fountain in the park against the morning light. A flight of birds passes as the shutter closes. Unwittingly, he has fallen asleep, become light-headed~ temporarily beyond the scope of the normal and prevailing gravity in these parts~ and momentarily escaped the present. He may not remember having fallen asleep when he wakes. A man in an outdoor kiosk, selling second-hand books and assorted literature, looks up from arranging his stall to recognise him.

'Ah the man who passes this way every weekday,' he thinks. 'What is he up to now? That man is so eccentric. He stands out. He is on my list of characters to watch, most definitely. Not the top of the list, but not far off perhaps. He visits the kiosk to browse and buys on occasion too. Friendly and polite, and tips the change from his purchases, even when handing over large notes~ he knows how to charm a poor street seller. His taste is for photography and artists, as I recall. It was him that bought the expensive Franz Felix monograph. If he were a character in one of my books here, who would he be?'

The street seller looks over the stall, perusing the covers, the authors, admiring his selection of titles, scanning for the section in which to place the man he is thinking of.

'I just can't put my finger on it. Is that man anxious? If so what about? Is he depressed, sad, lonely or unhappy? His sensibilities are different, in some way hard to define. Does he suffer with his nerves? Maybe he has had a nervous breakdown, although his general demeanour does not seem weakened in that way. He seems to suffer, but perhaps no more than a normal or clever man might in a foreign country. Although his strange detachment, where it is perceived, might lead someone to assume he is suffering bereavement perhaps, or has he been traumatised? Is he fatigued by life or simply 'Ferme pour deuil', *closed for mourning*. There may be some form of neurasthenia here, some nervous debility, but in spite of his actions there is no real substantive evidence to prove any of this. He might be hypersensitive and thin-skinned though, perhaps yearning for a past that had vanished for him or a form of 'anomie,' caused by a perception that there had been a disappointing break down in societal codes, or a perceived lack of purpose in a world only just discovered to be strange, with rules that seem hostile or arbitrary. Maybe this is getting closer to it; he is suffering from a sense of intolerable world sorrow, 'Weltschmerz'~ *the most romantic sounding form of melancholia to be found in the German language. A world-pain or world-weariness, describing the sort of feeling experienced by a person who recognises that physical reality can never satiate the demands of the mind.* There may be a morbid dryness in his soul. Is it a nostalgia for missed opportunities or lost chances that may have changed futures~ an irrational Proustian longing for some imagined mythic past? Is this a patriot's yearning for the country of his childhood? Do we distinguish here a deep-seated, all-embracing sadness of the psyche or the soul, or both, if they are indeed different at all?'

53.

The elegant and formally decorated Mannikin building is breathtakingly white in daylight. Light bounces off its smooth, bright exterior; it might be a blank piece of paper in need of an English watercolourist to add glory to its glowing, translucent surface or else the discriminating scribbling hand of a creative writer. It stands, majestically regal, next to other buildings in its vicinity, their natural stone facades grey and dirty by comparison, dulled through long exposure to the city elements. The gleaming building is the famous house of playing cards. The front façade is edged with gold ornamentation, using symbols to represent the familiar suits in the style of the Viennese Jugendstil~ each appropriately depicted in matt-black paint or glazed, ceramic red. The doorway is lined with caryatids supporting the epic and large portico, each one representing their own chosen suit. They are each the sister of the lady represented on the Ace of Spades. They hold their symbol in one hand and in turn, respectively, display a sword, scales, a mask and a bright star with a tail suggestive of a meteor, in the other.

Mannikin arrives at the front entrance after his morning walk through Warcapest and its parks, and hurries up the short flight of steps to enter through the doorway, anticipating that he is late or possibly early for something~ *as ever.* He turns briefly~ to see whether he might have been followed~ but there is no evidence of a tail~ or a line following his line~ or anyone else who is reading his movements.

The grey, oaken, striated doors are opened by saluting and formally suited attendants dressed in 'Mannikin Ruby', the familiar colour associated with the firm. Their commissionaires' caps are emblazoned with charming enamelled badges. Mannikin enters the building and begins to move decisively along corridors, stretching his legs out as he travels over parquet floors, past doorways, through the reception areas. The details of his passage are a blur as he walks. The fresh-faced executive appears detached, as though collecting thoughts for the day, perhaps preparing his head for work, or finding ways to be focused and single-minded for those events that business minded people might anticipate. The prime event of the morning is to be a board meeting, due to convene at 11am. Mannikin moves through the building with intent, passing the typing pool, stopping briefly to collect papers from a typist's desk. He then proceeds onward, pushing through the building, finally arriving at the main stairway, a wide, white, marble edifice, ornamentally edged with gilded ironwork made up of playing card motifs. The banister of polished walnut curls opulently and winds winsomely as it spirals upward. Mannikin speeds up the stairway, taking the steps three at a time and four for the odd set at the top of the flight. His office is on this floor. The smartly suited young gentleman walks a short distance before entering the anteroom to his suite. The day secretary, caught off guard, immediately stands, proving herself to be unusually diminutive as she formally greets her boss. She is new; he does not recognise her and so takes particular note of the nameplate on the desk. She informs him that the hotel has returned his cloak, which has been delivered to his father's house. Xavier continues to walk past as she conveys the information, causing her to have to turn her head at speed, through a wide panorama, whilst addressing the man. Mannikin acknowledges her information distractedly and briefly as he moves quickly into his office.

Once inside, Xavier stands in the alcove behind the closed door for a moment, suddenly smaller, swaying very slightly, as though on the deck of a ship. At last, he falteringly moves into the room. There is a tangible release of tension. The young man orientates himself, surveying the office to ensure it remains as it was, before moving to the window where, by chance, he glimpses a faint sunlit reflection of himself. He is intent on ensuring that the exterior view lines up with the interior one remembered in his imagination. Mannikin is surprised to discover that the windowsill is sodden. Leaflets, featuring emblematic depictions of raindrops, collected a week earlier, have become soaked. The hardwood sill is water-stained and the grain has risen. Puzzled, his gaze moves upward to find where the flood had gained entry. The lintel above the window is wet, having leaked during the recent and unusual bout of inclement weather; there are drips hanging on the underside of the grey stone. He is immediately anxious that the office should have been breached in this way. Mannikin glances towards his desk, newly concerned for the safety of papers that lie there. He scrutinises the surface for water splashes and damage. His hand involuntarily dips into his pocket and removes the camera, which he makes ready to use, attaching a flash unit taken from the top drawer of his desk. There is an overwhelming impulse to record what he sees. Mannikin focuses the viewfinder on the window's edge and presses the button. Simultaneously, the flash jumps into life~ radiating light, brightening the room with its intense magnesium glow. The bulb sizzles and crackles in the air. The brilliance replays for much longer in Xavier's mind than it does in reality. *As the aperture closes, so a moment becomes fixed and frozen.* He begins to move around the office, camera in hand, taking more photographs, looking closely at details, examining aspects of the space with forensic precision, intent on finding other minutiae that might describe or indicate subtle changes within the fabric of time that he has missed. He is unnerved, his train of thought overwhelmed by an immediate sense of uncertainty, wondering if the world around him now means something different, apprehensive about how these new circumstances might inflict themselves on his consciousness or spoil his current appraisal of reality. What is he looking for~ maybe an infestation of spiders or wood lice, or mice, something of that sort? Possibly more. Perhaps a little invisible tree has begun to grow in the carpet, bearing golden fruits on its miniature boughs. Or could there be curious, unknowable creatures that might infect, strange moths that might bite, or glowing radioactive worms from some previously unknown subterranean cellar? Is there something lurking at the foot of that bookcase? Or has some unwelcome alien brought in strange dirt on footwear? Maybe an unknown person has trespassed in his space and dropped something awful! He checks the walls for cracks never noticed before, looks to see if light in the room has changed or begun to shine in a new way, or maybe paint on the walls has suddenly darkened with age. Are the clouds moving towards the wind that is racing away from them? There might be something he needs to see in order to understand. He briefly remembers that he has placed something, which is not his, in a secret compartment at the back of his desk, a thing that needs to remain hidden from all others and which he is loath to acknowledge, for a reason he cannot explain.

Unusually, and contrary to common practice and tradition, Master Mannikin had turned his desk and chair to face the window, allowing for views of what lies beyond. He can see the gardens at the rear of the building and much further to assorted, municipal buildings, church spires and a monumental tower. Here, Xavier spends time at his desk secretly daydreaming into the view. The most immediate topography however, is right in front of him, being the surface of the large desk; gilt-edged, worn, distressed, ink-stained, with cracked grey leather~ water marks forming the latest addition to its patina. He knows the surface like the back of his hand. The central area of the desk is generally clear of objects, although at present it contains a few papers. On the left hand side are two venerable electric appliances, a brown Bakelite telephone and an intercom to his secretary. On the other side stands a meticulously placed water jug, with an inverted drinking glass serving as a stopper; it casts an abstract shadow and area of changing, magnified light on to the desk, the diurnal permutations of which Xavier is expert.

The central area of the room behind contains a low, Formica coffee table featuring a glass 'Senior Service' ashtray. Four low-back, wing chairs are arranged around the table for informal meetings and conferences. Mannikin turns his chair around to face the centre of the room to conduct or take part in discussions. A bookcase stands on the wall behind, adjacent to the short corridor leading back into the secretary's office. The bookcase houses box files to a height of two metres, above which a stuffed parrot, protected within a dusty, cylindrical glass dome is centrally placed. The walls to either side display paintings by Franz von Stuck (1863-1928) hung centrally, 'Innocence' splendidly depicted on one and a lavishly gilt-framed 'Sphinx' on the other.

Mannikin detaches the flash from the camera and returns it to his desk drawer. He rewinds the film and removes the cassette before loading a new one. The camera is placed into his pocket. He flicks a switch on the intercom.

'Excuse me, Ms. Schreker could you come in please.'
'Yes certainly, Master Mannikin. Mr. Towers is just here to see you.'

'That's fine. Please escort him in.'

Harry Towers, the CEO of the Mannikin Playing Card Co. walks in. He makes a smile at nothing in particular, whilst flattening his unruly hairstyle. The petite secretary follows the large man. Mannikin steps forward, hand extended.

'Harry, good to see you. Come in, take a seat.'

Mannikin turns to the secretary and passes her the film, imploring that it be processed in the usual way, whilst also requesting a meeting with the senior photographic technician, for later that morning. The woman makes notes on her notepad, curtsies with studied precision and exits. Harry remains standing and signals, by touching the face of his watch that this is to be a quick visit.

'Xavier! Things are fine for you, I trust?' He appears to be addressing the cuff of his shirt as he speaks. 'I just wanted to catch you before the meeting this morning. Is there anything to think through before we meet the board?'

Mannikin shakes his head and then, on impulse, continues.

'No, although we should declare the arrangements for Count Zapik to assist in our marketing~ if we haven't already shared that news.'

He looks closely at Harry to see if this had already been done. Harry responds by suggesting the time is right and that it is on the agenda, should Mannikin care to look.

'Also~ and this is important to me Harry, I would like to oversee the liquidation of the old factory premises, including the 'moth balling' and stripping of the remaining assets.'

Harry moves forward to see what it is that Mannikin might possibly find interesting in his view from the office window.

'Yes, that's fine. I remember, as we discussed last week. That's no problem I'm sure.'
He responds in a perfunctory manner, turning again to face Mannikin. The intercom buzzer sounds.
'Master Mannikin, your fiancée is here to see you.'
'Thank you, Ms. Schreker.'
Harry Towers is already making to leave, sliding sideways along the wall towards the door.
'Thank you, can you send her in please.'
On his way out, Harry meets the young beauty and with an air of supine gallantry, kisses her hand. His parting wobbles a little.

Once alone, the lovers embrace and enjoy a moment's intimacy before separating to seat themselves opposite one another. There is an air of expectant pensiveness.
'Darling Xavier, how are you? I have missed you. You are so elusive. I begin to think you tire of me~ we have nothing planned. Why is there nothing in our diary?' She looks at him intensely.
'How could I tire of you? Not at all, my little minx. I simply have work to do and things to organise. That is all. We will go out soon, I promise. We have invitations to the Franz Felix von Eissenstrom exhibition of paintings.'
Alyesha pouts petulantly with protruding doe eyes.
'Oh him! That Franz Felix man; he is such a bohemian! His work is too depressing for me~ he is a madman for sure! And can we please <u>not</u> go to the opera either? Do not make me go, darling. We do not want to do that, do we? Say we don't have to! You know I do not

like opera. You will never make me like it~ it is so old fashioned. The singers have big mouths, they sweat and they are fat and ugly. What do you see in it? Why do we never go to parties? You are not so much older than me, you know.'

Mannikin slowly raises himself out of the chair; he stands, filling his lungs and arching his back as if to achieve his full height before letting out a long breath~ determined to calm himself and buy time before responding.

'I should like to go to the exhibition at least. Felix's work interests me, and we can do dinner afterwards, at any restaurant of your choice.'

'Oh how lovely, thank you darling. You know Café Momus is my favourite, despite it being so close to the opera, or Ritzzio's even; that little headwaiter is such a flatterer. I knew it~ you do care for me.'

The ridiculousness of the situation causes a smile to pass over Mannikin's face. Alyesha is such a poppet and so much the naïve, self-centred, socially unaware debutante.

'It's settled then my dear~ we have a plan. What are you doing today?'

'Do not worry, Saviour darling, I cannot stay and I know you have a busy day. I must go and leave you to your grown-up things. Daddy is going to invite you to dinner on Friday; he is hoping to catch you at the meeting. Might we catch up this evening?'

'Not tonight, but we will soon, dear Alyesha. I need to stay late~ I feel sure.'

'My poor darling, you do work so hard and you neglect me too. I need more of you. You must come on Friday then~ to Daddy's dinner~ I need more dreamtime! I want you to play with me as you do.' She smiles knowingly at him. 'You are so handsome, gorgeous and virile. Today, I am going riding out at the stables near the summer palace with Sasha. I still hope that one day I might teach you to ride.'

'That would be nice dearest 'Bon-bon.''

She looks at him askance; he had never called her that before~ it had struck him as an appropriate term of affection for her.

'I'm unlikely to have any prowess at horse riding, unfortunately. However, my love, you must let me get on. I'll phone with details of how we might best meet this week.'

'Yes please, darling. I love you so~ I will do anything to be with you, even go to see that beastly man with his frock coats.'

'That's settled then.'

Mannikin escorts Alyesha to the door. He gives her a peck on the cheek. In return, she presses her high ripe breasts onto him and embraces him hard with seductive passion, her hand travelling into his jacket to squeeze his pectoral and armpit.

The morning moves on, steadily progressing towards 11am. Whilst waiting, Mannikin takes the opportunity to travel and wander the building. He saunters to and fro, between offices and areas, visiting colleagues and departments, catching up on a number of issues, during the course of which he strays into the typing pool. A feminine buzz travels across the space like a fever. Heads, of a sudden, point in his direction, like antennae alerted to a new presence; the change in atmosphere is palpable. Mannikin refocuses his attentions in order to survive the primal scrutiny, allowing the clocks in the room to capture his attention, providing a safe and impartial haven for his gaze for as long as he dare, and thereafter deliberates the high, painted friezes on the walls, intent on finding ways to avoid the penetrating gaze of others. These rapturous, inquisitive young women, aware of his bachelor status and potential availability, vie to see and hope to be seen. So many 'cabaceos' enacted simultaneously, every one a potential invitation to dance. He feels the need to look past or through all of them. Mannikin is causing a quiet sensation and is a notable distraction from the normal and otherwise laborious/repetitive routines enacted in the typing pool. Realising his mistake, he determines to move through the room as quickly as possible. His brief appearance will have provided a highlight for these female employees, something to talk and gawp about during the coffee break. The young man looks past the glare of those who wish to see or be seen and finally, in order to gain control over the situation, allows his eyes to settle on workers who are safely busy, or immune to his presence. There is so much hidden, secretive desire and teeming sex trapped, captured and contained within the large room. A smell comes into his nostrils, evoking a memory. It is damp, enticing and sweet, like bloodied meat. So many nocturnal, frustrated, feminine fantasies surround him, all restricted and curtailed in these moments by dull office protocol and institutionalised conformity. Many barely contain themselves as they sit, transfixed, seething and anxious to smile or shine, should the least opportunity arise.

Xavier finds himself disturbed by the intensity of the overpowering and subterranean desire lurking beneath the surface of the feminine psyche, like some desperate screaming beast seeking a way to vent itself ~ to give expression to its innermost needs.

Mannikin finally centres himself and dares to look around. Stories he had heard from Harry come to mind~ he wonders if certain infamous viragos are still in the employ of the company. His eye alights on some of the young typists, engaging young women with glowing complexions and eyes with black centres... but he quickly averts his gaze, looking without focus towards the far end of the room, where his attention becomes fixated on an institutionalised tea lady in bland uniform, trundling a trolley and distributing refreshments.

Mannikin arrives at the design department for the meeting with the photographic technician, an elderly and knowledgeable acquaintance who has known him since boyhood; he is a distinguished man wearing a blue, velvet pillbox hat and a broad, grey moustache. The men check and discuss the recent negatives and decide how they might best be printed. Next, Mannikin passes time, *drinking coffee*, with the Head of Design~ an avuncular man, never known to be without a pipe in his mouth. They discuss ideas for ways to use Count Zapik to market their products. A little later, Mannikin drops in on a dour, double-breasted, pinstriped executive, to request legal advice on company procedures. In their ensuing conversation, it transpires that both men had papers spoilt by water entering the building during the recent, uncommonly torrential rainstorms. They decide to mention this during the course of the meeting as 'Any Other Business'.

Mannikin creates an opportunity to talk with the generous and oversized Harry for the second time that morning, by visiting him in his large and ample office. Harry offers Mannikin a glass of scotch, which he accepts to avoid the older man drinking alone. They further clarify their approach to various items on the board meeting agenda and share thoughts and information on a number of issues:

~ There appear to be a few teething problems at the new factory.

~Mannikin discovers that the building's design had been nominated to appear in an architectural magazine.

~The success of the previous week's conference and dinner is discussed, including Zapik's magic which, they agree, had made a superb contribution.

~Harry informs Mannikin that the Count's agent, a Mr Dolonsky, had met with him to discuss contracts and that they had talked since on the phone. Harry details the confirmation document and contract details that Zapik had agreed, including the terms on which he was prepared to become an ambassador for Mannikin products. Contracts were being prepared for final discussion and eventual signing between both parties, but were unlikely to be ready for the meeting that day. Leopold had been very generous in his suggested remuneration for the magician.

~Harry informs Mannikin that Dolonsky had left complimentary tickets to Zapik's performance at the opulent and elite Villa Apollinaire.

~Dolonsky had also left a short story, written by Zapik, specifically for Mannikin. The younger man acknowledged receipt of this essay via the firm's internal mail the previous day.

~Mannikin explains the design department's initial reactions to the news about Zapik's involvement in the new marketing strategies. They were looking forward to organising a photo shoot for publicity purposes.

~Finally, the men agree a strategic plan for the sale or redevelopment of the old factory land. Mannikin again presses home his interest and wish for support to take on the responsibility. The old factory had been closed for a couple of years and lay dormant; it was sealed off from the outside world by high perimeter fences. Although derelict and mothballed, the factory continued to be supervised and maintained by its loyal remaining site employee, the caretaker, Mr Ryman Kilmit. He was afforded free residence in the main gatehouse as part of his remuneration. Mannikin has arranged for Kilmit to be in attendance and contribute to the meeting~ he would wait outside until the agenda item for discussion arrived.

During their conversation, Mannikin and Harry Towers collude to ensure the meeting confirms their ambitions, whilst avoiding conflict with other board members.

The meeting is due to convene at the allotted hour in the wood-panelled boardroom. Members arrive early to partake of coffee and pastries, as is customary, brought in by a tea lady dressed in a white uniform and concertinaed paper hat, sporting the ruddy Mannikin crest. There are approximately twenty attendees in all; they talk in small huddles or quietly circulate. Leopold Mannikin is the last to arrive and immediately takes up a seat at the head of the large table, a procedural marker that indicates to others that they should move to their own positions. Mannikin is to sit next to Leopold on the left and Harry Towers to the right. Other immediate members at the top end of the table include family, executives, and then further down, the department heads, followed by managers and lastly factory foremen, whose particular compliance with the formal dress code for the occasion leaves them looking awkward~ their hair unnaturally shiny and flattened with scented hair oil.

The meeting is brought to order by Mr. Towers sounding a desk bell. Quite independently and coincidentally, a cacophonous clatter of crockery is heard in the corridor; the unfortunate tea lady, whilst wheeling her trolley, has inadvertently collided with the apprentice post boy, who had not been looking where he was going. If the delegates within the room did but know it, pastries and cigars lay ignominiously strewn over the linoleum floor.

The secretary for the meeting records the time, before beginning a polite, but heady display of shorthand activity; she gazes around the room, taking note of attendees. Harry launches into the proceedings. Attention is brought to the agenda. He introduces each item in turn and proceeds to orchestrate the members of the board, inviting delegates to take part, speak, or update the group on unfolding events and items of interest. Points are queried when there is a need and the floor is open to contributions from all members, should they wish to partake. The ensuing discussions are smooth and uncontroversial.

Leopold Mannikin sits mutely back in his chair throughout, fiddling with his goatee, overseeing the discussion, making occasional, brief notes on a copy of the agenda. He looks around the table, his eye resting and dwelling on those he sees, remembering their stories and how he feels about them. The proprietor seems more interested in people than business.

At last, thanks are given by Harry Towers, on the behalf of the company, to those employees involved in the organisation of the recent conference week and annual dinner. Thanks are afforded, in his absence, to Count Zapik and the board is officially informed of his recent alliance with the firm. Murmurs of approbation and polite slapping of the table greet the declaration. At this juncture, the gift of tickets to Zapik's magic performance is mentioned. Mannikin asks if he might be allowed to represent his father, with his fiancée, at this event. Leopold acknowledges that he prefers not to go out in the evenings these days and willingly supports Mannikin's request, suggesting that it seems right that Mannikin take the lovely young woman out more often. There is a nod of approval from Mr Oezza, a senior executive, who is Alyesha's father and long time friend of Leopold.

The meeting concludes with discussion on the possible redevelopment or sale of land on which the old factory stands. Mannikin's declared interest quickly allows the responsibility to become his. With the permission of the board, Mr. Ryman Kilmit, the caretaker for the premises, is brought in to discuss the viability of the site and report on its state of dilapidation. He stands, hands tightly clasped in front of his body, to offer his account, in a suit that may have been fashionable once. Mannikin occasionally interrupts to support the caretaker's observations and emphasises the need to find a solution to issues within the year. He agrees to keep an eye on progress and explore how the land might be best used. Leopold interjects to reminisce, recalling how the young Xavier used to play for hours in the factory and grounds, and became a favourite amongst the workers. They were happy days. Leopold pauses, and then continues in a new vein, inappropriately mentioning that, whilst a student, Mannikin had his own rooms created for him somewhere or other in the building, so that he might learn to live more independently. These were the years when his increasing maturity made it seem like a good idea. Leopold concludes his reflections by saying he had a great regard for the blackened and dilapidated factory building that lay in the thirteenth district of the city. It had generated much wealth for the firm, its employees and the city over long years. It was a success story that had added much to the world; he felt sure that all around the room would agree. The 'room' becomes silent for a moment.

The attendees are perhaps remembering the once noble but now blackened, four-storey factory building. The frontage (originally the Mannikin offices with the printing works behind) remains a glorious pastiche of the Italian Medici classical style, built in grey stone with columns and cornerstones. The upper floors of red brick are less ornamented, with the top tier of the building returning to grey, ornamented stucco.

Taking his cue from Mannikin's nod, the caretaker takes a step back and asks permission to leave. Upon his departure, there is discussion of the options available to the company and whether there was any advantage to be had from keeping the site, with a view to redeveloping it within the business.

The precision and specificity of the ensuing conversation strikes Mannikin as uninteresting and, in consequence, his attention wanders. He becomes lost to some other place in absentminded and light-headed thought. The caretaker had seemed remotely similar to Zapik as he stood giving his delivery. The two might be brothers~

but this would be impossible! The resemblance, in truth, was only in passing. He was making too much of it. Ryman was short, clean-shaven and thin-necked; a lifetime of poor nutrition had left him gaunt and meant he could not stand as upright or straight as the magician. Mannikin casts his mind back; he had known Ryman since childhood and had great affection for the man. There was a remote understanding between them and an unacknowledged desire to look after one other. During his student days, when Xavier had lived in the isolated room at the top of the high-fronted factory façade, the gatekeeper had kept an eye on the maturing youth and helped him through his formative years. As a student, he was frequently worse for wear, drunken or debauched~ as often befits a young person intent on learning about the ways of the world. Ryman would make sure Xavier got safely to bed, that he had proper food and his clothes were clean and things of that kind. A caring reciprocity had grown up between the men. By way of return, in recent years, Mannikin had helped Ryman and his family financially during their most difficult time. The man's wife had died in childbirth and left him the difficult and very daunting task of bringing up his young, retarded and disabled daughter on his own. The girl had now reached the age of sixteen and lived in isolation in the gatehouse with her father.

Mannikin brings his daydream to a close, brought back to the omnipotent present at the point where the recent storms and flooding in the Mannikin office building is mentioned. As part of 'Any Other Business' it is agreed that the estate's staff will look into the issue and report back at the next meeting. And so the meeting concludes. The tea trolley lady returns, sporting a large bandage on her shin. She limps, leaning a little too heavily on the trolley for support, bringing sherry and little sandwiches to conclude the meeting.

Delegates linger at the meeting table, or else move away to talk in groups or clusters. Leopold trundles up to his son, takes him by the arm and repositions his boy in front of him, wanting to delight in his clever handiwork, of which he is justifiably very proud. Leopold asks after Xavier's welfare and instructs him to pop into his top floor office suite that week, when convenient. As an aside, he also declares concern for the delectable Alyesha Oezza, counselling his son to make an honest woman of her sooner rather than later. In confidence, he reveals that her father is pushing to have her married off and the two elderly men would be delighted to see the match work. In addition, he is emphatic that Xavier should visit him and his 'profundis', Izziara Sphinx soon, at the family home on the Grand Boulevard. Leopold asks why Xavier doesn't stop over these days; he confesses that he feels himself to be turning into a lonely, old man. With crocodile tears apparent in his glistening eyes, he professes that his last remaining friend in the world is Izziara. In his declining years, the father would love to see more of his son. Mr. Oezza joins them to shake Leopold's hand and to embrace the young executive awkwardly; he too might be trying to secure a son. Mannikin, in desperation, excuses himself, as soon as he can, from the elderly, pasteboard ambassadors, identifying a need to keep an appointment with his tailor. He first returns to his office and unlocks a drawer in the desk, from which he takes a notebook. Towards the back, are the short stories gifted to him by Count Zapik, including the most recent. He has become possessive of the magician's writing of late and admires it, having chosen to emulate the style in his journal. Xavier returns the book to the drawer, satisfied with his recollection of recent entries and moves on. He leaves the building.

On his way to the tailor, Mannikin stops to look in at the window of a Gothic antiquarian seller, his attention caught by a small, winged statuette on a cylindrical pedestal; it immediately takes his fancy. Possibly quite old, but doubtfully as old as the seller subsequently attempts to make him believe. In any event, the item is purchased and carefully wrapped in a small box. It would fit well on his office desk; it might protect the room from invasion or be a signpost to other angels that the space needed guarding. These irrational thoughts seem to resonate within him~ he does not know why, nor, for once, does he feel a need to analyse the strangeness.

54.

And time has passed... the experience of 'Now' in this particular space has become the new present. A portion of night waits, trapped/captured/isolated. The lingering point hangs on a thread, unaware of its own silence or the yawning gap it has become by daring to endure~ a discreet pocket of brief consciousness, caught in an internal space. The air is pregnant with uncommon quiet~ listen! It is as if it listens to itself! There is no apparent sound; nothing can be heard from within that moves. There only remains a muted, distant sense of muffled reverberation arriving from a place beyond or somewhere adjacent, or nearby, that might contradict the attention to, or concentration on, internal detail. In this immediate space, it is the quiet that is palpable. Here, in this centre, but only invisibly, there are strange, 'barely perceptible', imagined resonances that fill the air~ they cause consciousness to reach out in wonder. Had a bell been recently rung and did the afterglow of its sound vibrate yet in some unknown ether? Might the faded strain of a once jaunty tune, distantly familiar but virtually lost, play itself again but too, too slowly, as if recognising it is only vaguely recalled~ as if misremembered but secretly hoping to continue to exist? Equally, this phenomenon may be something quite different, perhaps the anticipated striking of a sublime chord about to be played and perhaps heard again. It is relived in an imagination before it happens; the sound is so near at hand, eagerly waiting to be heard in order to be remembered~ but elusive and invisible in the ear in this moment. In any event, a mysterious tintinnabulation is, or wants to resonate somewhere close to the edge of conscious awareness. The sensation is comforting and settling. The invisible sound has been wrapped carefully in silk, gorgeously, unprepossessingly, just there, waiting to be unpacked.

The space, wherein exists this lingering and familiar 'Now', is identifiable and can be recognised. There are, *amongst other things*, signatures that lie, barely hidden, within and beneath the dust and patina of the apartment. The finest of particles have come to rest~ many had become airborne and moved like ships on waterless oceans as Mannikin moved around the flat, but they had since settled and found a harbour. Other miniscule matter, independent of his physical influence, had been active since his leaving earlier that day, borne on invisible thermals of warm air introduced by the sun's radiation as it passed through windows and into the room. Yet others were subjected to movement or agitation in response to electro-magnetic charges, initiated by their proximity to metal or appliances~ although they too, in this moment, have lost or fixed their energy and like all else, fallen back into negative or positive slumber. There are inexplicable latent energies and radiations only vaguely discernable, some larger than one might think possible for so small a room. Notwithstanding these secret things, the room is seemingly still in its foreboding. All is quiet within its jurisdiction. An electrical hum vibrates through the building from elsewhere. A generator in the basement has just been turned on and its presence punctuates the sound of human activity in the building beyond these walls. Careful listening identifies the discreet, distant bang of a door, the sound of laughter, the drone of a television turned up to become remotely loud. There are far-off noises from the city too, seeping in through the windows; the glass minutely shudders in thrall as it allows sound to pass~ in a manner that the dead moth that lies upturned on the sill of the window will never experience again. Is there anything happening in any of these rooms~ in this cautious space?

Who could notice that the paint on the walls is yellowing, but slowly, virtually imperceptibly? The action seems, and is, painstakingly insignificant~ although so beautiful.

The rooms had been subjected to a splendid invasion of light, during those now past, glorious, sunshine-filled hours~ such light as would delight the photographer whose life graces this abode. His silvered images describe a parallel world whose core and substance might be projected onto the eyes and into the spirit of others, in much the same way as light might enter a cave. Indeed, the orientation of these rooms and the positioning of windows along the walls produce an analogous effect in Mannikin's mind~ he considers the apartment to be a camera~ a cave that absorbs light. It is a light sensitive space, the interior possessing the characteristics of a pinhole camera obscura that, over time, reveals the longest exposure to which any light-responsive device might be capable. It has become apparent to Mannikin that diverse pigments and materials contained in the carpet, furniture, plastics and curtains, and other items adorning his apartment, are all fading and losing splendour in varying degrees, dependent on their sensitivity and exposure to phenomena within the fabric of time and space. The invidious process is most apparent and recorded notably in those materials that face onto, into or most prominently capture, or are naturally sensitised to 'Light'. The apartment has become a camera that contains Mannikin, the moving platform from which he can observe the minutiae of light as the entire building rotates, slowly advancing past the sun on its diurnal route.

Despite Mannikin moving through this series of boxes, he remains unlikely to have his shadow captured or recalled within the enormous, timed exposure to which the living space is subjected. There will be no shadowy presence representing him or the ghost image of a Mannikin caught within the recording device. He is invisible to everything that is sensitive to light in these rooms, as would be other beings who might enter the space for shorter times than he~ they are even less likely to be recorded or recalled.

In the present darkness of 'Now' the apartment rests, as though a temporary lens cap has been drawn across all of its apertures. The quietude suggests that Mannikin is elsewhere. Tonight, he is attending the private magic demonstration performed by Count Zapik at the Villa Apollinaire.

★ ★ ☆ ★

A wallop… an abrupt crash passes through the apartment, the result of force and deliberate impact; it penetrates and echoes loudly. A collision of some weight against the front door has broken the solitude and silence~ *arriving and departing in an instant, creating the wonder of whether anything at all actually occurred.* An intense, slow, sustained creak follows as the door becomes subject to increasing duress and force. A muffled crack finally rings out as the lock fails under pressure. The glass in the frame rattles as the door flies open.

The anguished door is quietly closed again and a dark figure, enveloped in shadow, enters the living room from the compact hallway entrance. It is a man, shorter than Mannikin, in a hat and long coat, treading carefully, unsure of his footsteps~ or his way in~ or what he might see in the gloom~ or possibly meet. The figure is vigilant, moving cautiously, intent on making no further noise after the breach of the front door. It seems implicit that the intruder will touch nothing as he moves deeper into the apartment. A pencil torch, in use to light the way, illuminates his white-gloved hand.

The rim of his trilby is pulled down and pressed forward on his head. The man is preoccupied, listening for sound, insistent that he should hear anything coming his way before it is made aware of him. He moves through the apartment delicately with a light step, confirming that the place is indeed vacant, as he suspects. He establishes the layout of the flat, checks doors and rooms, unlocks the French doors to the balcony, recognising the opportunity for a handy escape to an adjoining apartment, should the need arise. Within a short time, he returns to the main room.

The intruder unbuttons his coat and slowly removes it, laying it on the settee; then looks around and finally doffs his hat, throwing it down on top of the coat. A check of the man's credentials and wallet identifies him as Ponting, *a secret agent serving the needs of a foreign power.* He carries a gun in a holster on his back and is in possession of a pager to notify him should Mannikin decide to return early. His wallet contains a sizable amount of cash and his pockets contain a notebook, pencil, small camera and penknife~ there is a cotton handkerchief in his trouser pocket and a silk one in his top pocket. These details become apparent as the man finds himself bewilderingly startled, recognising that a peculiar and unaccountable energy had just passed through him. The spy looks around, surprised, and in the absence of any explanation relaxes, to prepare for the business in hand. The aim is to examine the flat he has breached, whilst searching for an unidentified object of particular interest, the whereabouts of which is currently unknown, but may possibly be here.

Ponting begins his search and investigation, noting that the apartment appears clean and is contemporary in design. He sees that the long picture window looks out across the city vista, set beneath the vast, blue, evening sky. Faint lines describe the very last vestiges of daylight, barely discernible on the horizon behind the city skyline. The shadows in the room are dense and black. Furniture facing onto the window is colourless, bleached by the white light of a full moon, impressively felt in this moment. The walls are pale in the jaundiced glow of Ponting's flickering torchlight as it passes over their surface. The room is sparsely furnished; a couple of sofas, a low table and waist-high book shelving seem to be about all there is. The end wall functions as a kind of gallery and is covered in framed black and white photographic prints. Ponting, recognising that he has as much time as he needs, takes on the role of voyeur and connoisseur and saunters up to take note of what exactly is on display. Carefully positioning his torch to avoid reflected light, his interest increases as he begins to make sense of the pictures. There are specific themes, some obvious enough to take hold in Ponting's unschooled imagination~ *numerous doorways, revealing a particular fascination for entrances and exits; a series of panoramic views of the same places, repeatedly photographed from exactly the same spot at different times, highlighting changes in light, weather, human activity; photographs taken with mirrors where the reversed reflection of an object appears alongside the object itself. In addition, he discovers photographs taken by Mannikin of his own trouser legs and shoes, the camera pointing down as he walks over diverse surfaces, or looks forward with his feet up as they rest on chairs, or with legs crossed on seats and benches as he sits. In some, his legs are suspended, dangling down from heights above the ground, creating the impression he is floating above a landscape or walking on air that exists below his view of his own feet.* Ponting soon tires of all this looking; the images are too self-consciously arty and strange for his taste. The torchlight reflecting back into his retina makes him feel nauseous and confused. He turns ~ thinking that for a brief moment he saw a figure behind him, reflected in the picture glass. There is no one. The prowler is surprised at how spooked he feels, despite the present task being particularly routine for him. Looking down, he notices that there are portfolios tied with ribbon stacked against the wall, their flaps open. He crouches to leaf through the collections, quickly establishing that they too are testament to Master Mannikin's obsession with the photographic image. There is a dogged determination to capture particular features found in the external world, using the art of the lens. It becomes implicit that Mannikin has a great need to check the credibility and provenance of all the things he chooses to see and experience, like a writer overly keen to describe details down to the last specific. Ponting cannot imagine the point or need for such emphatic interest.

The interloper stands and takes a step back, then turns to look behind once more. The opposite wall is uncommonly decorated with relief and shadow~ it takes a moment to make sense of the confusion, but then he sees it. The wall has been joyously festooned with an eclectic collection of hats laid out systematically on a grid across the surface, each selected for maximum effect and to offset the splendour and eccentricity of the one next to it~ the wall describing itself as a series of events. At the behest of Ponting's animated torch, yet stranger shadows are cast, moving and stretching across the wall, passing over and between the hanging forms. Much of the headgear might still be in contemporary use but for others, the suspicion is that they were out of fashion, indeed relegated to history. There is a fur melusine topper and a wool top hat; a fedora, a trilby and homburg of the type worn by the coachmen in the tourist areas of the city, plus hats for dressage. Straw panamas feature, as well as a bowler and a pork pie hat; chauffeur's caps with cockades, one similar to the type worn by the 'Mannikin' doormen, and sailors' hats besides. The apparel, it is to be supposed, had all been worn by Mannikin at some point, each being a perfect 7½-60cm fitting. Ponting is faintly amused by his evening's espionage.

He continues to investigate the apartment, checking drawers below the hat display and then peering into cupboards, discovering all manner of miscellaneous clutter thrown haphazardly into spaces, without any sense of order; autographed playing cards, tinned fish, food labels, decorative badges, Russian military pins, wristwatches, birds' wings, feathers, gents dance shoes, dominoes, fountain pens, cardboard boxes containing preserved and mounted moths. A large number of spectacles seemed to be owned by a man who had never been seen wearing glasses to date. However, it was the extraordinary abundance of false moustaches that intrigued Ponting, since he too had a natural fascination for disguise, so befitting to a man in his line of work.

Ponting is sensing that Mannikin is an uncommonly strange fish, not a particularly easy target to quantify or define~ confirmation indeed of the 24-hour surveillance reports he had read. Something within the pattern of things was simply not typical, perhaps not even right~ he sensed it more than he could see it. Nothing really seemed wrong~ but maybe it was! The thing he wanted to tell himself about the apartment's owner... was on the edge of his perception, somewhere outside his experience. Did it all seem straightforward? Increasingly, none of it was.

Continuing his search, Ponting checks for ideas and clues that strike him as significant. In due course, he moves into another room, which seems to be an office of sorts, although currently in use as a dump and depository for all manner of miscellaneous clutter, piled high. It resembles a junk shop of picture frames, portfolios, historic cameras, camera equipment, manuals, newspapers and reference books. There is an impressive display of shop mannequins from another era standing against the back wall, some from the 1920's and 30's, an ironing board and, most notably, on the study table~ a stuffed pelican, designed to be a window display, its mouth wide open with bow tie tails sticking out, resembling fish. Ponting goes through the space, thinking, exploring, deep in thought whilst testing out the potential for hiding places. Despite the strangeness of the things he discovers, there appear to be no particular clues surfacing. The sleuth feels the eyes of the pelican on him, following his progress around the room.

'This is all a little unusual and eccentric and not particularly easy to rationalise or explain,' he thinks. There seemed to be an underlying absurdity to everything being encountered, a discernable detachment~ a lack of fit to expectation. One might detect lunacy in the manner in which so many commonplace, but disparate objects had been brought together, possibly attempting to prove that reality was, in truth, different to how it normally appeared. The apartment was like a museum of unconventional thoughts, rather than a place in which typical living might occur, an environment in which physical existence had been allowed to bend into an unorthodox shape that he did not quite recognise. What did it all mean? The displays and collections of objects were like mini-performances designed to test out spaces or ideas. Maybe, in some discreet way, he should be enjoying himself as much as the owner of the apartment at that other performance elsewhere in Warcapest this very evening? But he dare not allow himself that privilege~ Ponting was working.

He wanders into Mannikin's bedroom, a comfortable space containing a large bed and the objects and furniture one might expect, with the notable inclusion of a handsomely preserved shop mannequin~ a life size, articulated male doll, sans clothes, from a gentleman's outfitter in Berlin, circa 1930. It stands ominously looking out from a corner, staring at him. Ponting walks up to it, to observe it at close quarters, in order to be completely sure it is as inanimate as he suspects. Its presence unnerves him somewhat. He turns away, and in so doing, notices an incongruous ormolu Rococo writing table prominently placed in front of the window. The desk top is cluttered and strewn with tickets, papers, notes, negatives, little found objects that might have been taken from pockets, all laid out systematically and recording the activity of recent weeks. He views them with disinterest, recognising that if they meant anything at all, the significance would be lost on him. Continuing to move around the room, Ponting soon discovers the top drawer of the tallboy and dares to rummage briefly through its contents. He has no logic to provide an explanation for what appears to be yet another nonsensical and bizarre collection. He jumps to the unthinking conclusion that the drawer and the desktop are lazy depositories for rubbish that ought to be thrown out. Ponting concludes that Mannikin, being strange, has a propensity to surround himself with worthless clutter that means nothing. The man was protean, mercurial, erratic... and annoying. The sleuth was beginning to dislike his quarry.

Ponting swings around to observe the large painting above the bed depicting an ancient and decadent winged sphinx in the fetishist, symbolist style of the very exquisite Franz Felix von Eissenstrom. He stops to consider it for a moment. This is not a work or indeed a painter with which the detective is familiar. Ponting is conjecturing wildly about the nonsensical clues being unearthed~ there is an obsessive thread running through the interests and activities of this man, although annoyingly he cannot piece the influences together or put his finger on what it is, or what any of this means. There are signposts here that he wants to recognise, but cannot label. He has a distant, primordial remembrance of something he has always known, but never been able to acknowledge. What is it he is feeling but cannot place, about this reality he recognises, but does not see?

He turns again, to face the tallboy, to give himself time to think... and at last stumbles across small, framed photos of Mannikin, accumulated over past years, on the wall behind. The uncertain man is variously represented, looking much younger, in social settings, school, college, family occasions, holidays, previous employments, appearing alongside disparate and anonymous sets of people. In each of the snapshots, Mannikin looks intensely out towards the camera, piercing the lens with a scrutiny and gaze far greater than the camera's ability to penetrate the world it records. In each image Mannikin seems vacant, unsure, caught unawares, trying to 'find himself' before the shutter captures his image in the fleeting moment. Ponting muses to himself.
'This man, most of all, is uncertain about his identity.'

The detective returns to the main room and stands looking out across Warcapest, still lost in thought. The pager in his pocket lets outs a low ring.
'Time to go,' he thinks.

And so the covert, sordid invasion of Mannikin's life is perpetrated, conducted with the most gentlemanly of manners. Ponting, the true professional, does not interfere or leave evidence of his intrusion at all; indeed, is able to leave everything exactly as he found it, or as Mannikin remembers. All is as it should be. Has he left any mark or disturbance that might be noted? Indeed not! Even the front door, so violent in its recent declamation at being breached without a key, will give nothing away. The door was cleverly levered ajar, caused to bend in a particular way and sprung open using a common burglar's technique.

And during the investigation, has Ponting discovered much? He suspects he has discovered little that will be of real use to him. The consequence of his disappointment has added anxiety attached to it. His team will need to gain similar access to the house of Leopold Mannikin and maybe even to the offices of Mannikin Cards, to seek out that which he is in search of. The risk of discovery will be greater in these other places. A clean job may not be so possible next time. He will need more men to monitor the risk. He needs more men anyway; the urgency of the tasks in hand is growing daily. Ponting is frowning intensely. There is some kind of secrecy attached to Mannikin that he is only just beginning to notice and possibly get a handle on. The man is more controlled and guarded in his movements than a typical person ought to be, so it seems to Ponting, in his professional opinion. There are issues concerning Mannikin that need to be addressed and accounted for. Mannikin manages to evade the men who tail him, too often, too consistently and it begins to look like more than simple ineptitude on part of his men~ maybe Mannikin has more self-awareness and control than he had assumed and is dodging them deliberately~ the poor saps lose him too easily. Increasingly, on analysis, Ponting recognises that he cannot account for where Mannikin is for fairly long periods of time. This man disappears. Where is he when he is off the radar? For periods of time he appears to be off the planet.

55.

Guests at the Villa Apollinaire had paid very high prices for their tickets. The reception rooms were straining with celebrities representing the cream of Warcapest society; faces were familiar from media or known to be the aristocracy of the region. Mannikin, with his complimentary tickets, had the distinct impression that he and Alyesha were punching way above their weight, *surrounded as they were, by such a giddy cocktail of elite glitterati.* Count Zapik's performance was a special and important event in the city's cultural and social calendar.

However, during the drinks reception, Mannikin was made aware of how very splendid and fortunate he was in the eyes of others. It was all Alyesha's doing. He was wearing a rare jewel on his arm and basking in the glow of her. Alyesha looked radiant, beautifully fresh and youthful~ distinctly dressed in red ostrich feathers. She was turning heads. The gorgeous woman leaning on him, who, it appeared, might fall without his support, was in her element. She chirped endless, sweet nothings concerning the assembled rich and famous into his ear, almost without need for breath.

Mannikin observed events unfolding. The spectacle was already interesting, even at this point before the evening had properly begun. There was a studied sense of individuality on show. So many of the well-known and eminent guests were self-consciously self-aware in a manner that struck him as ludicrous and beyond credibility. There was an absurd sense of the ridiculous in the air. Mannikin was altering his perceptions in order to explain the artifice and hubris of which he too was a part, looking into unexpected corners in an attempt to understand the other levels on which the reality around him was unfolding, or being presented. He was unsure what it all meant. Amongst this strangeness, this curious 'weird', this incomprehensible reality on display, he found himself experiencing an unexpected and uncommon nausea all of his own. He felt as if someone had walked over his grave or entered his space, filling him. It was as if they had turned on their eyes for him and he could see as they saw. There was unexpected brightness in the room, an uncanny ability to see. The sensation escalated within him to the point where he began to feel physically ill, with a need to retch and convulse, as if about to vomit. Alyesha moved quickly away from him and held him at arm's length, her face suddenly ugly in her determination to protect her costume at all costs. Mannikin glimpsed what appeared to be an intermittently fleeting but vivid, light-saturated image right inside his head~ it twirled and spiralled away from him and towards him simultaneously, growing and expanding~ like little wings or moustaches made of light. Looking down, he saw that the glow was escaping from within his chest and, in the next moment, the same light-infested vision disappeared up his sleeves and vanished.

Xavier staggered back, clutching his chest, explaining that he needed to briefly take his leave to visit the men's room. Once there, Mannikin tried to calm himself, checking his appearance in the mirror, discovering, much to his astonishment, that there remained an after-image of the recently imagined wings above his lip, where they rested, unwilling to allow themselves to be rubbed off, persistent in their ambition to look like some celestial, glowing moustache. Concurrently, Xavier remembered that he had a particular association with Count Zapik and was complicit in some ongoing adventure, the nature of which he could not recollect. The man stood motionless, watching himself in the reflection, waiting for the luminescence to subside. By the time he returned to Alyesha, the bell to announce the imminent start of the performance had ceased to sound. All other members of the audience had left the reception room to take up their seats. A desperate Alyesha called upon him to hurry, for fear of missing the spectacle. Ushers quickly hastened the two latecomers into the performance hall.

The time they spend at the Villa Apollinaire and the performance itself will become a memorable event in Mannikin's mind; he will repeatedly return to it in order to make sense of the experience, suspecting it to be a turning point in his psyche. The oddness in the air and his reactions to the sensations he was exposed to ultimately left him confused. The whole evening proved to be strange and bewildering, especially on reflection.

At the end to the evening, Mannikin took Alyesha home to her parents' house and then, on an impulse, returned to his office in the Mannikin building. The night caretaker was pressed into service to accommodate his late entry into the premises at a nocturnal hour~ yet again. Mannikin endeavoured to remain awake throughout the night, to think and reflect on the events, inspirations and ideas that were welling up inside him. In an attempt to explain and make sense of his experiences, he composed an account of the performance in his journal, capturing his remembrance of the moment and the order in which events occurred, and how everything had affected his awareness. His head was swimming; he remained intoxicated and delirious with the strange passion that had overwhelmed him during the evening.

Mannikin borrows an anglepoise from the outer office to provide low, ambient light by which to work~ then sits and readies himself to begin. He heads the journal's page with a doodle, a drawing spanning its width of, what appears to be, a large curling moustache~ thickest at its centre, whirling outward in tight curls, moving into some unimaginable infinity, travelling towards an ever-decreasing point, spiralling away into ever tightening and paradoxically widening centres~ daring to invade some unknown oblivion. He begins to compose his ideas, deliberately laying out the page and writing in a manner that parodies the style of the Count's stories. Ahead of him, is the little gilded angel recently acquired from the strange, Gothic, antiquarian shop.

Pages taken from... Xavier MANNIKIN's Journal.
An account of an Evening Performance of Magic by the Count Zapiko.
Warcapest. July 19--.

We find ourselves quickly ushered through the classical State Rooms & along the corridors of the Villa Apollinaire. A remote bell, somewhere, has stopped sounding.

The room we enter is illuminated by points of light, each a candle flame, every yellow brilliance held aloft in one of eight magnificent, gold, baroque 'standing' candelabra, in the style of torchères, evenly distributed along the side walls of the room. The ceiling above our heads is high & remote, lost in the darkness that the little flames fail to penetrate. The only other furniture in the room consists of five centrally placed rows of gilded chairs, laid out for the assembly (of maybe forty-five persons) who have already taken up their places. The room is strangely organised & much space seems to be wasted. There is a large expanse of floor that contains nothing all around the chairs. They might be seen to form a small floating island amidst an ocean of parquet in this very grand room.

We, arriving late, move to take up the two remaining seats. Alyesha seats herself next to Princess Aelita, whilst I (Xavier Mannikin) find a position in the row behind, somewhat disappointed by our separation, but happily sat next to Franz Felix von Eissenstrom, the painter, a distant acquaintance & as I later discover, the artist responsible for what I see next. As my eyes slowly become accustomed to the dark, I perceive, as I peer in to the expanse around me, that the perimeter walls in front & behind are painted with an enormous fresco of uncommon size & subject. The painting extends into the ceiling above our heads. I pierce the gloom with my eyes & view the representation of a woman; her legs travel up the height of the wall behind & then, in the shadows, as I look up, I distinguish that the torso of her feminine form is moving across & filling the entire ceiling. An enormous gold ball hangs from her navel on a chain. Her pendulous breasts hang down in response to the thrust of gravity. Her body then continues on & falls neck & head first, down onto the wall in front of us to the level of the oaken floor where her outstretched arms & fingers support the weight of her effort. The quality of the image is hypnotic; the painter's art bewitches in its handling of the subject & the tender care apparent in the execution of this immaculate & bizarre image. I look intently, transfixed, consumed with interest.

My deep admiration for this alluring artwork is, however, cut short & my concentration broken~ as next, by some invisible coordinating force, the oaken entry door behind us, so snuggly situated between the giantess's legs & feet, closes with a thud. Simultaneously, the large, mahogany, library doors ahead, bordered by the stout, athletic arms & delicate hands of the feminine leviathan, open amidst an audible clunk & blaze of light from the room beyond. In this way, the new moment heralds the entrance of the Count in evening attire, accompanied by his beautiful assistant, Nadja, the Star of Mystery. It becomes immediately apparent that she may be the very person depicted so favourably in the image that adorns the space above our heads. Her dress of glittering gold shines brilliantly, in imitation of all the glowing candles around the room, each sparkle as bright as each flame & appearing to be illuminated from within. Uniformed stewards in red velvet close the doors behind these newly arrived entertainers.

The reserved, yet flamboyant, Count Zapik comes forward, holding a large, silver coin. The maestro presses it to his trouser leg, whereupon it appears to dissolve into the very fabric & vanish in some unfathomable fashion. No applause, it seems, is expected & none is offered. Zapik's discernable air of indifference to the moment is replicated in the audience's response; however, there can be no doubt that not one of us within the audience understood or might explain what we have just seen.

The mood in the room changes, altered by virtue of this tiny, seemingly insignificant act. There is slight shuffling on seats, uneven chair legs rock on the parquet flooring, chairs creak, intakes of breath are perceptible, air is expelled from tight chests, muffled coughs try hard to contain themselves in order not to disturb the atmosphere. The audience's concentration has become focused. Next, with assertive vigour~ his arms outstretched & extended~ the Count imperceptibly produces a pack of playing cards amidst an unexpected flash of light from his fingertips. He smiles broadly into the audience, effectively releasing all the accumulated tension in the room, indicating to everyone that they have permission, at last, to also smile. In response, we offer polite & grateful applause, during which time the playing cards are casually unboxed, the case thrown to the floor, the cards shuffled & passed to Nadja. She proceeds to distribute them in small packets to guests seated along the front row.

Using a soft voice, the Count asks that each of the six persons think of only one of the cards in their possession & without removing the card or bringing any tangible attention, or notice to that choice, shuffle the packet. Next, Nadja, stepping forward, collects the packets, reassembles the pack & reaching over, hands me (Xavier Mannikin) the deck, gesturing that I might shuffle the cards further. Despite my profound anxiety that I might appear clumsy, I do endeavour to rearrange the condition of the cards as instructed. For my pains, I am rewarded with a smile that is to linger in my memory.

On completion of the task, Nadja takes the cards & gives them to the Count. The magician reads off the cards, throwing each one to the floor as he does so. After a dozen or more have been dispatched in this manner, he asks whether anyone has yet heard their card mentioned. No one has. The Count proceeds to throw cards to the floor as he names them, & again stops to ask whether anyone is conscious of having heard their card called. Two guests raise their hands & are then promptly told of the card they were only thinking of. Applause ensues, amidst looks of bewilderment from the audience. The remainder of the cards are then thrown into the air with gusto & allowed to scatter as they drop to the floor. The mind reader, with hands in his pockets, proceeds to walk amongst the scattered cards whilst continuing to determine, with the highest degree of accuracy, the cards trapped in the thoughts of the four remaining minds. An amazing demonstration of mindreading! How can this be done!

We have to suspect trickery~ few of us are naïve enough to believe that magic is real, but there are no clues to suggest where we might direct our suspicions in order to understand. There appears to be nothing dubious to accuse. We sit enthralled, but confused, aware we had missed something that had eluded our gaze or understanding. All we might now do is sit back & look forward to the next, puzzling spectacle. Each new effect escalates towards a higher level of incomprehensibility, yet another skill that Zapik is particularly good at coordinating~ what, we wonder, are we about to see next...

At this point, Mannikin takes a brief rest from writing to view the night through the window beyond the desk. He finds himself producing a second doodle whilst peering into the gloom; a little sketch of a woman on all fours, with bended back, arching her head and hips~ in the act of raising her bottom to the sky, as if to make her sex available. The dark outside remains intense and his reflection glares back at him from off the greasy, glass pane. The image is well illuminated, his shirt and Pellican bow tie brilliant against the dark. His forehead is glossy and shiny, his hair flat to his head. He is surprised to see himself looking so much older; the man he sees appears lined and aged~ the image being distorted by a double reflection hitting his retina from a dual image, the first on the inner surface of the window, competing with a second one coming back at him from the outer surface. The slight blur, caused by the thickness of the glass, seems to be confusing, but no more than life itself.

He makes ready to continue writing.

There is a consequence to seeing these apparently irresolvable things. They are illusory~ no doubt. Nevertheless, they have an effect on our consciousness & undermine our sense of reality~ despite the probably simple artifice on which the deception is based. Such tricks affect us at a level that is primordial or ancient in some way. At the very least it serves to remind people of who they were when very young. In a childlike way...

Mannikin pauses to casually add a few lines to his drawing of the crouching 'calling' woman, whilst reminding himself of the ravishing sensation of looking up at her from beneath during the performance, seeing her dark pubis in shadow and rotund breasts and nipples hanging just for him.

...we feel smaller, aware perhaps that the universe is bigger & certainly more complex than we are likely to ever comprehend. So much is beyond our understanding & even, in truth, beyond the scope of this clever, conjuring Count too~ he cannot know so much more than anyone else & yet has, in a few short demonstrations, convinced us all of our own insignificance. This strikes me as uncomfortable, Faustian meddling dressed up as entertainment. I might even wonder if there are aspects of nature that man ought not play with.

During the performance, it is somehow implicit or subtlety implied that the best is yet to come.

Next, Nadja the Star of Mystery steps forward. The Count hands her a golden blindfold. She puts it over her eyes, after which, he carefully guides her away from the audience to face the torchères along one wall. We see her delightful face in profile, its contour illuminated by a soft, flickering candle glow.

Count Zapik then invites us (the audience) to take into our hands personal objects from around our person, they might be items or articles from pockets, purses or handbags, anything at all. The selection is to be held secretly; it may be shared with others in the audience if we wish, for entertainment's sake.

The blindfolded Nadja is then invited to use a 'Sealed Vision' to determine the objects members of the audience are holding & about which we should be thinking & concentrating.

The Count requests that anyone who wishes to take part should raise his or her hand. He moves between the rows of chairs & touches volunteers on the shoulder in turn, before inviting Nadja to speak. In each case she reveals the hidden objects with uncanny precision; the secret talisman, the lipstick, the key & its use, the letter & its author, the library card & its number, the lover in the photo, the charm, the scent & its secret ingredient, the secret wish, the departed whose hair is in the locket, the lucky coin & its date, the memory trapped in the concert ticket.

The demonstration is uncanny & faultless, more so than previous effects. We, the audience, become high-spirited & voluble. We now want to believe. We have become part of the moment. The night has become enchanted. We lose connection with time. It might be that some obscure change in gravity has allowed us to feel lighter.

Nadja, tired after her exertion, slumps. Fatigue has paled her complexion. This moment of relaxation between effects is short-lived however, as...

Zapik, with a controlled & measured authority walks towards the passive woman. Whilst moving, he procures a short stick, a wand, from his pocket, which immediately bursts into flame, burning ferociously at one end with an intense chemical brilliance. He uses the rod to draw an indecipherable shape or text in the air above his head, the traced line of which lingers, floating momentarily before fading & dying. On reaching his assistant, the magician throws the remains of the now spent, smoldering baton to the ground.

Then, taking her in a secure grip with both hands, he swings Nadja with considerable force and energy and begins to turn and rotate her. She flows out from him, at some distance. She circles his centrally spinning outline, as a satellite around a planet, moving vigorously through the air~ orbiting. The gold dress ripples, as if flowing, catching the light as she revolves, her shoes fall from her feet, first one then the other~ thrown off & caused to slide across the polished floor unceremoniously & indiscriminately. He continues to increase the momentum, pivoting confidently at great speed. The forces are dynamic & centrifugal.

In the next extraordinary & confused moment he lets go of her; she flies out from him. Her hands leave his. There are audible gasps & cries of desperation from the audience & thereafter, startled disbelief as she inexplicably continues to circle widely, without evidence of catastrophe. Incredibly, her figure traces an arc that spreads out around the room as she travels away from the performing area & wondrously passes around the centrally placed chairs on which we are all seated. We follow the floating Nadja with our heads, straining & craning to see behind ourselves as she mystically sweeps through the air, on the lightest of invisible winds, close to the room's perimeter. One circuit is hardly enough to register the mystery & our incredulity at what is occurring & so thankfully, amazingly, she is allowed to continue her circumnavigation for a second time~ gliding, or maybe truly flying past the standing maestro, who salutes her passage~ & yet, too soon, & at last, as we watch gaping, now most certainly lost in a space outside of time, we see the suspended Nadja approach her starting point once more~ having traced the line & course for two perfect circles. As she advances towards him, the magician stands braced, preparing himself to finally interrupt & intercept the woman's route, in order to capture & return the floating spirit to earth. This he manages to do, with studied & dexterous, fleet efficiency, despite the prevailing forces sliding him backwards some distance. In the blink of an eye, Nadja miraculously appears before us again, upright & standing, attached to the earth as before. I, & all others in that audience, are completely astonished!

The Count, without missing a beat, calls for applause, demanding a standing ovation for the 'Gifts of Nadja.'

We rise to the occasion, unable to know what has happened but prepared to respond automatically. The dangling egg above our heads adds to the confusion, as it unexpectedly bursts open, showering glitter into all corners of the room.

Next, the doors at both ends of the hall are thrown open, flooding light back into the space. The uniformed stewards in red velvet quickly reappear, dashing & rushing with intent to serve drinks & canapés from silver trays. The formal entertainment is now over. Indeed, it has vanished!

During the post performance reception & high-spirited party that follows, a curious, perhaps whimsical, three-dimensional 'neon projection' appears, suspended above the Count's head. Projected from some indeterminate source, perhaps from the gallery, it follows him around the room for the remainder of the evening as he talks & mingles, reversing itself as he turns; it moves with him. It reads~ IMAGINATION IS ALL!

Postscriptum~ As the remarkable evening drew to a close we witnessed a spectacular firework display in the company of the maestro & his assistant & other honoured guests. The event was viewed from the magnificent room's exterior balcony~ a homage perhaps to the expanding universe in all its glory.

The evening was memorable; I wish it could have been shared with... SPx

FINIS.

As dawn approached, Mannikin was able to finish his journal entry. The tired man rang for a taxi to take him back to his father's house for the first time in many weeks. He is not expected there, but has a key with which he will let himself in.

56.

Xavier Mannikin had been brought up in the house of his parents. Unusually, for a boy supported by such parental wealth and background, he had not been sent off to a private boarding school~ his father would not entertain the notion, despite his wife's request~ the man loved his son too much for that. He had wanted to see his progeny grow and selfishly wished to relive his own childhood through their shared experiences. Leopold doted on the growing boy and derived great personal joy and satisfaction from their time together~ the boy's mother was less effusive and, in truth, somewhat intolerant of young people, in spite of one of them being her own. She was of a nervous disposition, needing much rest and quiet. In part, and in consequence of such domestic circumstance and the expediencies of home organisation, Xavier was allocated remote, isolated rooms on the top floor of the family home. They were out of the way, distanced from the normal running of the house and conveniently as far from his mother's boudoir and day rooms as possible. His father, who was undoubtedly a demonstrative, enthusiastic and caring parent, was also an easily distracted and overly busy man and hence visited the boy less often than he initially planned or might, or should. There was a growing problem here waiting to happen, inexplicably compounded by the boy's apathetic mother, who had been unwell since the birth of the child. In short, she refused to set foot on the dusty, narrow staircase that led to the top of the house where her offspring's rooms were located. The sensitive Xavier, perhaps unwittingly or worse, had been relegated to a separate world and marooned in a place that, in his isolation, slowly and increasingly became infested with traumatic, anguished and indescribable thoughts more than anyone, including the nanny who looked after him, might have realised. The storm in his developing consciousness was great, overpowering and titanic, even then. When confined to his room as was too frequently the case, *often for not observing the needs of others or his mother's tiredness, or as punishment meted out by his nanny or later governess~ for the tiniest of misdemeanours,* he would cope and dismiss the materialising terrors from sight by altering or dismissing their reality. There was a preferred release, which took him away from these surroundings and isolated him from even himself. The little Xavier Mannikin gazed out of the window for extraordinary long periods of time, both day and night, in order to forget what was in that very room and the tormented and tortuous world he was forced to occupy, all of which began to lay like a secret, invisibly behind him. He would press close to the cold glass, imagining the dark energy that pushed him onto it, fearing that ideas, which lay dormant in the back of the room, were about to consume or contaminate him. He willfully escaped by embracing and loving the view from the shiny, smooth window, polishing its surface with a favoured, green, satin cloth endlessly and obsessively. The window became his salvation and delight~ he became transfixed as he observed the movements of birds on the sill or in the pollarded trees on the boulevard and eventually came to know all the common species, and discovered, because they nested near, that blackbird eggs were turquoise. *These things were learned through picture books and with the help of his father, who at last came to realise that the boy, like his mother, was unusually sensitive.* The child frequently looked out across the boulevard to see and wonder at the rich variety of buildings~ or spent time watching the people below going about their daily business. Even at night, when strange dreams woke him, young Xavier might access the benign and friendly window to see the world he thought he knew reinvented afresh. In time, the lad learned to orientate this glass aperture onto the city and the world beyond, identifying the geographical whereabouts of spires, towers and grand buildings, recognising them to be peculiarly fixed points in his sliding consciousness. Xavier grew to revere the fascinating and ornamented rooflines, and developed fantasies about what it would be like to live in the different high locales without any prior knowledge of what they might truly be like inside. In such ways the boy became proficient at moving out of himself into different places. The awareness of how the world looked from the window and how he experienced it when travelling with his mother or governess, left a deep impression~ this was a thing intangible and difficult to quantify. The views and how they altered in types of weather and differing light conditions fascinated him. The child loved the elements in all their glory. Rain on a casement was a magical effect and 'moustachioed' frost patterns on a glass pane during winter were a rare beauty. The window was a special place. It was his frontier. It moved in the direction where there might be an escape at least, or with yet greater yearning, the place where he might find himself.

Xavier Mannikin wakes after 11am. The sunlight streams in through the window in a way it never has before~ the moment is original. The man lays blinking, thinking and wondering about the brightness before him, distractedly watching the rays of brilliance spread across the carpet, wondering if he might see the gleaming shafts move if he concentrates for long enough. Mannikin, too soon, is defeated in the quest; he moves to the edge of the bed, sits up and stands. His shadow passes over the floor as he collects a green satin dressing gown from the back of the door. He slips the garment on; distractedly looking for proof that time is not standing still as he ties the belt. The watch on his wrist informs him it is 10.55. For a moment he hesitates, briefly unsure whether the second hand is moving. His heart misses a beat before continuing; he feels the sensation of its pounding deep inside his chest cavity~ like the point of a knife buried deep, invading delicate flesh. Still sleepy, gummy-eyed and lightly flustered, he faces into the mirror and begins to comb his hair, unsure as to why he should be thinking of Harry Towers. The morning was proving to be more complex than he wished~ or liked. His thoughts were all anticipant, as if he were ahead of himself. Xavier moves to look out of the window, pressing his body and the fabric of the green dressing gown onto the glass. He examines the view, experiencing the intensity of the outdoor light smarting in his eyes. It is a clear day and the spires, far into the distance, are full of bright, scintillating detail. Things are not so bad after all. He leaves the window reluctantly, to wash and dress.

Within a short time, Mannikin makes his way through the house, descending deeper, invading its layers, journeying along ever-widening corridors and down progressively grander flights of stairs, travelling into an increasingly opulent underworld of gorgeous colour and fabric, of ever more velvet, flock wallpaper and gilt framed paintings, of chandeliers and wall lamps. He walks, checking objects as he passes~ abundant memories and former associations free-flow into and through him. He notices mirrors, delighting in the spaces and images they capture, examining the reality they attempt to so obediently reflect. The man is acutely aware that mirrors have never become a commonplace experience; the beguiling dual reality they describe has always resonated at a deep and subliminal level. On arriving at the ground floor hallway he pauses, captivated by a spectrum of light radiating onto the geometrically tiled floor. Since boyhood, he has delighted in the stained glass windows to either side of the main door~ the source of these rich effects. He soon continues, walking along a corridor to the kitchen where, at last, feeling himself to have arrived somewhere, he begins to make tea. The room wraps itself around him, seducing him with its charm. The smell of coffee and vanilla enters his nostrils. There are newly-baked cakes and bread lying on cooling racks. Birds can be heard chirruping in the garden beyond.

There is an ambient and timeless quality to the day that he is beginning to savour and enjoy.

'Master Mannikin! Oh gracious! No one told me you would be here today! It's so lovely to see you, sir. Your father will be so pleased. He pines for you. Are you well, darling?'

Mrs. Scripture, the housekeeper, is returning from the large walk-in pantry, where she has unpacked groceries delivered earlier that morning. Mannikin nods and smiles broadly at the short wide woman; he does not know her well but she is friendly and he likes the no-nonsense and refreshing air she brings to the place. Xavier has no youthful memories of her, little that can disturb his sense of the present and therefore she remains constant and cannot shimmer too far in his imagination.

'Your father is in the dayroom; he is with Izziara. Take your drink in to see them, why don't you. They will be so pleased. Are you staying for lunch?'

Mannikin explains that he will stay for the day, although he has an engagement to attend in the evening. His fiancée will arrive later that afternoon for tea, before they leave.

'Would that be alright?' he asks.

'So delightful, sir~ I'll start preparing right away. Is Miss Oezza still on her diet may I ask?'

Mannikin smiles in response to the question and shrugs his shoulders, to declare he has no idea, whilst retreating from the kitchen with the teacup and saucer in hand.

He wanders down the corridor, past sketches and historical paintings of oriental worlds now lost to time and history. Mannikin turns into a darkened room; *the door to the dining room having been left ajar,* double doors at each end are closed, leaving the internal space without windows depressingly gloomy. He passes through, his attention captured by the soft, silky gleam of the dining room table, surprised by the layer of dust encountered as he sweeps his free hand across the beeswax-scented surface. He fleetingly questions the efficiency of the housekeeper. The teacup and saucer is gently set down in order to shake and clap his hands together, *to rid them of the fine dry particles.* Ahead of him, the double door at the far end of the room leads into the living rooms beyond; these are the best rooms in the house~ the front rooms. He advances, opening the nearest door using his still dusty hand. Mannikin reconnoitres, to remind himself of the look of the meticulous space before him. Light floods into the cheerless dining room as the door opens, driving a wedge of brilliance that penetrates and invades the gloom. His inconspicuous and hidden self looks back out of curiosity to see the effect, surprised at the copious amounts of dust newly released into the air, like miniature, floating universes, his own long shadow stretching backwards across the carpet helping to illuminate the bright particles. The man minutely observes the languid tranquility of the suspended moment, looking to see where its secret lies. He turns his gaze and attention once more to the room before him and is struck by the sweet smell of citrus fruit and lilies. The room, painted yellow, is fresh in the glorious light of morning, with Persian carpets that match the wall colour; a sense of orange and mustard abounds. The furniture is light rosewood, bright and, although the entire room is awash with ornament and clutter, it is distinctive and delightful. Well-placed flashes of red catch his eye as his gaze moves across the vista. Xavier can see that not much has changed; the room remains as appealing as it had always been. It is spotless, clean and charming. The door clunks shut as he pulls the brass rim lock towards him, before turning to walk back through the sombre dining room, this time towards the double doors at the other end. Xavier Mannikin knows that beyond these doors is where he will find his father. A frail, faltering voice from within the room calls out, 'Mrs. Scripture, we need you please, dear.'

Mannikin opens the door and is confronted by a grey, colourless space, which smells of the musty life that is to be found in it. The curtains are closed, denying light access; there is nothing here to convince one of the vibrant daylight that exists in the front room or of the immediacy of any pressing world beyond any of these walls. The heavy net and curtain simply hang like an impenetrable weight in the window space, curtailing all hope for light that might have design to penetrate this dominion. The space exists, cut off like a small island, a grey light, like fog, hangs over the dim, ebony furniture. The shadows are low, smudged and muted, adding little weight to the forms that describe the mass of books, files and boxes that are piled on tables and chairs around the place. A seated and worn day bed lies empty, but for blankets, which resemble petrified waves tossed to one side against a harbour wall. None of any of this would be seen at all, were it not for a solitary source of radiance within the room. Bathed in a little oasis of light, illuminated by a Gothic standard lamp of convoluted design that remains on, despite the day, is an old man. He sits in a high back, winged chair next to the open fire which, regardless of the summer, is lit~ his finger isolates a word on a page in a book, as if to retain the thought during this moment when his attention has been distracted. His expression suddenly changes.

'Xavier, my Mannikinboy! It's you! This is marvellous. Am I dreaming or am I dead, or are you an angel visitation? Whichever~ I embrace it all~ with all my heart. Izziara, look who it is.'

Leopold addresses a carved, ornamental post standing within the hearth of the large fireplace, the brass base of which overflows with lime. The top of the shaft has a thick cross bar, on which rheumatic claws clasp. A large bird sits atop its perch. It is an ancient, scarlet macaw of extraordinary beauty and elegance. If it once had shoulders, they are slumped and drooped like some old man in a coat too bright for his years. The bird raises its head and lets out a squawk; it realigns its plumage, as one might straighten a crumpled jacket prior to seeing an old friend.

'Who is it Izziara? Mr. Sphinx, sir! Tell us, who the devil is this, tell us, tell us please?'

The bird listens. It puts its head to one side, opening its mouth to caw, but stops; its tongue lolls. It begins to sway and then bodily moves a step to each side of its perch.

'Good morning gentlemen,' says Mannikin, 'it is so wonderful to see you both. Sorry to have interrupted your matchless, flawless morning.'

'My boy, you must have arrived in the night. I trust you slept well. I didn't hear you come in. We have been downstairs for a couple of days~ since my leg got bad. I have been sleeping here with dear, ancient Izziara. We are become two old boys. We only have each other now, have we not, Mr. Sphinx?'

'Pick a card pick a card, Leo-cold, poor old Leo~ it's the leg,' says the bird.

'Are you still him teaching poetry, father?'

'Good morning Master Mannikin, caw! Look at you please, caw-caw! Look nice you look nice my love, Jack of Spades' interjects the bird without warning, as though having just found the words to deal with the moment. He adopts a wide stride on the perch and begins to bounce his head to each side, dancing, to be noticed, or to show appreciation.

'There seems little need to teach him new tricks these days, he knows so much and is such a clever bird at reciting...'

Leopold brings his hand to his mouth to make an aside, beyond the bird's hearing and continues.

'...although, I do believe the poor soul's brain is going. He remembers poems in the wrong order and takes potluck on which lines to recite from his full repertoire. The effect lacks meaning or sometimes makes new meaning. I no longer know which. He can appear uncannily clever sometimes and when he does, I look at him carefully and always, just as carefully, with an even greater, penetrating beady eye, he looks back at me! Sometimes I wonder which one of us will fall from off our perch first. The bird is a fool, but too clever by half. Never have I met a fool so deserving of the coxcomb he wears, by dint of his own birthright.'

'Caw, caw, call me a bird Nuncle,' screams the macaw, in a voice that might be redolent of Mr. Punch.

He parades his bright feathers in the glow of the yellow light, declaring the beauty of the rich, scarlet plumage around his neck and primary colours of the feathers worn like clothing. The bird reaches out and strikes an exotic-looking Tibetan bell that hangs above one end of the perch... it rings out with a piercing resonance that continues to float in the air following the thump from the old, gnarled beak. Izziara collects a large brazil nut from the bent, brass food crock hanging next to his water jar; both hang from one end of his perch. The parrot dunks the 'brazil' momentarily in the water and then places the nut against his beak, with no intention of eating it~ as an old man might place a cigar to his mouth for effect.

'How are you my poor boy?' says Leopold. 'I have seen so little of you in recent months.'

Mannikin cringes slightly, recognising the dig that is implied and the truth it describes.

'You have your own life now of course, but forgive me, I mean no harm at all, I just think of you so much. I can't help it, it's the legacy of my lifetime to have to remember the things I love most. These days I live so much on my own. I find it easier to remember through you; there is no disrespect in doing this. It is the inclination of my age to revisit the best of my past, when there is less future. Where else can I go?'

Leopold becomes animated, suddenly remembering.

'Do you recall the pedal car you had as a child? We have it still you know. I was so surprised to find it again, about a month ago, whilst rooting through old furniture in the outhouses at the end of the garden. I have been waiting to tell you. That old teddy bear you were fond of was sitting, looking the worse for wear, in the driver's seat, wearing a battered, old Christmas party hat. It was a shock to find it again. I could have jumped out of my skin the way I discovered it. Apart from the rust, the car still looks grand; you should go and have a look! It will make you smile.'
Leopold tries to look deep into Xavier's eyes.

Mannikin averts his gaze to look around the room, hoping to gain time and opportunity to change the subject. He redirects his father's question back at him in internal dialogue, '...and how are you too my poor boy?' The room he sees is out of control, adorned with interests that clutter the place; everywhere there are boxes full of mementoes and reminders from the past. Leopold is wrapping himself in a world he once navigated, intent on pulling it all closer, with a view to revisiting his glorious and most precious moments. 'He is coming to the end,' thinks Mannikin, 'he is closing down, his adventure is diminishing, he is beginning to die before the event itself; he is preparing himself for a future that will live on without him.'

Xavier could barely call to mind putting the teddy into the old pedal car. He had all but forgotten. The episode was conveniently placed beyond his recall. However, events flood back as Leopold's prompt causes him to remember. The remains of long-perished apples, placed under the bonnet of the vehicle, seem to be absent from his father's description. Xavier winces, realising the apples do little to sweeten the memory. In truth, he had placed the bear hoping to never see it again, sending the toy onto an adventure without him; he recollects there was also a golly~ the playmates had been relegated to a perpetual holiday in a corner of the garage that Xavier was to subsequently avoid. He would not have voluntarily brought the memory to light had it not been evoked by this meddling intrusion into his childhood. He searches for an explanation. The picture of a pyramid being sealed on the death of a pharaoh comes to mind.

Mannikin continues to survey the room, noticing a cut glass, cognac decanter and a half-empty glass on a silver tray. The items lay on a low pedestal table next to where his father sits. Birdseed has spilt across the tray from a brown packet and fallen further onto the floor. Pushed, partially out of sight, to the side of the chair, Mannikin can make out a box lying with its contents strewn; he recognises these to be some of his mother's letters. She briefly sits in the far chair opposite his father as she once did and smiles tenderly at her husband~ but not at Xavier~ before vanishing as though she had never been there at all. Mannikin resumes the visual circuit of the room and sees old photo albums, jumbled playing cards piled high, some precariously placed and about to fall, some already slipped and lying on the Persian carpet. And then, quite suddenly, impulsively, Xavier pulls his head away, experiencing an unexpected stab of pain in his chest, immediately followed by a mortifying sense of unease and remorse. He recalls lacerating the toy bear's body with a sharp implement. He is shocked by the involuntary remembrance and recollects he had hidden the knife and a small mirror, on which he had left one final image of himself, *intended to be the last thing the mirror ever saw,* in the torn chest cavity at the very heart of the teddy.

Mannikin is surprised by the strength of the dormant emotion still attached to the memory. It hits him, alongside a sense of his own embarrassing naiveté. He briefly resents his father for the reminder. This is why coming home is so difficult. This is why parents are the undoing of their children. This is why Xavier disowns those once realities; Mannikin does not wish to be reminded of what he has been~ that anomalous and vulnerable beast which, try as he will, he can never fully shake off or escape. Establishing a new framework to reinvent 'the self' had proved to be very difficult, especially when the existing patterns insisted on tumbling right back in on top. Thinking in radical new ways required a peculiar partitioning of the mind, an ability that was an invention in itself. Man might indeed be self-determining and free to make himself into the being he needs to become. However, it wasn't proving to be an easy process for Xavier or his virtual alter-self, Mannikin~ or even for the whole of mankind, on the closest of inspection.

'Oh for the wings of a dove...high above the clouds so high, Polly wolly doodles...'

Izziara sings in shrill falsetto and then ceases abruptly. Both Mannikins stop to look. The macaw turns to face the other way as he picks up a hot chilli from his crock. He begins to chew, securing the delicacy on the perch with one talon.

'It's not hot is it? says the bird, into the dying heat of the almost empty fireplace.

'I see you've been rooting out all manner of things, father.'

A cardboard biscuit box has caught his attention. It reads 'by appointment' to the late emperor. Sweat-stained, leather handles stick out of the torn and faded box.

'The old tennis rackets have found a life again, I see. Have you and Izziara been reminding yourself of the rules? Have you been playing?' He smiles at his father in an attempt to dispel the mood currently running through both their heads.

'What summers they were, boy! You never took up the game, but you should have~ you have strong legs for it and the height for an effective service. You would have been good, like your grandfather. Now, there was a player. That man coached professionals in his day. He was the District 9 champion for years you know…'

Leopold waits a beat, hoping for a response, hoping that a conversation might ensue, preparing should it come.

His son had anticipated the 'tennis conversation' and the role he is meant to play. He knows the stories well and has no need to revisit any of them. Leopold has moved up to the plate and is suddenly rejuvenated, keen, reanimated~ his youthfulness, *in spirit at least,* restored. The old man is remembering, engrossed and lost within his own epic past. Might the years continue to roll away, leaving him as he once was? Xavier remembers his father; the man of those hours returns. He is proud of these memories and knows that he loves his father still.

However, the younger Mannikin is loath to relive any pasts, having been too close to a few already today. He artlessly cranks a handle that lies somewhere invisibly hidden between the two men, enabling time to return to the present, then daringly attempts to roll it a couple of teeth further, into an unknown, but anticipated future where there might be something new. His father may well be old, but might yet be cajoled to view futures with vigour and may tip, become inclined or persuaded to embrace new things, despite it being late in the day for him. The son is preparing a tête-à-tête that may mean something to them both. It should be memorable for the new ground it breaks. Such would be better use of their time. Mannikin is intent on posing a question, as an antidote to his father's indulgent exploration of a moribund past. Xavier comes forward to face Leopold. The men take stock and look at one another properly for the first time during their encounter. Leopold is made anxious; he already knows he will not understand what is about to happen. The younger man speaks.

'Can I dare to ask you a strange question, father~ a question that you have never heard me ask before?'

'Yes go on, I recognise the infernal mood you are in, go on,' he replies.

'Can you tell me something important that I need to know~ about things that you feel should interest me? But, in doing so, try to tell me something you have never shared before~ something you have never been in a position, as my father, to allude to. What you say should be surprising to me and maybe to both of us, so important as to be the thing that needs to be said before the opportunity is gone. My question is challenging I grant you, but tell me, in such circumstances, what is it you would say?'

Leopold looks away, then shyly looks at the bird and then returns to see his son setting him adrift into a deep, waterless chasm beyond his understanding.

'It is possible to do this father, if you want to. I too am a man now, so you can step out of your role as my parent, if you so wish. We can obscure the embarrassing blood-tie and the restrictions it imposes, if only briefly, before you safely return to your chosen twilight space, but first~ share a secret! It would be a wonderful gift, were it available or possible. Can you see it as I do? What is it you wish your father had been able to tell you? This could become a defining moment, made possible because I have dared to push a boundary to pose an audacious question.'

Xavier lowers his position and moves to kneel aware that Leopold's neck is becoming tired with the effort of looking upward. Mannikin continues.

'You are at your furthest edge and can better glimpse into that precipice that lies before both of us and, whilst there, you can see back again into this world, the one we both know and, before long, will soon have both known. Such is the certainty of the ongoing story. You might yet be able to tell me something new. As my father, you would want to, if you could. I know you would. Let's not dwell on sentimental reminiscences of past worlds; glory days should all lead somewhere. They do not need to only lead back to themselves. Do you have anything at all? Where are you now? Do you have any sense of what you have made yourself into or allowed yourself to become? After you have gone, what do I need to know that you will wish you had told me... about any of this?'

It is as if the air becomes very still.

The bird ruffles its feathers and lets out a low murmur, then puts its head deep under its wing.

Leopold, recognising something of what Xavier has said, desperately looks around, whilst looking into himself at the same time. He moves to speak.
'What can I have that you ask for? You are such a strange one, you ask for the impossible. I only make playing cards; I cannot deal them or play games with them. What have I done on the planet? No more than anyone. I have helped rearrange the furniture that is all. I recognise myself to be a plain man. You know this. Why then ask me, of all people, the million dollar questions best suited to the intelligence of a physicist, a philosopher or a scientist? You are a curious boy, an enigma unto yourself and that is where your answers lie, deep within the conundrum you have invented for yourself. We might be the same blood, be travelling at different

points along the same line, but I cannot know the answers you seek. This is not a hereditary madness you suffer from, you are beyond me; we are not sharing the same ideas. This is a sensibility of the time you have created for yourself. Perhaps my sense of pride and the notion I have wisdom should give me the ability to know the answer you seek. But in truth, I have come to learn that it is you who should inform me, and my old bones of the things that I have missed. Surely to God, this is more accurate. This is how it is. I have watched you carefully and this is the conclusion I have arrived at. However, as you no doubt know, this is information I do not want to hear. Let me alone. Why don't you humour me in my dotage; that is all you need to do. Do I really need to know life will go on after my death? Is it of any consequence to me what happens? If there is any telling to be done, it is you who should tell me, but do remember I am not listening to your crazy ideas. I only want to be left alone, with enough comfort to not hurt.'

Izziara's bell rings out. It swings wildly on its chain; the bird's beady eye admonishes both men in a single sideways glance, like the all-seeing eye of God disguised in the breast of the ornate beast. Leopold reflects, shaking his head.

'I will tell you what I do. I listen to Izziara Sphinx more than I should~ more than makes sense, even to me~ more than a sane man ought! We are two old creatures making do, helping each other, are we not, Mr. Sphinx? .... What do you say bird?'

Izziara strikes the bell, but gently this time. The tone rings out prettily, like a soothing charm, quietly floating across the room. Xavier reflects a moment.

'You are right father, this is good advice, thank you.'

Xavier decides to retreat, recognising the glorious ambition of what he had tried to do and the foolishness of his question, simultaneously.

'You need to sort your life out boy. That is what I think~ where is that lovely woman, Miss Oezza? She is a beauty; you will not do better than marry her. You must do that. Bring her around more often. Marry the girl; she is your match~ such legs on her too. Marry before you begin to lose your hair, whilst you have your own teeth.'

'I will come back this afternoon father. Alyesha will be here too and we can have tea together and cake… and nuts.'

He says this whilst looking directly at Izziara, caught holding his head in a talon. Xavier rubs his father's shoulder tenderly as he moves to stand before taking his leave.

'Xavier my boy, bring me more of your photographs, I always enjoy them. They tell me where you are.'

'Yes father, I will be back.'

'And so, off he trots! He leaves me here, surrounded by my delightful chaos, without noticing any of its charm~ these worn out trinkets of an old man. That is how he sees me. I have become useless. Can he not see the worth in these objects, the descriptions of my time and how it has been spent, the markers of my experiences and nobility, the treasure in these dilapidated, torn, cardboard boxes, the beauty behind the dust, the memories long vanished, but enshrined within? Even without me a meaning would live on, but only as long as there is someone to see it, I suppose. Maybe this is why my son is important. Although, without a doubt, I do love him. I do love him, but is it only as I love myself? Now there is a question and one that I dare not give him sight of. He is right, there are things unsaid, things that are not known, impossible to recognise between people. In my absence, he is the nearest thing to my continuation. But none of it makes any sense. I have Izziara here with me. If he goes first~ God forbid, what then? I have the radio I suppose, that's an alternative, but not really a bird at all. It won't fly, although like Izziara its ranting will seem to come through from some external ether. What would then become the bird? Maybe I could get a cat. Not that Mr. Sphinx must ever know that... must you, my fine feathered friend, sir?'

'*Say Cheese, my poor boy, you is a clever boy, my poor boy, eat a nut, eat a nut, want a nut.... make you better.*'
His tongue lolls and then, by chance... '*the cat walked alone along the briny beach, the sunset behind the most starless of nights never seen.*'
The bird moves to sit in his water bowl and flutters.

'I must make an effort. Xavier must not see me like this. I will call Mrs. Scripture and make the front room ready for our refreshments this afternoon. He must not see more of the old me. I will put a good memory into his mind of his old dad; we will talk fondly of his mother. I will convince him of the worth of the union with Alyesha. Hers is such a good family and her father and I go way back. I must put on new clothes. He must not see that someone has spilt soup down my tie, or that the hair in my ears is a thicket. I will wear a hat, one that will spike his interest. There is life in the old bird yet. What do you say, Mr. Sphinx?'

The bird looks at the old man 'sideways on' and winks at him. Izziara Sphinx brings his foot up to his mouth and bites on the bangle and chain that shackle him to the perch.

57.

The air is filled with the sound of traffic~ the last of the day's commuters are moving through Warcapest on their way home. Mannikin and Alyesha Oezza are out for the evening. They walk arm in arm, engaged in idle chatter and sporadic sweet nothings, oblivious of people, unaware of the noise in the city. They hold hands at busy crossings to walk faster, at one point dashing for a tram. The afternoon spent in Leopold Mannikin's front room eating polite sandwiches, cakes and drinking tea, had been very pleasant. Mid-evening was now approaching~ the softening light heralded the end of the day. It is the evening of Franz Felix von Eissenstrom's private view. Alyesha becomes quiet, seemingly passive, in part lulled by the soporific nature of the afternoon. Mannikin leads her along streets that begin to fall into shadow. Her world has temporarily paused as she endures the journey's dead time, waiting for something happen. To her, this is empty space, down time, dull time, dead time. Mannikin is more aware, his perception functioning and questioning, despite being tired. He takes interest in the metropolis happening all around and reflects as he confronts its complexity. As they walk, he sees himself moving through the city with her, against her, next to her. Their journey is like watching a film. What, he wonders, should be his response to the enormity of the unfolding events of which they are a part?

Their journey to the gallery takes a little time. As they tread their path, following an invisible line, they are moving through their present space in a partial fog. The world is experienced as a series of 'soft focus' events that simply pass by. Mannikin has no wish to make memories. He denies any cognition of what has led to this moment and is disinclined to anticipate what might be coming next. That larger thing around him~ the 'It' that it appears to be~ is running away with itself, in transit, like him, just happening. Without him, without Alyesha, without all these other simultaneous travellers, everything would disappear completely. The thought is almost too difficult to grasp. Without life there could be no awareness.

What then?

Would everything be damned to be equal and the same forever? The diamond in the jewellery shop window would become as dull and as irrelevant as the broken glass bottle in the gutter or the lump of coal that lay fallen from the back of a lorry. There could be no empathy. Is this what was meant by nothing? Without life, who would there be to see colour? The world might as well be a uniform grey. What an unimaginable emptiness. Contrary to expectation, he begins to feel comfortable, liking the sense of detachment these ideas generates. It feels warm and sits prettily within his sense of being. There was something here he identified with. There was an implied freedom within the scope of such hypothetical notions. Mannikin is functioning automatically, without thinking~ less of an individual and more of a cipher, a marker, a label of what a person is, or might be, although in truth he would prefer the description to read, 'this man has escaped and made himself invisible in the moment.' He feels anonymous and unknown in the world he inhabits. He might not be here, but for the fact he is being watched and observed. They are in fact both being followed as they walk down the busy, bustling street and, without knowing it, are serving an outside purpose to an agency of which they are not aware.

Mannikin intermittently looks across at the petite figure walking next to him, quietly spellbound by how gorgeous Alyesha looks again tonight. She has made special efforts to please him, wearing an haute couture, off-white, silk cocktail dress and cream shoes that match. Her hair is up and looks fresh and well groomed. Her face is radiant, in spite of, or because of, the artistry with which she has applied her make-up. He knows that the effort is for him, but recognises that her delight is in getting the response that confirms to her how ravishing she is. Everything starts and finishes with Alyesha. She is unable to see herself, unless it is through the look or approbation of another. It had been so important to the success of the evening that he confirmed to her, during the afternoon, how desirable she was and how beautiful. She only knew she existed if she saw her reflection in the eyes of others.
'She assumes this to be enough,' he casually thinks as they pass a large shop window that reflects their appearance back at them. He seems plain by comparison, casually dressed in a lounge suit.

At last they descend into the metro, where they wait for the next train. Mannikin contemplates the ornate, over-painted, green, cast iron pillars, enjoying the convoluted pattern of their exaggerated Corinthian design. His eyes drift thereafter onto the glazed tiles~ opulent patterns that describe abstractions he has no vocabulary to label. Behind the window of the little ticket office, a fat uniformed woman sits disinterestedly reading a celebrity magazine, whilst stroking a kitten that presses itself against the pane~ its moulting fur sticking to the greasy glass. When at last the train arrives, a number of people exit carriages and three people step aboard.

He wonders how long existence can go on like this. Was it all going to endlessly continue in this vein~ and if so where was the rationale that might give rise to a reason or an answer? The alternative seemed the easier concept to reconcile within the reality he perceived. Everything was a pointless series of events, forever tumbling over themselves, following the least line of resistance. And, without the absurdity of life and existence cluttering the equation, everything would be so much easier. He began whispering to himself.

'Can it really be, that without consciousness, nothing knowingly exists? Is the cosmos so blind? In such a firmament, even the decomposed, petrified corpses of angels could not be imagined floating forever throughout eternity ~like ships, once haunted, passing over the infinite and continuous progress of events, since time itself would lose all meaning in such a context. The present would become all encompassing and indefinite, the beginning and the end enabled to transpire in the same instant.'

Mannikin and Alyesha finally emerge from the station three stops further on, at the far end of the long street on which they had begun. They walk swiftly to the tram terminal, following the best route to the gallery. A long coat is an ill-defined and almost invisible presence in the distance behind. The unnamed man's task is made harder due to Mannikin's preference for walking, and his use of public transport.
'Why doesn't he drive everywhere, as one would expect, or avail himself of his father's chauffeur at least!' The man mutters to himself, adjusting the collar of his light summer coat.

Mannikin and Alyesha arrive at the private view late, perhaps fashionably late~ although it turns out that the artist is yet to arrive and the opening is delayed, pending his appearance. Franz Felix is ultimately in command of what will constitute 'fashionably late' this evening. The gallery is situated in a quiet street, a cul de sac. The day has all but completed its diurnal visitation, and illumination from within the gallery strengthens, as electric light spreads out across the pavement, making long shadows of potted ornamental trees, all carefully placed to aggrandise the cultural event. Guests and art lovers are milling about, spilling out into the street, poised with wine glasses, and smoking cigarettes with cultured affectation. The young couple pushes past the throng to enter the gallery, where they are immediately invited to partake of a glass of sparkling wine and offered a catalogue. Alyesha moves closer to Mannikin; he feels her warmth against his chest. The gallery is full of bodies and tightly packed~ which accounts for the overspill of patrons onto the street.

On the way to the gallery, Alyesha had held on to Mannikin's arm and sat very close to him on the tram. Proximity seemed to be a key issue with her wherever and whenever possible. The bubbly debutante had engaged in small talk about fashions, her weight and what he liked her to wear and how in love with him she was, and did he love her too? And could they make love again soon? Would that be all right? She so loved being next to his skin and was in awe of his touch. It took her breath away. Her breasts were only for him. She had never known her nipples to be so hard, except with him. He humoured her and indulged all these things. He had enjoyed the frisson and the 'daring' of their intimate sexy exchanges. They were talking 'bon-bons'. She had, however, shrugged and lost interest completely the moment he altered the conversation to declare his enthusiasm for the work of Franz Felix. He tried, in vain, to engage her attention in the topic. When asked, she declared it to be decadent, existentialist and twisted. Not nice at all. She fired off a fusillade of questions.

-'Why does he not use lovely colours?'

-'Why does he not make his work appealing?'

-'Why does he make pictures that look so unhappy and are impossible to understand? They hurt my eyes, they are uncomfortable.'
-'Surely an artist's job is to delight, to give pleasure, to make me smile and feel good.'
-'He should entertain and glamourise the world. He only thinks of himself.'
-'My shoe designer knows more about art than that man.'
-'I know what I like.'
-'A painting should look as if it smells beautiful~ if it is to have any worth at all.'
Alyesha was pleased with all her pronouncements; Mannikin seemed to have been unable to contradict her. She felt she had made statements in a way that should please him. She was concerned with effect rather than the meaning of what she said. Alyesha was so sure of everything she didn't know. Mannikin resisted making a response, realising anything he said would seem platitudinous.
The phrase, *'Surely every smell has a potential to be the perfume that tells us something of who we are...'* crossed his mind so briefly as to have almost not existed.

Alyesha continues to hold onto Mannikin's arm as they move through the exhibition; it has become a vice-like grip. She looks ahead, anticipating what they might have to see next and leads him away where possible, or holds back, attempting to avert his and her gaze from the inexplicably strange world of a creative beast~ one who possesses the power to paint and describe the unimaginable~

with the insight to imagine those things at or beyond edges~ those unseen places where there might be hidden danger or anarchy lurking~ where a reality in nature conflicts with the pleasant artifice of blind, pleasure-seeking, human existence.

'Alyesha, I really want you to look here!' Mannikin points out the direction he wants them both to move in.
'This must be some of the man's best work. He is a law unto himself. He dares to twist reality to suit his vision of what might be possible; he is inventing a new edge through which to see his and our predicament. Yes, he is decadent and daring and insolent, as you say, but just try to see what he is saying. Should he only make paintings to confirm what you already know, want to hear or are prepared to accept? Should it be a thing that only entertains and diverts uneasy attention away from contentious issues, or should the creative endeavour enable and encourage us to question our understanding of the universe?'
'What are you talking about?' she says turning to him. 'I love you, that is all there needs to be and that is enough. Love is all you need!'

He finds himself agreeing. Annoyingly she might have arrived at the answer to the equation without doing any of the work. However, he finds himself suspicious of her notion of love, heavily suspecting its authenticity and ability to cope with everything it has never thought of, or been inquisitive about. Her love comes with a selfish belief in self, a thing that those who truly love her must always overlook if they are to prove they can love her on her terms.

Accepting those terms would make a slave of any suitor. She might indeed be gorgeous now, but there was a tinge of self-serving, shortsighted prejudice attached to Alyesha, or so it seemed to Mannikin. His anxiety was that she made no attempt to understand herself, or him, and never would. He gives her a peck on the cheek, causing her to radiate. Alyesha was spoilt and selfish, but innocent. She was beautiful and sexual. He did like her very much in truth, in a carnal, lustful way. She was exciting and knew it, but she could not engage the depths of his mind.

He moves away from Alyesha, momentarily, to view a particular series of paintings, believing himself to be in the presence of something important.

Mannikin felt there was a bigger picture implied, but never quite declared in Franz Felix's work. It therefore became part of the viewer's imperative to make sense of a thing that could barely be envisioned and perhaps made no sense at all. The paintings depicted figures within dark or subdued landscapes, or mysteriously appearing in expansive interiors. The suggestion was that they might be floating in space. There seemed to be a lack of shadow to suggest how they were fixed into their environments. Each spirit radiated varying degrees of light from within, some much more than others. Perhaps an irrepressible energy at their very core was discharged through the pores of their skin or escaped through the apertures of their eyes.

His concentration is broken as Alyesha reminds him of her presence, by sliding her arm through his once more. On looking around, he notices that Count Zapik has arrived~ Caruso Maelstrom is embracing him with gusto. He had noticed this other man at the Villa Apollinaire, where his prowess as a dancer had been unmatched during the after show party; Mannikin recognised a gifted dancer when he saw one. Zapik seemed drained and tired or maybe, in the full glow of a gallery spotlight and without stage make-up, was simply looking as real as any other person.

Mannikin returns his empty glass to a passing tray and takes another that is full. He hands this to Alyesha, in process of which he returns her glass and collects another for himself. At her insistence, they continue like 'lovebirds', arm in arm, perambulating slowly around, taking in the paintings and the atmosphere. The sound in the gallery soon begins to sing a new song; the ambience in the room changes, at last denoting the anticipated arrival of the maestro for the evening. Franz Felix has set foot in the space. He enters the gallery with an entourage of associates. Everyone becomes quiet as the gallery director shouts for order and then begins the late introduction to the exhibition; there follows a brief discussion of the work between a member of the gallery staff and a critic.

During this time Mannikin looks to see where Zapik might be, wondering whether he might move nearer the magician to conveniently catch him for a chat, but he seems to have vanished from the room and is nowhere to be seen. The director steps forward again.

'...and so, ladies and gentlemen we are here to celebrate the extraordinary genius of a great painter~ not all the world knows this yet, but we here tonight are the advance guard.'

Applause ensues.

Franz Felix steps forward to offer thanks to the owner and his gallery staff. The man is flamboyant, unaccountably singular and, as appearances would suggest, made of the same odd stuff as his work. Sartorially, he is quite out of keeping with every other person in the room, sporting a unique and lavish dolman, not unlike some kind of opulent smoking jacket. The body colour is of a glistening crimson, Italian thick silk cloth, cut and decorated in the Hungarian style of around 1680. On top of this, patterned embroidery down the chest front and back is lavishly raised in ornamental gold wire decorations, inlaid with coral beads that curl, *redolent of organic growth*, into elongated spiralling forms across the garment. Between this, atlas silks are interwoven into and over the fabric, with gilded silver and gold thread bobbin lace~ the antique lace is tightly bound and meticulously embroidered. The opulence is breathtaking and anachronistic, the splendour faded. The fastenings, to the front and at the neck of the garment, are gold enamelled clasps in the shape of wings, grouped closely together and finishing at the navel. The deep cuffs and each of the five sleeve buttons, *again in the shape of wings*, are made of gilded silver thread. Beneath, he wears a pair of black, close fitting trousers and bench made, black leather, laced shoes.

Mannikin realises he is missing everything of what Franz Felix is saying~ the look of the man and his garb has demanded so much of his attention.

'...in addition,' he continues. 'I do thank you all for coming tonight. There are more people here than this space should be holding, in truth. This is good and it is bad. My work is that of a private man and to be seen amongst so many confuses how I would most like it to be viewed. I wish each of you to come when there is no one else here and then, in the quiet of your mind, see again what is before you. It is in this way that you might best discern what has happened during the course of building these paintings~ if anything at all! We deceive ourselves better than we deceive those around us, do we not? You must decide, and I am happy to be at your mercy. Even if I~ or you, were to understand what it is you see here tonight, it is not my role to inform you of what you most naturally choose to see yourself.'

'Re-living memories and imagining futures is essential to all our lives. Yet, the very nature of imagination impedes and disorientates those same memories. It diversifies reality to the point where almost nothing can be known unequivocally. As a species, we make use of this to define multiple truths. In so doing, we keep reinventing our own past and anticipating our preferred futures, both collectively and individually. These things all coexist side by side. Are we unique in being able to dream ourselves into imaginary spaces, those places where our spirits would like us to be seen, travelling mentally in time in the direction of our own choosing? I suspect not. Are we the only ones in a turbulent universe to question the ontology of existence? Now there is a question!'

'For me, painting is not about art or an artefact, or a book in which characters might only appear to exist, it is the encounter between the conscious mind and the worlds it locates in its perception. I have discovered this~ if there is 'time', we are it. Take me apart and learn my constituents and you will realise I do not truly exist, only your prejudice in this moment refuses to allow you to accept the truth of what I say on behalf of all of us.'

'We wonder about ghosts.... we all are.'

'I hope the work on these walls is the endeavour of an inquisitive artist. It is yours. Please enjoy.'

Franz Felix von Eissenstrom looks slowly around with concentrated focus and intent, seemingly into every face of the large assembled group, as all clap to herald the grand opening of the exhibition.

The group of associates Franz Felix arrived with presses forward and surrounds him once more. Amongst their number are youthful men, possibly artists themselves and a couple of young women, one of whom most conspicuously seems to be the familiar of the man in the exquisite dolman. She is a breathtakingly beautiful, bohemian beauty~ bejewelled and bewitching, wearing lavishly embroidered clothing like the master she stands next to. She adopts a pose, strangely coquettish and beguiling, appearing somewhat shorter in stature than those around her. Could one anticipate her look to be that of a lost soul, a character in a fiction who may forever be destined to look out to sea, mesmerised by the beauty and tranquility of a line where water meets air?

Franz Felix appears surprisingly different tonight, or so it seems to Mannikin. The painter is fresher and more dynamic in appearance than he had seemed at the Villa Apollinaire so recently. Mannikin sees that the man has become smooth skinned. Previously he had been unshaven, sporting facial hair. For a man in his late fifties, he looks deceptively young. His unusual leanness accounts for this. He might be a Zapik without a moustache, only slightly taller, towering over most of the others in the room. His silver-grey hair is worn very short and his eyebrows are thick and black, his skin without blemish, but for a large dark mole in the centre of his forehead. He leans into the bohemian beauty and tantalises her with an unexpected comment made into her ear. A look passes between them~ an indication of some indecipherable, but intimate bond.

Mannikin looks around, disappointed not to see Zapik in the gallery. He should have liked to make a comparison between the two men~ their opportunistic proximity might have allowed for a direct observation in the same moment. He was wondering whether his interest in Zapik was developing into an obsession. Something about that man, or a particular detail to do with him, occupied his thoughts at some deep level in a place just slightly beyond his reach. There were things about him that Mannikin kept almost remembering and then totally forgetting.

Just beyond his gaze he notices a man in a long coat at the doorway~ seemingly denied entry to the exhibition, perhaps because he lacks an invitation. The stranger cranes to look around the gallery, maybe searching for an advocate or someone he might recognise to vouch for him. Alyesha, meanwhile tugs at her chaperone's arm and asks, in a baby voice, if they might go for dinner now~ with a view to walking past some of the exquisite clothes shops in the central district and looking in at their window displays. Mannikin agrees to her request, but expresses a wish to briefly converse with the artist and congratulate him on his work and endeavour before they leave. He moves towards the painter at an opportune moment.

Mannikin has to wait his turn, as an elderly patron takes precedence. The man asks Franz Felix whether he might buy the key work in the exhibition and whether that would in addition, buy time to talk to the maestro-virtuoso about future commissioned work. Felix encourages the man to buy whichever work he likes, whilst informing him he no longer undertakes commissions.

'You may buy anything of me from the walls. Negotiations for sales should be directed to the gallery owner.'

Franz Felix changes the subject to compliment the man on his homburg and then turns his head to face Mannikin.

The men look at each other and then Xavier realises, in so doing, he has been provided with an audience and should speak first.

'Excuse me, Herr Felix,' he collects his thoughts, wondering what it is he wants to say. 'I am so pleased to be here this evening. You may remember me. Indeed we were seated next to one another at the Villa Apollinaire recently.'

Felix smiles warmly at Xavier, which encourages him to say more.

'I like your work very much and find it so unusual; it is uncommonly intense and although absorbing, is difficult to look at. Your work, correct me if I am wrong, seems to be obsessed by your personal sense of being~ but in addition, there is a thing beyond that, is there not? Something I, like so many others, only imagine I vaguely recognise. What might it be? Do you know?'

The tall figure now turns fully to face Xavier and in so doing politely acknowledges Alyesha, whilst clicking his heels. He smiles broadly at them both from his little bird-like mouth.

'Thank you both for coming this evening~ it is lovely to meet you again. I recognise you, of course and moreover know you as a gentleman who already owns examples of my work; we have indeed met previously, as I remember, on a number of occasions. Sir, you ask~ what do I know? Very little in this moment, I assure you. I am the last person who can talk about my work. I do what I can. I try to find better ways to do it. That is all! As I look at these paintings tonight on these walls, I suspect they are shallow and ultimately meaningless. They have merely assisted in the passing of time and helped deal with an unaccountable and deep yearning within my poor, demented soul. To tell you more is to engage in deceit, to impress you with ideas that may not be real. What I do is all I can do. What you see is the total of the phenomenon that is me. Tonight, in this place, these works, as I look at them, all seem to mean nothing and make me wonder whether all of me is a deceit. In truth sir, all this seems absurd to me. That is what I know now, ask no more~ or ask again when my former, grandiloquent sense of reality returns and I will speak like a mystic or a magician of strange, inexplicable things~ however that too will be a deceit, no doubt. So, more interestingly, tell me what you see in these works.'

Alyesha moves in closer to the group, apparently interested at last and wanting to be looked at a little more. Thus far, Franz Felix has not taken enough notice of her, in her estimation. Xavier continues.

'I doubt I know, Herr Felix. I do empathise with all your work. I would like to own more should it become possible. Your paintings explore those edges for which I also feel a great affinity. They demand my interest with their sense of illusion, mysticism and yearning for a thing that cannot be described. More formally, I simply love the decadent use of colour and texture, the turbulent intensity of the images and the anarchy in the pattern making; such descriptors suggest possible or proposed meanings, before any analysis of the iconography begins. Thereafter, I cannot help but notice that the expressions of the figures describe an abandoned, vacuous look, a desolate emptiness~ and yet, from within their very core, your figures gush with a spiritual and emotional energy that is in process of releasing itself and dissipating. Might they be batteries running down and dying? Is it something like this? Have I got it right?'

Franz Felix smiles briefly as he looks away momentarily, before turning his head back.

'There is no right, but if I were to know, I would say we are talking along similar lines. In this moment, we are become brothers. Let me give some advice. Do not buy any of these works. Come and see me later~ next year would be good~ if you are still interested, if we are still here! Here is my card. I will remember you, I promise.'

Xavier thanks him and gives assurances that he will indeed be in touch, sooner rather than later. The artist smiles in acknowledgement. They turn away and move on. Alyesha has to take one further look back as they walk away.

'He is a strange one, telling you not to buy his work! You can do what you want, he can't tell you. You are the customer, right! You are in charge. You do what you want~ buy one of his silly pictures and show him. How dare he tell you that they are rubbish! I quite like the frames, actually.'

'Alyesha, you missed the point, that is not what he is saying. There are different realities here; you misunderstood him completely.'

'Why has he given you his card, what does that mean?'

'I think neither of us know. He is seeing an opportunity that might be interesting, that is all.'

'What do you mean, what opportunity?'

'Simply the chance to move in a direction that has potential, for sharing ideas perhaps, being inquisitive, testing our diverse sensibilities to see if we are the same or different without fear of reprimand or need for commitment. I don't know, its just a door into another potential future, I suppose.'

'Will you go to see him?'

'Who knows?'

'You must let me come too. You need to be protected, I think.'

'Yes I am sure you are right, darling. Lets go look into shop windows and find you a dinner.'

The rest of the evening unfolds, following a pattern that might be predicted, adopting the most convenient line of least resistance through to its conclusion. The debutante pushes food around on a plate, eating little whilst her beau only has a small first course. Little is said. Mannikin is quiet and contemplative. Alyesha is in a mood at the tedium of the evening. She was looking so beautiful tonight and has not yet had a proper chance to show off. Her opportunity to be glorious has been stifled, if not wasted. They soon decide, by mutual consent, to leave the quaint little restaurant, feeling slightly annoyed with one another. Mannikin is tired and impresses upon Alyesha his need to spend the night at his father's. They make their journey by taxi, first returning Alyesha to her father's home.

On arrival, her inamorato offers his protection by escorting the piqued Alyesha to the front door and into the safety of her father's house, where he lingers a moment to give her an affectionate peck on the cheek and an intimate caress. In return, she looks up adoringly into his eyes and presses herself onto him. After this, Mannikin returns to the waiting taxi driver, where he instructs the man, in a perfunctory manner, to drive on to an outlying area of the city.

Far from returning to his father's house, *as he had intimated to Alyesha*, Mannikin took the taxi to an address in District 13~ the site of the old Mannikin Playing Card factory. The dour, desolate street was, as he expected, dark and dismal at such a late hour~ barely illuminated by an ancient, gas lamp. The taxi slid to a standstill, its headlights picking out the brooding woebegone buildings beyond dilapidated railings and an imposing gateway. He paid and tipped the cabbie. As the car drove off, leaving the street in dense gloom, Xavier felt for, and pressed, an ancient cobwebbed doorbell on the face of the tired, brick wall next to the gatehouse. Within moments, a yellow floodlight made itself known, throwing the wrought iron gates, high railings and extensive use of barbed wire into sharp relief. Ordinarily, the buildings that lined this abandoned street appear empty and forgotten. No one would suspect the quiet, secret and continued use of the defunct premises.

Ryman, the gatekeeper, was quickly on hand to open one half of the gates to allow the visitor access. Thin smiles passed between the men. It was enough~ their brief salutation, it seemed, needed no spoken words.

Xavier walked through and stood adjacent to the gatehouse, waiting, whilst Ryman padlocked and chained the ancient, cast iron gate behind them. The original gate lock had rusted beyond its utility long ago~ only the ornamental handles, cast in the shape of spiralling cephalopods, remained. Xavier hovered a moment longer, as a courtesy, to ensure the man had secured the premises and was safe and then, as Ryman waved and began to return to the gatehouse, he took his leave. They were a little distance apart when the men turned again to look at one another. This time Ryman nodded to suggest that everything was fine. There was a brief return acknowledgment. Xavier walked away from the gatehouse, by degrees becoming enveloped and lost in the black night. He walked up to and through a grand entrance arch on the front of the large factory building, feeling his journey to the unassuming and hidden side entrance to be longer than he had previously remembered. The blackness insinuated itself into everything, it pervaded, entering his heart. He felt strangely detached~ more so than usual. A large hawk moth fluttered a little distance above his head, becoming briefly illuminated, before vanishing. The heavily worn pathway seemed to be taking an eternity to traverse. Such intense blackness consumed both his image and his soul. He moved into a space away from the light.

★ ★ ☆ ★

58.

Xavier's thoughts wander.

Inexplicable images of Ryman's gatehouse drift in and out of his consciousness. The building stands surrounded, immersed in a nocturnal, murky gloom; a dank mist lies in the air. The man finds himself glimpsing the interior of the house like a voyeur, having to stand on tiptoe to look through windows, intent on seeing past shabby nets and ill-fitting, closed curtains. Within, there are half-glimpsed poorly lit images of Ryman's skinny, invalid daughter dragging her poor, twisted feet from room to room. He catches sight of her strange, inarticulate movements as she disappears around corners or exits through doorways into internal corridors. He moves from one grime-streaked window to another to find where she has gone.

Xavier is in a dream.

Then, the world is newly bright, it is daytime and a dusty wind blows as fleets of lorries pass continuously through the factory gate. Xavier, *struggling to adapt to the unexplainable searing light,* is talking to Ryman Kilmit, who leans against the faded, paint-peeled front door of the gate house~ it is slightly ajar. The old factory appears to be in commission again or is he remembering how it had once

been? He counts banknotes into Ryman's hand, raising his voice to be heard above the din of the engines roaring past. The thin, pale girl peers around from behind Ryman and looks up at Xavier with wide eyes as she holds onto her father's coat, then moves back, merging into the narrow hallway of the tiny house where she remains in shadow, leaning against a wall, staring into vast emptiness. Xavier finds he is shouting the same thing repeatedly.
'This is to help. This is to make things better. This is so nothing changes. This is to keep things the same. Do you understand... you do understand, don't you?'

The scene fades and the darkness returns. Xavier discovers he is driving through the factory gates in an ancient, black limousine with running boards, its chrome yellow fog lights blazing, forming conspicuous cones of light in the surrounding mist, illuminating squid patterns and nautilus shapes in the wrought iron. He mouths words to thank the gatekeepers as he enters, his voice lost amidst the roar of the engine and the whirr of his mind. Ryman and his daughter stand in the lurking fog as if haunted or bewitched, hollow-eyed and staring, their blank, drawn-faces bleached of colour in the yellow lights of the car. Ryman beckons the man to keep coming~ and then once through the gate, Xavier glances up into the rear view mirror to see the gate-keeper's lank figure illuminated in the red glow of the vehicle's rear lights. He turns to regard the man's daughter on the far side, strangely illuminated in a way that confuses him. She is no longer crippled, but stands poised and made perfect.

The scene unaccountably changes one last time as Xavier begins to resurface from his slumber. He sees that he has parked a few streets away in an old garage and walked to the factory, entering the site through a side gate that, in truth, has never existed. *Might this be a warning about the potential of being discovered?* The image vanishes, leaving a benign trace, a marker of its meaning in his consciousness… for later.

Xavier wakes in the night~ into the still, still of night, into the quietude of an expanse of what might be mortal emptiness, finding himself disturbed and disorientated. He imagines birds in the air, flying in slow motion at the strangest of speeds, aware that there are wild cats looking on. He might be floating or suspended, lost in the arms of an indescribable moment, entwined within dynamic energy, close to a place in which he feels comfort. Who is this weightless dream person surrounding him, arousing his interest, taking her pleasure, stealthily sucking him in, intoxicating him with passion, stretching him out, filling herself whilst lost amidst a miasma of sensation, enveloping him in erotic energy and physicality. The woman is astride him, moving slowly and with the tiniest of movements, creating the largest of sensations possible. He is trapped in an enclosed, warm space, unable to resist, with no wish to escape. He gives in, abandoning himself, losing time, without the need to exist other than to feel the moment unfold for as long as it will allow... before falling back to sleep.

It is some hours before Mannikin awakens once more into the continuous sleeping heart of night. The voluptuous siren lays next to him, vanquished, asleep and docile, a sleeping cat, a sphinx perhaps. He can feel her soft warmth, her body smelling of scent and salt. The last flickering glow from a depleted candle next to the bed blinks, prior to its imminent oblivion. Xavier looks into the gloom scarcely moving, so as not to wake the woman. A stemmed glass half full of red wine, begins to change its position, apparently of its own volition, moving imperceptibly across the pitted surface of a low table near him, perhaps transported by tremors or a disturbance in the atmosphere, or an earthquake. He hears thunder crack and listens, imagining where above his head it might be. On returning his gaze to the glass, he sees that it has not, moved at all and is, in fact, quite empty. Xavier raises himself from the mattress, taking up the brief flame to guide him through the murky blackness. His naked outline, little more than a silhouette, walks across uneven floorboards sparsely covered in dilapidated carpets and worn rugs. Dancing shadows on the walls indicate that the room slopes inward towards a flat ceiling. There is plaster missing, exposing wooden slats like ribcages that lie beneath. Narrow, classically styled window alcoves appear at the centre of the four sides of the room, their wooden, painted surfaces peeling and the window frames rotten and dilapidated. This space is the interior to what would have a once been a lavish, ornamental pinnacle at the top of a building. What furniture remains is old, worn and in poor repair. Internal curtains divide and partition the room. Xavier moves into an area pressed into service as a kitchen, where he pours water from a large enamel jug into a saucepan and begins to heat it using a stove connected to a gas canister. Purring cats appear at his heels and rub themselves against his legs. The improbable bohemian space is both a camp and a hideout. Indeed, it was Xavier's childhood den, later made into a flat during his student years and remains a place for clandestine rendezvous. The room exists, hidden at the top of the old factory.

Whilst water is heating, Xavier dons a knee-length, fur coat to keep warm. He makes tea and with a steaming cup in hand, gingerly crosses the room to ascend the spiralling staircase that leads to the small, flat roof. After stepping out into the night air, he carefully closes the little door behind. Soft billing and cooing breaks out where nestling doves in wall recesses have been briefly disturbed by the man's intrusion. The perimeter to the square rooftop is edged with a waist-high, brick parapet below a rusted, black, ornamental balustrade. This is the highest point on the building and the best vantage point for miles. Xavier is greeted by familiar and spectacular views across the ebullient, electric city in front of him and by the brooding, foreboding countryside and mountains behind. Moving to the middle of the space, he steps up onto a raised, wooden platform; at its centre a redundant flagpole rises yet higher. From here, the view into the night in all directions is most dramatic. This is Xavier's lookout post across the entire world and from where he can view the firmament above. A light wind passes and there is dampness in the air. Despite the glow of the city in the distance, the view overhead reveals the sparkling path of the Milky Way in all its glory and the night sky's cosmos of stars. Xavier reminds himself of all the times he has spent on the rooftop over a lifetime. He pictures and remembers himself as a boy, then as the student he became and the long summers that fill his memory. And now, at last, he has arrived, filling the space in his maturity.

This is the place where it becomes possible to think without restriction; it is the only place in which Mannikin allows himself to know he has two, independent, parallel existences.

Xavier Mannikin has two lives and has learned to live, and even enjoy, both. He compares them to the rivers that run through Warcapest. The first is the Dula. It is shallow, slow and sluggish but dependable~ trustworthy, used for formal state occasions and has pleasure trips that run up and down its course. People are married on its banks and there are funeral barges that take the dead to a place of rest further downstream. Its photograph appears in brochures and on postcards everywhere, and is universally embraced as the acceptable face of the great city. It describes history and the prestige with which Warcapest wishes to surround itself. In consequence, the Dula has the best bridges and the grandest buildings lining its banks. This is the river that Mannikin finds himself travelling most often. It is safe and proper, ecclesiastical, pompous and ceremonial, so sure of its own tradition and importance. It is insistent on never changing its route. It blinkers the world to other possibilities and can only be seen in this one way. He knows it to be universally preferred by his fellow denizens and is the common standard by which a noble river, with a good course and sound banks, is judged.

It is so easily contrasted and contradicted by the other.

The Vienop, by comparison, is dynamic and full of motion. Fleet-footed, fast flowing, determined~ forever altering its course to undermine buildings and cause bridges to fall, it consistently breaches Warcapest's most delicate underground systems~ the wayward energy is intent on running deeper and further than expected. The structures along its route have been built in contemporary styles that vainly attempt, *using modern technologies,* to outwit its obduracy. In this river, there is, in some indescribable way, a more discernable truth, a rebelliousness that intimates true spirit and raw physical nature. It is also the river of the suicidal. The Vienop, however, does not elucidate a tangible reality for Xavier~ it seems more akin to his dream world, made as real as he dare make it, for fear of censure. There is comparatively little water traffic that uses this river. If it is access to another place, few people know where to, or what for.

Each of Warcapest's rivers lives alongside the other. Both are perhaps indispensible and joyous. Being part of and not being part of, are necessary aspects of who Xavier Mannikin is. However, there is more... having a life that is lived on more than one level simultaneously reveals truths that might otherwise go unnoticed. He feels it acutely, the artifice of one is revealed in his analysis of the other. His life is constantly informed by living on more than one level at the same time. Two streams of separate water, like two rivers, flow through him. More than one life being lived, more than two lives being understood, providing insight into a profusion of different realities.

His secret factory hideout is decadent, morbid and the antithesis of the world he formally occupies. It is for him a real space where he can ebb and flow without restriction.

Come the daylight Xavier sleeps late, due, in part, to his midnight, nocturnal visitation and the time spent glorying in the splendours of the world from the roof of the old factory. The siren, his lover, the woman from the night, the elusive Sara Phielnx, wakes him~ having prepared a light breakfast. They eat and relax amorously in each other's company, before returning to the comfort of the bed. Time is spent idling the morning away in sensuality and deep conversation about all and sundry. They frequently become animated and laugh uncontrollably~ indulging the passing hours and playing like children.

Later, the young woman gets up to start work in a partitioned corner, where a little workshop has been constructed. Xavier decides to browse and enjoy an old book on moths and butterflies he has had since a child. He wanders the space, distractedly looking out of windows and notices Ryman, far below in the distance, doing his rounds~ he spends a moment absent-mindedly and poignantly watching the gatekeeper. He recognises that he and Ryman are in cahoots, intent on keeping the old factory in existence for as long as possible; they need it as a relativity point and a thing to hold onto. Xavier understands his own need, but is left wondering about Ryman's. This other man undoubtedly has a bond and a deep-rooted connection to the site and its grounds. The factory is so important to him that he cannot see beyond it or see himself being anywhere else. The man has buried himself here, perhaps more so than Xavier. In Xavier's imagination, Ryman Kilmit is become a boatman, a ferryman into this secret place, which they have both agreed to share and maintain~ there is a need. They have a symbiotic relationship.

59.

Xavier, wearing a vest and trousers, lays drowsily on the raised platform next to the flagpole. Perspiration trickles from his armpits onto the warm, slatted surface beneath, the salty moisture absorbed into the porous, weathered wood. His consciousness examines the line of where he finishes and everything else starts.

He attempts to look up into the daylight, into the vast sky above, but it is far too bright for that; instead he closes his eyes, covering them with a forearm. An airplane, he recalls, had leafleted the city with raindrops recently. He finds himself trying to make sense of the memory~ then reminds himself of the summer storms. During the most recent and unusually tempestuous deluge, the whole roof had been engulfed. He had seen it, witnessing the event. Water had collected and 'backed up', unable to escape into the gutter and, in consequence, overflowed in a torrent from the open-mouthed downpipe. The world was so miraculously wet then. He had never known the heavens to be in such turmoil or so loud in their declamation. The roof seemed like the bridge of an ark that floated above some biblical flood. Today however, the world is warm and smooth again. He opens his eyes and imagines Sara Phielnx before him. He looks at her intently. She returns his look and is heavenly, her demeanour bewitching. She looks away to indicate that the sun is too bright for her. She shields her eyes and looks back and beams, her mouth opening as her smile continues to grow, and then she laughs, without any sound coming at all. This strange, hypnotic woman, who is she? She fascinates him. He is bewitched. What does he know of her? He reflects…

Images of her keep coming.

He sees her in the room below in the workspace she has made for herself and carved out of nothing. Xavier had never anticipated that the room might one day become a studio or that he might have access to such a prize~ this gorgeously, enchanting, enticing woman, brimful of creative thought and beauty. Who might have guessed? Sara Phielnx occupied her time for hours, in deep concentration and activity, making maquettes and constructions of weird and wonderful design. She would tie found objects together with string or wire, or use glue to make magical, abstruse figurines and little sculptures, which were delicately painted, and often hung from the ceiling. Sometimes she modelled shapes in wax or clay, for casting. Sara was a secret poetess, capable of giving form to bizarre ideas and flights of fancy.

He catches a glimpse of her decorating a hinged cigar box with a striped pattern, designed to be worn as a necklace, like the artefact that appears in the surrealist film, 'Un Chien Andalou', by Buñuel and Dali. She intimates she has something important to place inside it. Xavier concludes that the interest and joy she extracts from such creative endeavour has evolved out of the pleasures and frustrations of her occupation.

Sara works in a city museum as assistant curator and researcher of ancient artefacts and collections. She is highly qualified in her area and has a passion for handcrafted objects from all periods in history. Her position, and the responsibility that accompanies it, is full of protocols that restrict the joy and abundance for life that is so apparent in the objects she deals with and handles. The museum service cocoons the objects in its possession from the life they were once intended to live. Perhaps her personal artwork reinvigorates the passions that her job curtails.

Protocol demands that she demonstrate reserve, good sense and be deliberately understated in the workplace. Most often she wears simple, classically cut suits and court shoes to the museum. Despite a passion for living, she has few expensive clothes and avoids make-up. A range of her garments and other possessions are kept in their room at the factory.

Most curiously, Xavier does not know where she lives outside of this, their shared world; she disallows him all knowledge of her background. He has no contact information for her; the woman wishes to remain an enigma. In spite of the curious arrangement, their relationship is well established and the lovers have been secretly meeting for years past, since their early twenties, when they were students together. Their romance is unorthodox and atypical. They agree the days to meet in their factory nest, often two or three times a week. Other than this, they attend exhibitions or go to cafés, or the city centre where they encounter one another, but only ever from a distance. She is very particular and will rarely allow them to fraternise in public. She is impenetrable. He only knows what he has seen of her through their shared experiences.

'Don't ask me who I am out there; its no part of what we are, it's not your business to know. I only want us to be this; what we have is 'this'. It is fragile; expose it or me, and we will die.'

He had once asked whether she had some horrendous back-story or dark secret, but she was vehement that this was not the case. She simply would not allow anything to spoil their fantasy~ there was no need to recognise the rude mechanics of the tedious, independent life they were both forced to lead outside of this, their shared dream. In the past, he had followed her to see where she went, to discover where she lived in the external world. He had waited for her to finish work, never knowing at what time she might leave and when he saw her, would follow, but could never keep up with her movements along streets, onto and off buses, through thoroughfares or shopping parades. He soon gave this up as a poor job. She changed patterns on a regular basis, as though she knew he might be there waiting, or knew that one day it would happen and therefore was always prepared. She moved with the stealth of a cat, a leopard. He had once phoned the museum to ask for her when he knew she would not be there, in the hope of talking to a friend or a colleague. When she discovered this, she scolded him, became petulant and refused to talk to him for days for cheating on their

arrangement. He could not discover her family or parents anywhere in the equation. He had checked the city records office for evidence of births, deaths and marriages, all to no avail. Her name was unlikely to be her own, he decided. She was an enigma, like the sphinx statues that glory the entrances to the museum. When he saw her at the end of a day, she was tired and weakened, her skin worn and pale. Her time each month left her ashen and white lipped for the duration; the pain bent her double, making her vulnerable and soft, and drained of life. He imagines her then, as a figure lying supine in deep, newly-fallen snow, the blood within her draining away. She could be so weak and when she was, he lifted her up and protected her, and then she would be strong again. She was, for the most part, dynamic and irrepressible, vivacious and electric. She thrilled him. They were dancing life's adventure together in each other's company, calling out to the moon, as if to say,
'Look, we are here... we are... see this... you thing... you whatever!'

He often wonders if keeping their meetings clandestine and secret is the reason why they seek each other out. Doing it any other way might break the spell of a thing they both needed. Life must be kept mysterious and vital for her, for them both it seemed, in accordance with her steadfast view that this was the way it is, or has to be. To allow it to resolve itself and become normal would somehow be a lie and the death knell.

Although, he had noticed recently that subtle changes had crept into the conundrum; she had become increasingly erratic. Their relationship seemed to have shifted and become, if anything, of greater dynamic intensity and somehow desperate. She had told him that she feared she would not live long. It was her lingering apprehension; he knew this. She had told him before, but the anxiety had intensified lately. She had cut her hair, without explanation, for the first time he had known. This saddened Xavier, as her long hair was so lovely to him. He had pleaded with her to grow it back. She had merely smiled benignly at him, in slow, impenetrable response.

Their shared passion and sexuality, which had always been hypnotic and intense, was become wild and eccentric. Usually she preferred to hardly move at all, seeking out his shapes and revealing hers to him. She now gave way to frenzy and wild incoherence, made big sensations and would bite and scratch him as a wild animal might that was escaping capture. She would dig her fingers into him, deeply invading the muscles and sinews beneath the surface of his skin. Tears would fill his eyes at her wild desperation and unease. She would tear and beat at him, as though fighting back demons that were attempting to devour her.

He turns on his side to shield his eyes from the full brightness of the sun.

Her 'writing wall', comes to mind; a magical place, vaguely reminiscent of the great cave paintings of prehistoric peoples. She scrawls graffiti and makes strange marks using all manner of implements and knives, *accessing high parts of the wall from the spiral staircase in the room's corner.* She makes repeated use of the same words and letterforms, frantically depicting them in bizarre texts and expressive scrawls. They are frequently gouged out of the plaster using a vicious energy. She writes 'Ariel' and 'Sphinx' endlessly, *[Sara **PHielNX**]*, without ever attempting to explain the meaning of why she does this. And then she goes on to passively and delicately draw hands that look like wings.

Xavier alters his gaze to wake from his reverie, wondering if he has invented her, whether she is real.

The flagpole sways gently in the light breeze. The world seems to have stopped momentarily. The top of the pole has a blackened gilded star at its point, its surface depleted and worn, the wood grain standing proud in peaks~ the gold that remains is heavily distressed. A bird, high above, floats into view, then a second one appears; both pass, gliding in and out of the picture he sees. The sky beyond is magnificent but empty, apart from the paleness of a crescent moon that remains almost hidden in daylight and, more surprisingly to him, a barely discernable, tailed comet.

He stands at last, stretching to his full height and then elevates further onto tip-toes, expanding himself and feeling his calf muscles lengthen, enjoying the sensation. He looks out across the city~ in the distance there is another large star, a red one, rotating slowly on top of a commercial building just half a mile away. In some way, everything is connected~ it is joyous and bewitching~ it's just all too strange to figure.

★ ★ ☆ ★

60.

'I must get more cigars. I know I am about out.' Harry Towers flicks the switch on the intercom.

'Mrs. Stefanz, could you send the errand boy out for cigars, please? And Mrs. Stefanz, tell him there's a five florinz tip in it for him, if he does it before his break.'

The bulk of Harry Towers stands, raising its immense self from behind the desk to walk over to the window. Such a large girth makes it difficult for him to keep his shirt tucked into his trousers and Harry uses this opportunity to push the garment back beneath his straining belt. He removes a black, plastic comb from the shirt pocket and combs his hair against its natural inclination to part from the other side. He is thinking about the events of the day before and is running particular incidents through his mind. He frowns out into the sunlight. There is a knock at the door as Mrs. Stefanz enters with documents she places on the desk.

'Excuse me, Mr. Towers. The boy is on his way to get your cigars and Master Mannikin's secretary has informed me that he will be a few moments late for your 10.30am appointment.'

'Thank you, Mrs. Stefanz.'

The overweight man smiles past the woman and returns to look out of the window, casually placing the comb back in his pocket. The door closes, he begins to mouth words, talking quietly to himself, under his breath.

'Xavier will be late. H'mm, that's pretty usual~ it's what I have come to expect. That boy is getting weirder and more eccentric the older he gets.'
Harry continues thinking about the time spent with Mannikin the day before.

Harry and Mannikin had made an official visit to the new factory, travelling across the city in an ancient company car~ one so old it had running boards. It was Harry's preference and passion; he had adopted and nurtured the company vehicle, at the firm's expense, for a long time, over many years. He had driven slowly, indulgently, languorously, soaking up every passing moment, enjoying the walnut interior, the leather seats, the changing views of the various districts as they drove through them. Amidst the joy of such splendour and revelry, Mannikin had thwarted the elder man's unbridled rapture by requesting that he desist from lighting up his cigar until they got to their destination. So, Harry had politely placed the cigar on hold in his top pocket, sticking out just enough for it to be a constant reminder that it was still there and could be looked forward to and enjoyed soon enough.

The job in hand and the task for the day was to examine the running and organisation of the factory, checking to see that systems for governance and oversight were in place, and that all was working, as it should be. There had been a number of tiresome interruptions to production lately. These hiccups had been viewed primarily as teething problems associated with various newly adopted procedures and although annoying, were unlikely to be signs of underlying malaise. The day's work was to be routine, a management walk-about and inspection of the site, and a check on the roles of department heads and the rank and file.

There had been an unexpected surprise that began the day however. The unforeseen incident had occurred before they had even started off. There had been a 'break in' during the night; the Mannikin offices had been burgled~ although nothing seemed to be missing, for sure. Harry had been informed of the crime when he entered the building that morning. The reception staff explained to him what was known. The police had already made an initial inspection of the damage caused by the forcing of a window on an upper floor, close to a balcony, near a down pipe. The night caretaker had related how he had discovered the break in, disturbed the burglars and single-handedly raised the alarm to chase the interlopers out of the building. Other than the damage that occurred to a window, nothing seemed to have been interfered with or had obviously been taken.

Harry had casually explained the incident in an offhand way to Mannikin when they first met that morning. It seemed to be simple opportunism and Harry wasn't necessarily too concerned, however the elder man was taken aback by Master Mannikin's reaction. Xavier seemed unusually disturbed at the news and needed to know which areas of the building were breached or compromised. There seemed particular worry on his part when it was revealed that the burglars had passed through the management corridor and its suite of offices. Harry pacified the man by saying nothing had been damaged or stolen, and no attempts had been made to breach the company safes where sensitive information was stored. A few typewriters were about all that could easily be taken; the lead on the roof had been checked and found to be intact, and the company's paintings were untouched. These comments did little, however, to subdue Mannikin's anxiety.

In consequence, the start to their journey to the new factory had been delayed. Mannikin was insistent that he had a chance to check over his office to ensure nothing had been moved.

Within ten minutes, he had returned and seemed happy enough~ things were undisturbed or at least those things he had been anxious about were in place and unharmed. Harry took this to mean Mannikin's cameras were okay.

The journey to the new factory took them in the direction of the bridges that pass over the city's rivers; they travelled through Warcapest and the cultural centre and thence on through poorer residential areas, which led to remoter districts beyond. They sped through the outer ring roads to the north. Their trip was slow, due to the density of the traffic, taking almost forty minutes. They had talked of this and that during the journey, pleasantries for the most part, although Harry was surprised, *despite knowing the boy to be naturally inquisitive*, that Mannikin dared to delve into aspects of the Towers' personal life. The young executive had asked Harry about his family. The big man let out a long low whistle to hide his initial discomfort, but followed through by grasping the nettle and deciding to open himself. He declared that he only saw his 'loved ones' infrequently, mainly at weekends, because so much of his time was spent at work. It was common knowledge that Harry enjoyed his job and was proud to be the firm's key worker; his were the brains and organisation behind virtually everything. He was invaluable and that was the way he liked it. The position afforded him privileges, the car for example, and an office larger than Leopold's. Over the years, Harry had piled his office brim full of work and with his 'take' on life. The stout man didn't think he was simply working whilst at the office; his view was that he was also living his life somewhere he wanted to be. His collection of American jazz recordings, his large kipper ties of gaudy design, his drinks cabinet of Johnnie Walker scotch, the resplendent collection of cigar boxes on his shelves and his desk drawers full of lighters, were all testimony to the privileges afforded, due to his indispensible position in the company. The CEO was careful to never overstep the mark though. The eccentricities he brought to the work place were primarily there to allow others to more easily place him and know what he stood for. They were all key to the success of his operating base within the firm and with clients, especially when he needed to impress or bond with others, or the situation warranted that 'personal' touch. It was only ever in secret ways that he took his own pleasure from these innocent diversions~ in no way did anyone suspect they might be vices~ or so Harry assumed.

On this particular day, young Master Mannikin had pressed home an advantage though~ Harry had been wondering since, what he had inadvertently given away during this exchange, by being as open as he was.

'Harry! What do you actually have at home? I have never known. What do you go home to?'
The large man looked intently into the rear view mirror and whistled, taken aback, surprised by the question, despite knowing enough of Mannikin's nature to expect something personal or left field. The best way to deal with such questions was to be plain and simple, he felt.
'I have a modest maisonette, where my darling, little, skinny wife (a third of my weight) looks after our kids. We are simple folk. We have three children, two girls and a boy. The youngest is six and the eldest twelve. That's it!'
He pulled a wallet from his inside jacket pocket and revealed a photo of his progeny, all of whom had partings combed in the opposite direction to the one that might result in less turbulent hairstyles.
'We want for nothing,' he said. 'We celebrate our religion once a week. I manage to be there every Saturday night for a family meal and that's about it. We are a close family; believe me, although it

might not look it. It works for us, boy. No one's complaining, *....so nothin' needs fixin',*' he said with a mock American drawl.
Glancing across at Mannikin, he chuckled before continuing.
'That's my little family, my personal family, my 'loved ones'. My big family is the firm. That's where I live, but hey, you and Leopold know that don't ya?'
'Your dedication is amazing and much appreciated Harry, you don't need to worry about that.'
'I know I am a bit strange, when you look into stuff. Not many see it though~ at least I like to imagine that's the way it is, although <u>you</u> see don't ya, boy? I see you looking. I remember you looking at me when you were a kid, playing in the old factory. Look! There are things I tell no one and stories I bury deep, the war and what happened to my folks, mainly. Seeing people die and be killed has cut me up in ways that its best not to dwell on. I move forward. Your old Harry is doing okay~ don't you worry.'
Harry looked across to discover Mannikin staring at his own reflection in the wing mirror, only half listening. Good job as well, otherwise he might have noticed Harry's eyes glistening a little. Xavier had missed the moment. He was too engrossed elsewhere, rubbing the area above his lip on either side of his philtrum with his thumb and forefinger, checking out stubble growth under his nose.

The new factory was prominently positioned on a recently developed green belt industrial estate. On arrival, they were afforded a guided tour of the facility and its modern working processes. They were led by the works foreman~ a man in his early forties, whose pride in his position was evident. Both Mannikin and Harry were impressed by the cleanliness and efficiency of the new factory; its processes were exemplary. The printing presses were immaculate, faster and more efficient than either man knew possible. The print operatives were well coordinated and knew their roles. Quality assurance procedures ensured that misprinting was kept to a minimum. The production of 'seconds', where cards were poorly printed or misaligned with their edges, had been reduced considerably. In addition, the workers had dedicated working areas and proper facilities for the first time ever, a thing not possible in the old factory, which was not purpose built and never big enough. The Company had been able, at last, to demonstrate its concern for the welfare of its employees whilst engaged in and at work.

Mannikin photographed those things that particularly attracted him and took a keen interest in the preparation of presses for the inaugural print run of two new editions of playing cards. The exhaustive visit proved to be a long day for both men. Harry remembers that both he and Mannikin were pleased by the efforts of the workers and their 'team determination' to improve methods and productivity further.

They had said little to each other on the way back to the Mannikin offices and had simply relaxed and enjoyed the journey in the old jalopy. They finally parted, once they were back in the Company garage. Harry hung back to talk to a mechanic about an engine noise that had disturbed him. During what little remained of the afternoon, they returned to their respective offices. Harry noticed that Mannikin soon left the building, within an hour of their return.

Harry Towers continues looking out the window, reflecting on the previous day's events, standing, deep in distracted thought, an unusual activity for him since his general rule is to keep moving~ it saved time and got more done. The intercom clicks into life... 'Mr. Mannikin Jnr. is now here to see you, Mr. Towers.'

Harry springs into action, momentarily startled, reaching for the respond lever on the machine.

'Do please send him in, Mrs. Stefanz.'

Mannikin enters within moments. He smiles briefly, tall and upright, wearing a new suit.

'How are you Harry? I trust you slept well?'

'Fine, my boy; we had a good day together yesterday. What are your thoughts? Things seemed to go well.' The elder man notices an uncommon shadow above Mannikin's top lip.

They begin a discussion, debriefing each other on observations made the previous day, talking in leisurely, measured tones. Once the exchange has run its course and become exhausted, Mannikin raises the topic of the break in, explaining that he has talked to his father, whose office shows no sign of being harassed by the thieves.

'How about you Harry? Noticed anything missing in here?'

'Nobody in their right mind would steal jazz records, boy. How about your office? Is that okay?'

'Well, it seems untouched; everything is where I left it, nothing is gone or even might be missing. This is all so strange. What do you think the break in was all about Harry? Were they burglars or merely trespassers or what?'

Harry shrugs his shoulders.

'It's a mystery,' he says. 'We have little that others might want or need to take. We only make playing cards here.'

'Indeed,' says Mannikin. 'The interesting thing for me is, I have a suspicion my flat has been recently tampered with in the same way. There is nothing missing as far as I can tell, I only suspect that someone has been in because the front door opens differently. The door sticks in new places and there are minute wood splinters and paint shards from the doorframe on the floor~ also a balcony door was unlocked. I am wondering whether it is something to do with me that has warranted this intrusion. What do you think Harry? Am I being paranoid?'

'No idea dear boy, I would have doubted it. This isn't a detective story you know, this is real life or something supposedly close to it.'

Both men smile at each other, in a manner that is momentarily out of character.

'What have you to hide that others might care about?' Harry asks, showing concern for the flash of unease he detects on Mannikin's face.

'I am not sure. Like anyone I have thoughts and a few things I keep to myself, but nothing that I imagine anyone else would really care to know. My anxieties are my own; they always have been, although there is a strange thought at the back of my mind that I can hardly dare access. It seems to be deeply hidden and just out of reach of my conscious self. I have been forced to remember it, and it may be this that someone is after.'

'I think I have something someone wants.'

Harry Towers has no idea what Mannikin is talking about. He is not paying attention. He is preoccupied, trimming the end of a new cigar, imagining the dark-skinned beauty that once rolled the perfect cigar for him, in exotic, far off, light-filled Cuba.

61.

So, Mannikin has the Egyptian key; the break in caused an unexpected panic to manifest in his brain, enabling him to recall he had hidden the object in the first place. He found it in his office and realised that he had secreted it there, deliberately and without being aware of what he was doing.

He has an instinctive need to protect it, without understanding why, without even knowing what it is. It's a new mystery, another one that doesn't make sense. He is unsure how it came into his possession, whilst recognising his duty to protect it at all costs. A subliminal hunch suggests to him that the strange device is tied up with Nadja in some way~ and more than likely with Count Zapik too. Xavier has a suspicion that he has been chosen to protect secret information~ he conjectures this much.

The key was in a secret drawer at the back of the desk. On reawakening himself to its existence, he had checked to make sure it had not been stolen and, in the process, re-discovered what it looked like. He didn't like remembering that he knew about it, feeling somewhere, remotely, that it was supposed to be confidential, even from himself. He was relieved to discover that the item had not been uncovered. It meant he had protected it well, done his job~ the hiding place was a good one. The chance of burglars returning was remote, or so he felt. Does lightning strike in the same place more than once?

What has he been protecting? A precious metal box, skillfully engraved with geometrical patterns and spiralling moustachioed shapes of curious design, which contained something. Mannikin felt the contents move when he shook it, but it did not rattle; the thing inside had perhaps been wrapped in tissue or thin cloth to protect it. The box was tightly sealed and could not be opened without excessive or brute force. Whatever was inside eluded him; he had no idea what it could be. He was a messenger, a curator and a custodian of… something. Was he taking it to someone or waiting to be contacted? He was more important than he realised; he had a mission. Indeed, he could not help conjecture that this strange box was inextricably tied up with his whole being and might explain his underlying sense and need for meaning and purpose. Xavier could not stop himself from believing it was part of his personal history and he was an instrument of a force greater than himself. He felt it might be an omen or key; it might allow him to understand the unfolding conundrum that existed all around.

And yet he could not know.

He was curiously comforted by not knowing. The need for a rationale was elusive, had not been supplied and he was simply a willing participant in a scheme of things bigger than he was able to comprehend. This though was enough! In a sense, it provided comfort to know he did not have to own the understanding of the mystery. Somewhere, he sensed he was doing it for humanity or for something bigger than the sum total of his insignificant parts. Not that he felt insignificant, indeed, of a sudden, he felt more alive than previously. A quest had materialised, apparently out of nowhere.

The fantasy excited him. The rational part of his consciousness however, recoiled at this new absurdity and would, if it could, reprimand him for his light-headedness.

After talking to Harry that morning, he had returned to his office to think these things through. The young executive sat behind his desk looking out of the window, gazing into the light. He knew the metal box was safe, hidden at the back of the drawer; he did not want to look at it again and dare not violate its sanctuary. It was not for him, he did not own it; it was not his. Should he move it to a better place? Was there one? Should he even be thinking about any of this?

So, burglars had been in his office; he more than suspected as much, although there was no apparent evidence that he could discover. Someone had definitely been to his flat though; there was proof of that. Xavier recognised the premeditated invasion into his privacy, being sure enough of his consciousness to know he was not imagining any of it. Should he tell the police?

He was hesitant to go so far, fearing that the attention might undermine his secret sanctuary and place of clandestine rendezvous. He needed that sanctified reality containing its bewitching siren too much to allow it to be jeopardised. That had to be protected at all costs; it was the truest part of his existence, after all. He doubted that the burglars could know about it, since he and Sara went to such trouble to cover their tracks from the entire world whenever they went there; they always had. That had been one of the rules of their shared reality in that place since its inception. Perhaps he should hide the silver box there? It would probably be safer, despite the fact that such a move would contaminate his safe world, by allowing the two worlds he lived in, to collide. That could be dangerous~ maybe most pressingly to his psyche.

Of a sudden, his life seemed complex.

However, he was left feeling euphoric, unusually aware of his being, indulging in a kind of metacognition, second guessing his responses to everything that seemed to be suddenly unfolding and happening all around. The world most often felt wrong to him and at last he wondered whether this was the turning point that might allow him to take control and make sense of the absurdity. A silly aphorism pops into his head~ *'Our greatest blessings come to us by way of madness.' Socrates.*

★ ★ ☆ ★

62.

It is the opening night of the Warcapest opera season. After the long summer closure, the splendid opera house is again open for business. During the break, the interior had been given over to inquisitive tourists and sightseeing tours, whilst essential maintenance was undertaken and the building rejuvenated and made pristine from top to bottom. In this way, the sparkle had been re-energised~ the grand floors had been waxed and made to shine~ everywhere the marble looked glorious. The lighting, chandeliers and ledges had been wiped of dust; an anachronistic wonderland was created anew.

Xavier arrives back at the luxurious opera building, this time as a theatregoer, dressed in a lightweight, black, lounge suit, paisley Pellican bow tie and black leather Oxford shoes. He enters the building, having turned up early and alone for the evening performance. His 'early bird' zeal is predicated in order to absorb the ambience of the building's interior and to enjoy its grandeur before the arrival of others. Xavier's greater enthusiasm is for the building itself. In truth, he is somewhat ambivalent towards musical opera, uncertain of its charms although, despite his natural antipathy, he has acclimatised himself to what he considers an eccentric and strange art form.

Such occasions were used to allow Xavier and Sara to view each other in public. She adored opera and was keen to attend first night performances whenever the opportunity allowed. He went primarily to be near her. A woman of her means would not ordinarily be in a position to afford the opera and certainly not in the quality seats she was perpetually gifted. It was Xavier who bought the tickets, enabling Sara to indulge her passion in style. This was his lover's gift. Importantly of course, they were <u>not</u> to be seen in each other's company. The agreement, as elsewhere in public, was that whenever they attended outside events, they did so separately. She would watch the opera from a reserved box, whilst he, from a safe and discreet distance, would watch her, most often from a cheaper auditorium seat nearby. These were <u>her</u> conditions; it was their arrangement and had been in place for what now seemed a long time.

Sara will arrive just in time for the performance. She always cuts it fine. Whilst waiting, Xavier purposefully likens himself to Aladdin in a treasure cave, as he wanders and imaginatively indulges in the opulent environment, seeking out its splendid features. He is *as ever*, overwhelmed by the grand staircase and the epic grandeur it portrays; it is a bridge, a conduit to another place. At the bottom of the imposing curved flight of steps, *a truly gorgeous flight of fancy*, stand two large bronze torchères; they depict angels brandishing burning flames of man-made, electric light above their heads, arms extended. With their free hand, they hold long-necked trumpets to their lips. The stairway between these dynamic beings leads to the first level of the three-storey circle seating. Here, there is access to foyers, adjoining rotundas and the long salon. Every surface of the exceptional interior is ravished with lavish and sumptuous embellishment. The plethora of classical features is made notable and wonderful through the intelligent and skilled use of exquisite stone, rich marble, mosaic and sculpted forms of mythic and epic proportion. The richly decorated and stunning painted ceilings are abundant with flying creatures, further emphasising the use of wings as decorative motifs; they also appear on capitals, doorknobs, friezes and windows. The man wanders slowly, indulging in the heady magnificence and before long feels the need to take breath. He releases himself from the intoxicating fervour of the claustrophobic interior by purposefully wandering out through high, external French doors into the simplicity of the early evening light. This is the first floor balcony beyond the grand foyer. The day is still hot, the canopy of sky above his head is liberating, although there begins to be a slight cooling breeze, smelling faintly sweet~ *of apricots?* An impish looking waiter approaches, a round tray tucked under his arm. The steward smilingly asks if he might provide 'a pre-reception drink?' Mannikin requests champagne and orders refreshment for the intervals~ for both himself and his remote guest.

The glory of the opera house inspires him. The elegant architecture is all 'chocolate cake and champagne'~ a joyous artifice dedicated to delight, designed to enchant imaginations with fantasy of epic proportion. He moves to speak into the breeze, wondering what it is he is about to say.

'It may be true that the streets and gutters of Warcapest are where real lives are lived, where the human condition exists...' He appears as though on a stage, looking out into the world before him.

'Out there is where the weaknesses of the body and the reality of the flesh, and existence are repetitive daily occurrences~ all celebrated without celebration. Such a harsh world is so consuming as to minimise contemplation of the sublime by all but a possessed few, it seems.'

He turns his head to look up at the resplendent opera frontage that rises behind him, epic and gorgeous in its confidence and ability to delight in the intellect of humanity. He turns back to face onto the world again. This time he whispers, speaking to himself under his breath, perhaps trying not to be heard by the sweet breeze.

'And yet, by contrast to all this splendour, I can see that there are wet ditches in which wretched bodies lay decomposing in my imagination; I have seen them, or have I only guessed? There are gaping smiles on the fleshless faces that stare out. Their swarming, slowly moving insect eyes of weeping jelly have no lustre. The bodies have poor broken limbs, all akimbo, bones appearing through the flesh. Such humiliating nakedness is muddied and orifices are all slowly filling with wet clay. Such beautiful sex~ mutilated beyond pleasure. Everywhere there are horrendous deaths~ everywhere. Do we deceive ourselves by not recollecting them? Do they deliberately make themselves easy to forget? Why is the sadness of all this so hard to remember and yet, in rare moments of clarity, as

now, impossible to shut out? There is inconsequentiality to 'being', no time ahead is certain, nor can it be presumed to be sustainable. There is an indeterminable point looming somewhere in every future that is invariably allowed to remain silent…invisible.'
These thoughts, curiously instigated by the magnificence of the opera, cause tears to appear in his eyes. Xavier has mortified himself. What immense inconsistency the world tolerates. How contradictory and hopeless he feels himself to be.

By and by the opera audience arrives. The evening is establishing itself and moving forward. People wander out onto the balcony and in so doing, disturb and de-sanctify his sweet breeze with their respectfully inane laughter and chatter. The man is no longer so able to present himself as the lone and solitary figure he most often is, and prefers to be. Xavier nonchalantly regards the congregating people on the balcony and the changing/transforming scene before him, looking to observe and take note of what everything is in process of becoming. He looks out at the streets beyond the balcony packed with pedestrians; the traffic congestion circles the roundabout~ this is the hurly burly of the world. There is so much of it. He takes it in, watching without awareness of anything in particular, simply regarding all of what is there as if it were one, as if everything was joined. It strikes him once more that, perhaps, everything is seamless and equal. The hidden object, for which he is the lonely custodian, briefly materialises before him and passes across his consciousness; it strikes him as being some mysterious object of hope in a desolate place. In the next moment, he banishes its memory from his presence.

Xavier soon shrinks back into the building, re-absorbing himself into the shadows where he immediately feels at home and comforted~ simply wandering through the interior of the opera house calms him. As the evening's audience at last begins to find their seats, he too slips in to find his place in the auditorium. He notices Sara's arrival, whilst purchasing a programme from the usherette~ her appearance causes his heart to miss a beat. He looks up as her head bobs in and out of view a couple of times; she seats herself, looking out from the box. Her eyes scour the auditorium, intent on finding where he might be. At last their eyes meet. There is a brief flash of recognition, then no more. She is wearing a tiara, a response to anxiety about her short hair no doubt. He imagines she too wants to feel less vulnerable.

The audience has taken up its place and is sitting in readiness for the spectacle. Soon, houselights dim in preparation for the performance. Sound in the theatre evaporates to silence...

The overture begins; the drama starts immediately. A cloaked figure, shrouded in shadow, dashes across the front of the stage, stopping momentarily to look behind; he strains his neck to see, telegraphing the chase of which he is the quarry, and then rapidly scampers off into the wing. Soon after, the stage curtains open to reveal the interior of a large cathedral in Rome. Xavier's fascination in the optical glory of the set designer's subterfuge is immediate. All has been directed with intent to divert and tease the imagination of the observer. *Such tricks and artifices, used to create fantasies and impressions of worlds in other places, enthrall him.* This is a reality that does not truly exist. Music intensifies the dramatic experience further; it contributes to the entertaining bewitchment. The audience is transported to a new place. This truncated and economical attempt at classical perspective fills the mind with the very thing it is intent on describing. The visual shorthand resonates. Rich and gorgeous lighting charms the scene, adding dimensionality to the stage painter's skill. The theatrical artifice is easy to accept and quickly embraced. The audience is no doubt aware that there is an outside world, more real, that matches these concise conditions. They draw on their knowledge to add credulity to the scene before them. What they see is not really a church, it is a pastiche, doing no more than evoking something of the essence of what a church might be. They are nonetheless happy to linger, where emotions, motivations and unfolding stories are humorously represented as flattened cutouts. These are rich stereotypes and clichés that merely pantomime reality in a pleasing and beautiful way. The essence of something enchanting remains without the hurt or the turmoil needed to bring it into existence as truth. Everything has become the essence of an idea stripped bare of authenticity.

The cloaked figure reappears, further back this time, entering from the left wing of the stage. He has arrived into this space, into this newly discovered thought that represents a cathedral. The figure moves carefully, eventually coming forward into a spotlight. Heavy make up emphasises thick stubble and a rough complexion. The character looks more like 'Bluto' from 'Popeye the Sailor Man' than any 'bel canto' singer, or so it seems to Mannikin. Xavier looks into the gloom on either side of him; the audience's attention is concentrated.
'We are longing for an experience to emphasise something splendid that we feel in our hearts, as though there were a thing here that has become necessary to discover,' he thinks.
A noise from the wings causes the actor to display consternation and quickly hide in an area behind a gate leading into a crypt. Another man enters, greeted by tremendous applause, although he has done nothing! However this actor/singer is recognised as the young, handsome, romantic lover. It is quickly established that his great weight, size and advanced age are no impediment to the audience's acceptance of him in the role. How well this heroic tenor sings of his love for an adorable young woman. He possesses a remarkable and rich voice~ the gift that signifies his suitability for the part, notwithstanding the truth of his appearance. A series of stylised actions, aided by his costume, a smock spattered in colour, quickly establish his credentials as an artist and painter. A character enters to join him, a man, in the role of a sextant or churchwarden. They sing a duet together. Patterns in sound rise and fall, emulating the singsong of speech, supported by rich and pleasing

orchestration. A delightful little drama is unfolding between these two, all in preparation for the appearance of the leading soprano. She arrives in time to meet with her lover, the artist. She is a mature lady, dressed and made-up to inspire the notion that she is both beautiful and young. The gravity in her bust, her immense cleavage and the rotundity of her figure all reveal the truth of her vintage. With blind disregard for these impolite anomalies, the production, without blinking, moves forward. Actors old enough to be the grandparents of the parts they play, pantomime the joys of young love.

Xavier maintains a cursory knowledge of the thin plot as it unfolds. He has little interest in the artifice of the simple narrative. There are so many aspects of the spectacle he finds ridiculous. In any event, he does not understand Italian. They might be asking each other for a glass of water, for all he knows. His preference is to listen to the rise and fall of the music and bathe in the colour contained in the instrumental and vocal lines. He imagines himself listening to a conversation without words, or experiencing thoughts unattached to language. Xavier likes it when he recognises a leitmotif. Such devices suggest larger themes that interest him more than simply following the worldly narrative. His interest is in the dynamic energy within the music and the way it reflects the emotional wailing of these wonderful singers. In truth, as these things are unveiled to Xavier, they are not words at all, but a series of sliding energies, electric impulses detonating across synapses, abstractions attempting to make sense of stimuli and responses. For him, this was where complex cosmic energies flowed. There was a spirit revealed deep within the performance and in the musical soundscape. He found himself attempting to decipher shapes and patterns, *or some such thing*, contained within the substance of what passed in front of him. He looked to see at what point any of this matched his own experience of reality~ or perhaps prompted new thought.

Mannikin suspected that for many in the audience, the appeal of the evening was simpler and required less concentration, indeed, was less centred on the glory of the performance than was necessary. There were those who were insistent to put themselves first, who wished primarily to be seen and were keen to swan around as egotists, in the belief they glittered as brightly as their surroundings, and were of great importance. They had the god given right to shine. Xavier wondered why Alyesha was so opposed to the place. Evidence of mammon appeared all over. He looked carefully to discover exceptions, to see where nuanced and subtle other persons like himself were lurking~ he looked for sophistication, defined by intelligence, in preference to the cut of a suit, the name of a shoemaker or the design of a fashionable handbag. Xavier felt he detected comparatively few other spirits within the audience whose sense of purpose or reality coincided with his. But this was no problem, he was used to being alone and feeling separate. The fact that Sara was here made it all more bearable.

Xavier becomes lost and absorbed within the production, increasingly picked up and swept along~ finally captured by a gloriously dynamic swell within the rich orchestration. Energy changes direction as a new musical theme emerges. An unfamiliar character appears. The villain strides across the stage. The composer's arrangement and sumptuous colours enrapture Xavier. Detonating cannon punctuate the score, providing evidence, *should it be forgotten*, that sound can travel in time over large distances. The device fills Xavier with a sense of imminent expectation. The man on stage, although menacing, has a dynamic energy that intrigues; he pitches his mortal strength against the gods, using the machinations of Machiavelli to achieve his will. Where the rules fail to work, he will change them. He is a man unlike others; he does not fear gods at all, it seems. The energy in the music conveys this, although Xavier is not sure what the man's part in the story is. Is the villain there looking to find Bluto? The cathedral bells are heard calling the faithful to vespers; they chime beautifully amidst the sound of distant canon being fired.

So the first act ends. The curtains close dramatically, swept across the stage by the music and power of the drama; their impressive swoosh indicating a temporary hiatus and intermission. Xavier makes to leave his seat, but is bewildered and adrift~ his eyes slow to acclimatise to the brightened auditorium. In a daze he sets out, following the congregation as they move en-masse towards the foyer. In the Grand Hall, he passes close to Sara, *by accidental design*~ these protagonists avoid direct eye contact as they collect their prepared champagne order, their fluted glasses standing side by side on the drinks counter in a way that they dare not. Sara wears a sparkling, Prussian blue, strapless evening dress. In his detached stupor he is aware of how beautiful she looks. His heart races as she moves with apparent nonchalance, away from him, back into the crowd; who might discern that they know each other? The subterfuge and artifice is exquisite and beguiling. The act of denying a truth of which one is conscious has a curious ring and taste to it. The pleasure in those instances where it is 'owned' is utterly subversive and full of delectable frisson. He wonders if it would be better to make an honest woman of her, what ever that means. His face twists a little, his bottom lip protrudes, recognising that she does not want this, will not allow it. Their thrill in each other is probably so strong, precisely because things are the way they are. 'What is not broken requires no fixing.' Harry's recent utterance returns to ring once more in his ears.

In an unguarded moment, he acknowledges that Sara and Alyesha coexist in his life. Mannikin invariably denies these two independent realities an opportunity to confront one other. The possibility of the two worlds colliding was difficult for him to reconcile~ as it would be for any man living in a city with two rivers running through its heart.

The eventual sound of the interval bell triggers the audience to return to the auditorium. Xavier lingers a little, long enough to hear the second bell; in the same instant a car screeches to a halt on the street outside. As ever, the coincidental event is of no consequence. Somewhere far away, in some outside space, it might be snowing. Somewhere a snow leopard walks. Somewhere an angel may be watching...

The second act commences. Xavier watches; he sees. The heroine visits the villain in his office apartment, part of a large Palazzo in Rome; he is evidently a high official in the city government. She becomes incrementally placed under pressure and is blackmailed by the power-crazed, bad man, who evidently lusts after her. The woman discovers that her lover, the painter, has been taken prisoner and may be executed by the villain's henchmen. She has to save him. Xavier sees all this and understands. The performance has come alive, he is held spellbound by the unfolding action. In an ensuing retaliatory moment, the woman cleverly takes her revenge on the corrupt, villainous official. She stabs him to his heart and ends his meddling. He is destroyed by a redeeming energy within the woman. Xavier feels the power of these actions. The tragic heroine is triumphant and with a cleverly obtained letter of release and safe conduct for the painter in hand, makes her escape from the building.

Xavier, absorbed and overwhelmed by the energy unleashed in the opera, forgets where he is. Or, more accurately, feels himself to inhabit the very room in which the drama occurs; the production has become a real space for him. He is captivated by the size, weight and ecstasy of the incidents that unfold and loses track of time, hypnotised and enraptured by the performance. It is too soon for him when this second act finishes.

'Oh, is it over already?'
He readjusts his vision and returns to the present. His surroundings appear to belong to some other simultaneous fiction, albeit more convincing. Everything seems impermanent or open to change or reinterpretation at any moment. All this might be made up, too. Xavier remains seated, dazed, as the audience around him begins to stand~ using the opportunity to stretch legs or revisit the foyer. Looking towards Sara's box Xavier sees her lean forward, her elbow on the edge of the balcony, staring out at him with an intent and mesmerising gaze. She caresses her lip in a manner that suggests she is blowing him a kiss. He looks away embarrassed at her behaviour, fearing it might reveal the sublime subterfuge they engage in~ anxious that should she persist too long, their deceit might be noticed. He looks back, suddenly deciding to smile in response, but too late, for like anything too briefly glimpsed in a mirror, she has gone.

★ ★ ☆ ★

The second interval is as the first, although by now the audience is particularly relaxed. The performance has calmed that savage breast and the beast within each aching heart. Cares of the day are vanished, allowing for the evening's enchantment to take hold. A kind of ancient necromancy exerts itself. Faces throughout the auditorium have become, or at least seem, younger. World-weary pressure has dissipated and in its place a new sense of sublime, easy magnanimity prevails.

On his way to the foyer, Xavier discovers that Sara has placed herself opposite and in front of the auditorium doors, at some distance across the shining marble floor. She is inconspicuously sat, looking demure on a white sofa, a snow leopard stole covering her shoulders and arms, for modesty as well as for warmth. He casually moves in her direction, deeply accepting a brief look as he walks past on his way to the grand hall to collect champagne~ and thereafter wanders out onto the balcony over-looking the city.

The last vestiges of daylight persist. The night is drawing in. Xavier chooses a spot and stands looking out onto the traffic as before, passively watching as it circles the roundabout in front of the opera house. Magnificent city buildings face him; their upper storeys fade into the darkening sky beyond his consciousness. At the level below the balcony, the pavement is decorated with lavish, ornamented streetlamps; their glare causes his eyes to smart. These large, multiple globes of light, illuminating the opera house's frontage, are unusually bright. Beyond this, car headlights by comparison, seem dim; they move directionally, white beams ever speeding towards him, red lights constantly chasing away. The traffic is mesmerising as it passes in fixed channels around the flood lit roundabout. An ancient verdigris fountain at its centre, even from this distance, dazzles and confuses~ lights hidden beneath the water's surface illuminate the ravishing, cascading liquid as it endlessly rises, tumbles and falls.

Xavier entertains the idea that he too is moving, imagining himself travelling in a rocket ship or on the bridge of some great vessel that is hurtling through space at colossal speed. The glory of the opera house is fully ascendant, brimming and alive. The darkening night surrounds the bejewelled space ship within a glittering universe.

Xavier stands straighter; he sips champagne, ennobling himself in the process. The refreshing liquid is cold and the outside of the glass has condensation on it. Light from the streetlamps shines into the glass, illuminating the exquisite elixir; the bubbles follow one another as they rise... like perfect punctuation. The evening has become ubiquitous; it seems to have the essence of other previously experienced evenings about it. There is imminent, precious timelessness infiltrating his awareness. He recalls the opera house on that previous night when he had thrown a stone into the air wondering whether it would come down or not. There were two boys walking past, arm in arm, wearing curious hats. Where are they now? He would like to see them again~ but doesn't know why; they had made a deep impression on him. He peers out to see them now~ looking out from the balcony in the way he does from so many other high vantage points~ from the balcony of his flat, from the roof of the old factory. The two boys can, *by some unexplainable coincidence that he just knew would occur,* be seen in the distance, turning a corner. He had almost missed them, but for the fact that he had not.

A slight, inconspicuous breeze passing across him alters. Broadening his gaze, he is made aware that light in his vicinity has also changed. A man is standing in close proximity, slightly nearer than Mannikin might consider appropriate, or would like. Xavier glances sideways, and then looks again. The man, of mixed race, is shorter than he, North European, with a generous helping of the orient pulsing through his veins. He, like Mannikin, stands in a black lounge suit with a glass of champagne; two penguins side by side, but not at the South Pole. The man speaks first.
'Are you enjoying the performance, sir?' The accent suggests that a Russian tongue may be his first language.
'Why yes,' answers Mannikin. 'Who wouldn't?'
Xavier checks the man some more~ *recognising that he has been checked out first.* The stranger's face is wide, maybe Mongolian.
'You must know about these things~ this opera. It is new to me, I am not sure I understand how to appreciate it,' says the man.
'Well, how exciting, just treat it as an adventure, let it find you; don't go out looking for it.'
Mannikin takes a sip from the glass and moves it into his other hand away from the stranger. The man continues, undaunted.

'It is not my culture. I should have started with the opera about the oriental princess. You know the one? I might feel more of an affinity with that story.'

The man casually takes out a cigarette, which he lights, using a Zippo lighter.

'I think you mean 'Turandot',' replies Mannikin, both surprised and delighted at his own knowledge.

'Opera is the old European tradition, is it not? I hope you don't mind me speaking my mind. I speak through ignorance, I am sure. I am surprised all this has lasted so long. I would rather go to the cinema and see a film these days. Do you come here often?'

'Namely?' says Mannikin, with an unexpected and incisive force in his voice, wondering if the stranger is being deliberately provocative.

'Excuse me?' says the man, not understanding the response and not expecting what appears to be a pointed jab. He seems bewildered by Mannikin's reaction, and moves back, very slightly.

'Which film? You say you prefer the cinema; what might hold your attention?'

'Oh yes, I see what you mean. That's an excellent question.' After a moment's consideration, he says '... a detective thriller on a train would be good... everyone likes films on trains. Although, being here tonight reminds me of an old French film I once saw, about 'Les Enfants' in Paradise or some such. Have you seen it? It has scenes in a theatre like this, if I remember correctly. I could enjoy that again.'

'What made you come here tonight? Something must have drawn you to this old-fashioned and anachronistic place. What stopped you following your nose and going to the cinema?'

'That's an interesting point. There you have me again'. The man's wide smile seems inappropriately relaxed. 'I have come out of curiosity, in truth~ and to break the monotony of some not very interesting... um ...insurance business in the city, that's all. And you?'

The two men look at one another, the happenstance encounter turns peculiar, neither man completely sure why. An element of mistrust seems to have entered their conversation. Mannikin decides to find out what is going on and looks for room to manoeuvre.

'That's easy,' he says, becoming flamboyant and effusive in his gestures. 'I come because I must. I am led by a need to be close to a spirit in this place. There is a great beauty here that I choose to be associated with. Mysterious and magnificent forces in this building have captured my thoughts and piqued my imagination.'

The gentleman doesn't react to Mannikin's bizarre, melodramatic openness. No emotion at all passes across his face. In an attempt to diffuse the situation, the stranger simply says,

'Have you come alone?'

Xavier looks at and into the man, determining that this operatic neophyte, this theatrical alien, is aware that his creditability and motives are being investigated. Mannikin's bizarre and larger than life behaviour has unnerved him. He exhibits a split second awkwardness that allows Xavier to see deeply and at leisure into his soul. Xavier slips into the space; time has temporarily stopped whilst he continues to move within it. In an instant, he sees the complexion of what is going on. This clever, oriental opportunist, although subtle in his approach, is after something; he is inquisitive. The conversation, Xavier decides, *finding himself on the defensive*, is no idle pleasantry; there is an underlying agenda somewhere.

He returns to the surface and time resumes. The stranger continues, unaware of the yawning gap that had just opened, during which time he had been invaded. Xavier Mannikin inspects the look of the man with intense scrutiny, quickly determining this is not a person one might normally associate with the opera; he complies with none of the stereotypes that one might typically observe in this exalted place. Without doubt, the man is outside of his normal jurisdiction, a temporarily misplaced person. Xavier looks at his hand as it holds the delicate glass~ it is large and strong. There is physicality, underlying power and strength in evidence. This person is fit, perhaps trained for a purpose; but certainly not as an office slouch or a soft businessman. The man is contrary to expectation in some way.

'I did arrive alone. I always do. It is not unusual. Do you have company yourself?' asks Mannikin.
'I am here alone, like you, just filling in the evening.'
The man changes the position of his feet, in an attempt to lean in as before, to regain lost ground. Mannikin recognises something in the symmetry of the man's motion from elsewhere. He steps up to the

bar, realising what is going on for the first time. The man becomes familiar. Mannikin looks at him, questioning his understanding. Is he standing next to one of the men in long coats? Such men had only previously been experienced or seen over great distances. Indeed, might this be the man who invaded his flat, or a compatriot of the men who gained aggressive entrance into the Mannikin building?

'Do you know me?' Mannikin says. 'Have we met before?' His gaze is fixed on the other man's eyes.

'I am not sure, no I don't think so,' the man says.

His eyes dart away, they widen, move sideways, escaping at speed into his head. He takes a sip of his drink. His movements have lost coordination and symmetry in an attempt to move the moment on. He is surprised at the offensive stance materialising before him and is resorting to lying~ his look and the averting of his gaze says it all. Xavier detects discomfort and sees artifice and opportunism in the man. This gentleman has been too clever by half and had not expected to be challenged.

'It's been nice meeting you, sir and very informative.'

Mannikin steps back, moving away, watching. The man stares as the figure before him shrinks rapidly from sight, surprised at the speed with which their conversation has come to an end. Mannikin's temperature rises; this is indeed one of the men in long coats; he had never assumed he might be confronted so closely by such a nemesis, or that the thing might change its appearance. He had met an enemy. Nothing must happen further that evening to signpost or reveal anything of Xavier or Sara's secret world together. There can be no stray threads connecting him to the beautiful siren in the opera box. At all costs, his world in the old factory and his close, intoxicating connection with Sara Phielnx must not be divulged or discovered.

★ ★ ☆ ★

Xavier returns to his opera seat, perturbed, feeling violated and invaded. He shrinks into the plush velvet, wondering if there is a vantage point from which the man in a long coat might be watching 'him' or 'them'. What was the man in the long coat's strategy meant to prove? Why had the fool dared to talk to him? Mannikin collects his thoughts and wonders what he gave away, if anything, and wonders whether in truth he was being paranoid. Could the poor, nice man who had talked to him have been entirely innocent after all? Mannikin tries to settle his mind and in so doing, recognises he may have overreacted. The lights fade. He sinks into his seat further, to rid his mind of an experience that has seriously disturbed his equilibrium.

The third act begins. Xavier is especially keen to be absorbed back into the fantastical world of the opera. The curtains open, this time to the sound of French horns. The stage set seems to depict a high place, one that looks out across the flat roof of some large circular building~ it is a castle. A skyline of Rome can be seen beyond; notable towers and domes rise higher than the roof's edge in the far distance. The scene is scarcely lit, indicating that this may be night. The view is reminiscent of Xavier's flat roof at the old factory, although the space depicted here, *using a cleverly distorted perspective,* is more expansive. The edge of the roof is at the farthest limit of the stage where silhouetted soldiers, arms at rest, walk slowly along a parapet. In front of this, at the apparent roof's centre *dwarfing the scale of all else* is a mighty six-metre, bronze, verdigris sculpture, depicting an avenging angel. It looks down on all that occurs below its gaze, its head almost disappearing beyond the highest point of the proscenium arch.

The large, inspiring, semi-lit sculpted prop has been impressively constructed to recreate the appearance of a formidable statue of enormous size and weight. Its authenticity suggests that it has been modelled on an object that may have existed in the ancient world. The vengeful angel, dressed in Roman garb and chest plate, brandishes a star-crested sword in process of being driven downward with great strength and determination. The weapon is perhaps redolent of a meteor with its tail moving in the opposite direction. Xavier wonders how such an immense sculptured form might have been brought onto the stage and looks carefully in the gloom to see if there are joins suggesting that the edifice had been assembled in sections. How else could such a large object appear in such a space?

The orchestra is playing the overture to the third act; the very one he had recently chosen to play on the gramophone in his apartment.

The simple folk melody sets the scene. A new morning is just about to unfold. Light across the stage slowly brightens, imperceptibly, to indicate the dawning of day. In the distance, *from off stage*, a shepherd boy sings out into the air, accompanied by the sound of goat bells. His simple, pure voice echoes across imagined distances. Mellow French horns and oboes are heard across the same presumed vista. Soon the tolling of distant bells begins, whilst violins glide an elevated theme across the entire stage, spilling into the theatre and filling an imagined sky above. The church bells grow louder and continue, calling a world of make-believe to wakefulness, as if into reality.

It is apparent that bells punctuate memorable scenes in this story, even now, in this very moment. Bells toll~ and then there is silence. The painter reappears, moving slowly across the stage in chains; he is a prisoner. His developing theme includes a new, tolling bell that sounds closer than those before. He sings in response to his reduced circumstances, as a convict in a cell, a man about to be executed. An orchestral breeze picks up on stage, he cries out with a new cadence, a glorious and mighty theme that is expansive~ *'E Lucevan Le Stele'*, at the end of which there seems to be nothing else that can be said...

The painter and his lover stand temporarily reunited beneath the shadow of the towering, winged statue positioned at the centre of the stage. The scenario develops further and evolves. Xavier sees the prisoner about to meet his end, *by firing squad*, watched over by the epic fury that has control over him. He wonders whether the still, starry dawn before him, *apparently no more than a staged illusion*, might go on forever, into infinity. He feels inconspicuous and vulnerable.

During this reverie, his thoughts wander, ferried by enchantment to a new place. It begins yet again, but with an unusual intensity on this occasion. Xavier sees the face of the man he has just talked to and feels he is about to become trapped or pursued by a malign energy. An even murkier place opens for him. He seeks sanctuary in an inner world where bells ring and distant sounds crash, punctuating the passage of an endless time. Alienation overwhelms him.

Xavier is gazing into the painted night sky, now brighter than before. The stars peek through into the accumulating morning light, illuminated like holes in a curtain with light shining from behind. Theatrical gauze implies an atmosphere that subtly distorts a perfect image of the very thing he might like to see with some sense of clarity. For the first time, as if newly conscious, he begins a dialogue with himself.

'In this surrounding gloom, in this still, quiet, unlit auditorium that envelops me, I am a lost entity, little more than a voyeur of events that unfold in time~ perhaps the same as and no different to any other spectator or participant. I might be individual and yet I doubt it. I lack control. I feel I am something and yet suspect I am nothing. Only consciousness makes me different from my surroundings; without that spark I am equal and the same. I might cleverly realise my separation from the matter that surrounds me, may choose to eulogise the human condition, whilst harnessing my skills to tinker with the edges of malleable things. I can do all this, but without any awareness or knowledge of why existence deems me necessary…'

'I recognise myself to be surrounded by an infinite, overwhelming helplessness. I realise there is nothing I can do about anything for sure. A deep sense of despair has taken hold. Might I have the ability to grasp control of this situation? Would it make a difference? Why should I bother? Occurrences are outside of my control and appear most often as opportunities rather than conscious decisions. Few events allow me unequivocal ownership for my actions. What happens is only seemingly within my jurisdiction and feels more like the gift of circumstances~ the results of serendipity. But this is hardly enough to keep me happy. Where might I exert individual control or independent navigation, have sole rights for my thoughts, acquire the autonomy that will prove I am free?'

'Even my death evades me. It is out of my hands, although perhaps only for as long as I feel a need to continue the story. To determine one's end is no more than a premature death indicating an abdication of responsibility.'

'Is it possible to truly disrupt the flow of time and the tide of humanity to really change futures~ not just the appearance of things, but the very fabric? There seems to be an inevitability to what is possible~ and what might lie beyond is dogged and persistent in remaining invisible. It is precisely into these regions I need to go. Where is the chance I want and yearn for?'

'I must deal with my destiny to determine my future. It has become pointless to continue waiting for an imagined cue to tell me when to move. Time moves too slowly; it appears before me like a story with no plot. I need to be decisive; now has to be the time, regardless of how strong willed or intransigent the colossal universe around me appears to be, and how small I feel by comparison. It is I who must determine that the moment has come. After all, *but only for a short time longer,* consciousness is mine. I will, if necessary, leave all others and move forward into a different space. I may become dangerous, maybe even to myself, but it is a thing that should be done. There is a future I need to meet. I feel it, if only within my subjective experience of thinking. The clues are all around. The immanence and presence of the things I suspect and feel are overwhelming, despite their apparent absence. Such notions are bearing down on me from within my subconscious. This sensation is more real to me than those tangible proofs of reality provided by my empirical and quantifiable mortal senses~ those common and garden sensations that allow for easy navigation and interaction with the world, habitually recognised to be real. I find myself more willing to believe the fantasies within my own imagination than the truth of what can be proven to apparently exist. These abstract and ridiculous imaginings offer a fantastical alternative, a madman's dream, a nonsensical possibility of ridiculous potential that might defeat the restrictive laws of nature, perhaps undermining the steadfast control, rate and manner in which the known universe is revealed and unfolds.'

'I will not be vanquished. There must be a way to be ingenious and I am crazy enough to want to believe it.'

The performance at last draws to a close and ends. Before the house lights are turned on, before the curtain call, Xavier makes a premature exit from the auditorium, intent on using one of his circuitous routes to escape back to the old factory for the night, knowing that Sara has every intention of returning there herself, using her own secret and safe pathways.

Their clandestine secrecy, without a doubt, would be beyond the guile of any man in a long coat to penetrate *or follow;* he knows this and is confident, or possibly naively arrogant enough, to believe so. He desperately needs to talk, to explain this newly discovered storm within his consciousness. Only she will understand.

★ ★ ☆ ★

Xavier rushes through the celebrated halls of the opera house and down the grand staircase, oblivious to the glories he had spent so much time considering earlier that evening. He passes through the main assembly room to the canopied entrance and then out of the building completely, determined in his zeal to steal a march on the man who ought to be wearing a long coat, the man who had talked to him, who had disturbed him, the one who he suspects of being a menacing presence. The sleuth had made himself inscrutable by talking to Xavier and revealing the complexion of his face. Why had he done such a thing? Xavier is confused and recognises this to be a sign that he needs to beware; the man's approach was unexpected. There are patterns here that Xavier had not anticipated and could not reconcile with his own sense of reality. Of a sudden, he feels there is something enormous happening outside of his control; he needs to be more vigilant than ever. He dashes into the now dark, but well lit, late night, city street~ finding it to be alive with the exuberant congestion of noisy evening traffic and the generic sound of a nocturnal metropolis. There is, in addition, that same constant passing wind, that passes for the sound of an imagination, passing overhead.

The opera's end had come after the ignominious and inglorious death of the poor painter. The beautiful heroine had no choice but to likewise end her own sweet life. She had jumped from the high battlements to her death, tumbling over a lofty edge into an abyss. Xavier was disappointed at the dismal end for the woman. He refuses to accept the grim finale and, as he rushes through streets, chooses to reimagine the conclusion. He sees a feminine form somewhere ahead of him, lifting into the air, high above the tops of the Warcapest buildings, carried on wings as impeccable and as splendid as the epic, sculptured fury beneath which, the action in the third act had taken place. The woman becomes some kind of an angel herself~ a kind of Erikhe, if he did but know. The concept of angels is increasingly pressing itself into the dull material out of which his body and consciousness has been formed.

63.

The journey through the city is complex. Mannikin has intimate knowledge of pathways that, without too much forethought, allow him to enter spaces, buildings, exits and underground passages using a variety of routes. All kinds of navigation, topographical and metaphysical, are his forte after all. It would require a team of well-placed operatives to follow his convoluted and inspired flight. He has this down to a fine art. His passage is a kaleidoscope of influences, landmarks and visual stimuli, all of which have meaning for him and act as external as well as internal markers to the emotionally driven Xavier. The journey is as inwardly inspiring to the cerebral Mannikin as it is to that exterior pedestrian copy of himself, seen passing incognito over the face of Warcapest~ dashing through the cityscape to avoid the detection of a potentially perilous force. Ponting, *the very man met earlier*, is lost early on, despite being superbly experienced in the art of surveillance. Mannikin has got away again; the protagonist has avoided detection~ much to the spy's annoyance.

Ponting has been frustrated similarly on a number of occasions. For reasons he cannot explain, he fails to predict or recognise the thinking and logic that informs this man's activity; those traits that might provide clues to how Mannikin will act or react seem to be beyond easy detection. His timing, for one thing, seems irrational. *Mannikin and Ponting are on different wavelengths in this regard. One is not more baffling; in truth they are both equally confusing to each other.* Ponting is vexed with himself~ he is, in addition, trying to identify or locate the mysterious woman of whom he has only the briefest knowledge. He suspects that his junior henchman, tasked with the job of tailing her from the opera, will have lost her too, by now. Ponting needs to be working harder and needs to get more operatives on the case; he begins to be sorely stretched. *The remainder of his team is currently engaged elsewhere in the surveillance of Count Zapik, the magician~ that work too, seems to be drawing blanks.*

Ponting walks through the streets of Warcapest, his quarry lost somewhere in the labyrinthine complexity of the city and its darkness. Mannikin and the mystery woman are uncommonly secretive and particularly good at being so. He is only beginning to realise the extent of all this. He had been a fool to talk to Mannikin as he did; he had sold the man short and had assumed he would be unable to handle himself. He had stuck too long to his initial impression of Mannikin as an unstable character, not fully in control of the things that happened around him. He often appeared to be awkward, misplaced, disorientated, perhaps not fully functioning~ maybe a bit of a buffoon! Indeed, Ponting hadn't even thought he was central to the investigation. However, of a sudden, he realises Mannikin has been underestimated~ his front is clever. Mannikin is hiding something rather well and, far from getting nearer to understanding, Ponting was heading in the wrong direction and making stupid mistakes. He had thought that an innocent chat with the suspect could have informed him and his intuitive self of new ways to approach the issue~ a way to gain insight into that which was eluding him. He might have gained behavioural or personality insights, maybe even made Mannikin uncomfortable or anxious in a way that could have caused him to inadvertently reveal more of his secret story. In this respect, Mannikin had completely outflanked him and effectively turned the tables. These were strategies Ponting had used before, in similar, non-life-threatening situations, to effect change. He thought of himself as being a bit of a behavioural psychologist, but this time his clever and ambitious personal self had screwed up big time and revealed much more to the world than he had discovered of his target.

Perhaps Ponting's faulty logic had been predicated on one simple fact. He didn't think he had been seen or observed whenever he had followed Mannikin; others in his team may have been glimpsed, possibly, but he thought his previous surveillance had gone completely unnoticed~ evidently he was wrong. He relives the point in their conversation at which Mannikin closed up, began to protect himself, reacted in a way that would, from now on, make Ponting's job harder, maybe impossible~ he had lost all of his advantage. Ponting coloured up, noticeably reddening, he felt hot and momentarily annoyed, but quickly resumed his cool, aware that in truth he was now more intrigued than ever; more was going on than he had anticipated. It was without doubt, that despite having an apparently respectable relationship with Alyesha Oezza, Mannikin, the cad, was seeing the mystery woman as well. Interestingly, in Ponting's view, this other woman had a greater ability to control her movements and knew how to keep herself secret, more so than the formerly, underestimated Mannikin. He needed to concentrate more attention on her. Ponting had only managed to encounter them together once before, in a park on the outskirts of the city, at a weekend. The woman, when it was time to leave, melted away and disappeared completely, leaving Mannikin a solitary walking figure; it was as though she had never been there at all. Indeed Ponting, master sleuth that he was, suspected it was the woman's skill in artful deception that had rubbed off on Mannikin. These people were working remarkably closely together, in cahoots, acting as one, like two deer stepping through a forest in unison, with only one set of movements; a tango animal with four legs and two beating harts, operating somewhere close to, but maybe beyond his own level. He felt outmanoeuvred and recognised he had a real challenge on his hands.

Ponting vividly recalled the day he first discovered Mannikin's connection to the mystery woman. Whilst tailing him, as part of a routine operation, he had stalked the man to a park on the outskirts of Warcapest, in the midst of which was an impressive late nineteenth century glasshouse. It hadn't been easy to follow his quarry; the journey had involved short train links and a fair amount of walking. There had been bewildering behaviours and eccentric activity on display that caused Ponting to question Mannikin's sanity on a number of occasions. To say he acted unusually was an understatement; at the time, the sleuth put the dalliances and hesitations down to the man's bizarre nature, suspecting him to be simply odd. Although, Ponting concurrently wondered if Mannikin was being deliberately vague in order to outwit the expectations of the world around him. In another life he might have been a magician, like Zapik, using subterfuge, feints, misdirection and sleights~ or so Ponting had idly thought. Mannikin and the woman, he was to discover, had secretly arranged to meet; he witnessed them soon after their initial rendezvous. They were embracing, kissing passionately in a quiet arbour and thereafter sought out a series of discreet places around the park in which to conduct their clandestine liaison. It had been Ponting's best encounter of the two together; indeed it had been the only one to date, the one that had alerted him and aroused his interest.

The small end of the park was, as he remembered, full of cone-shaped topiary and tall conifers that had been exotically pruned and sculpted. Amongst such Arcadian splendour was an impressive collection of stone statuary. The underlying theme was impossible to ignore, the landscape was inundated with sphinxes in every possible pose and attitude. The beasts adorned plinths at the end of pathways or presented themselves languorously, scattered across the lawns. Yet others were to be found in fountains~ where they vomited voluminous amounts of water, screaming at the universe with wild expressions on their faces. Some wealthy collector, or so Ponting imagined, had indulged his passion to exhilarating excess. The winged creatures stood, sat or lay reclining, strewn across the landscape, making it alien, like the surface of another planet. Their enigmatic, feral look~ their stance~ their underlying sense of wild, sexual energy filled the air with a brooding tension. The latent energy made Ponting fearful, anxious somewhere deep within his core. These bird-like beasts, with their proud breasts and standing nipples pushed forward, established their mass pouting of lips to be a signal of very obvious intent. Every stone animal was on heat, with eyes glazed, seeing only that which they were intent and desperate to receive. Could they move at all, their tails would lash fiercely, those tails attached to their rumps in such a way that each looked like a phallus entering the creature from the rear, perhaps serving to explain the severe over arching of vertebrae and stretched spines on every animal. Were they truly alive, were they real at all, there would undoubtedly be the primal smell of sex in the air.

On this particular day, Ponting was disarmed by his responses to the unfolding events he observed. He felt drawn in, sensing in some indefinable way that he had become part of what was going on, a participant rather than an onlooker. *In similar ways, his objective and detached surveillance of Count Zapik had become problematic also.* Had he accidentally and unintentionally become a character in the very drama, the peculiar fiction, he was meant to be investigating? His position seemed to be unaccountably changing around him. His attitude to his work had definitely altered~ he had wondered about it and suspected he was getting too old for this kind of toil and drudgery. He had been on duty on his own at the time, not his preferred way to work; his partner, a junior henchman, had flown back to Berlin temporarily on other business. Ponting had followed Mannikin from his apartment to the park on the outskirts of the city. The detective had bought fresh cigarettes, boiled sweets and a newspaper en route to help fill in the dead time~ the ever present occupational hazard of dull surveillance. Mannikin had taken the metro to a terminus and then overground trains to a stop near the old emperor's summer palace, from where he had walked the remaining distance. The once exclusive retreat was now open to the public; the grounds had become a recreational beauty spot, available through egalitarian largesse, for the benefit of the Warcapest populace.

Mannikin, despite seeming 'odd' to the conventionally orientated Ponting, was at least in good spirits; this was apparent in his demeanour. Xavier played with and amused a boy and his younger sister who sat opposite him on the train whilst the morning sun flashed by, streaming in through the dust-streaked windows of the carriage. The children's callow, fresh-faced mother giggled and laughed at his whimsical, winsome antics. It was all good-humoured fun. The enchanting gentleman shook her hand respectfully when he got off at his stop and began idly wandering through the station, moving slowly, without any discernable sense of purpose, letting everyone else pass through the station before him. The man stopped to check the time, synchronising his watch with the station clock~ he did this more than once, perhaps not remembering he had already verified the moment he was in, or was currently passing through. And thereafter Xavier loitered further, distractedly throwing a couple of small pebbles found lying on the platform into the air, taking some interest in where they landed. One in particular seemed to go up vertically, without subsequent evidence of it coming down at all. The sleuth took this in his stride, although the episode left the man perplexed. Ponting wondered whether Mannikin might have been early for an appointment since he seemed to be dallying so, with little intention of moving on, or any pressing awareness of time passing. The spy went so far as to suspect he had been rumbled, speculating that this could be the explanation for the hiatus in action. The spook moved back, hiding in a shelter, not daring to look out, his position partially hidden and obscured by glass partitions. At last, Mannikin moved to the other end of the platform where he purchased a chocolate bar from a kiosk. Soon after, he began the fifteen-minute walk to the park. His erratic pace slowed and sped up by turns.

Once in the park, the visitor relaxed his stride to casually wander past park benches, along avenues of cordoned trees and regimented high beech hedges in process of having a summer trim. Before long, his pace resumed its former anarchy and became erratic again. Xavier lost his balance whilst fumbling in his jacket pocket for items that evaded his attention, all the while checking hesitantly and nervously around and behind. Despite such apparent wayward awkwardness, it soon became clear that the young man was heading towards the glasshouse. The magnificent and enormous, green, iron-framed building loomed high and impressively above the hedges, in a remote and discreet part of the park. It stood redolent of some fabulous machine, perhaps an imaginative prototype for Jules Verne's 'Nautilus' submarine~ where, in this version, space between each riveted panel was filled with glass. The epic building possessed great beauty and nobility and seemed both heavy and light simultaneously. Mannikin began to walk decisively, his footsteps crunching over the pebbled gravel leading to the entrance. He moved swiftly past the myriad petrified beasts that lay scattered in every direction. On arrival at the ornate, riveted doorway, he entered the greenhouse, paying the attendant the small ticket fee, securing his opportunity to be enveloped and consumed by the damp, humid and rarified atmosphere of the magnificent and ancient space. Ponting, eager to not miss anything, entered very soon afterwards, having to catch his breath on entry, as he too experienced the newly challenging heat and humidity. It might have been a sauna; such was the tropical nature of the temperature in the greenhouse. Ponting, even in this short time, had lost Mannikin to the vast, green, verdant interior, and so had to tediously plot the layout and routes through the greenhouse in order to regain and find the man he was intent on following. It took some desperate minutes until he located the object of his deliberations~ his prey~ during which time he had opportunity to discover, and marvel at, the enormous banana plants, the ancient olive trees, coco de mer, large, stunningly-leaved trees of all kinds, as well as impressive selections of waterlillies, azaleas, cyatheales, and cliveas. Ponting at last halted abruptly, stopping in his tracks, for fear of walking into Mannikin's line of vision. The undercover agent had glimpsed that object he stalked, beyond a cluster of orange-tinctured flowers overhanging a reduced and overgrown walkway. There, sat on a bench, half concealed in an inconspicuous and shady arbour, talking to the unexpected and mysterious lady, was Mannikin. These two lovebirds proceeded to share an intimate embrace, caught in each other's thrall, enjoying a stolen moment and feeling magnificently alive~ this much was apparent. The lady was talking avidly, although she was too far away to be heard. She was full of joy, impetuous in her manner, sparkling as she gesticulated. Ponting detected a refined and educated nature. On moving closer, it became evident that the woman was both articulate and clever in her use of language and had the ability to draw abstract ideas into existence, through use of subtlety changing inflections. Mannikin was captivated, enthralled to be in her company and so amused by the beauty unfolding before him; he was liberated, unleashed and laughed uncontrollably. She overwhelmed him with her compulsive enchantment. He shared her ideas, visualised her imagery and delighted in her amusing points of view. He pulled her towards him, fascinated, bewitched and spellbound by her skills, her loveliness and her presence. Ponting recognised that he had stepped into a moment of love and union between these two beings. As a voyeur, he watched them kiss and fondle; she touched his crotch knowingly. Ponting quickly moved back, sensing that the next move would be for them to check they had not been observed. He moved out of sight prematurely.

The day had developed further. The humidity and heat in the greenhouse had been overbearing and, before long, Mannikin and the woman left the stifling atmosphere of the glass building. For the next hour they wandered the surrounding area, during which time Mannikin photographed the beautiful, young woman next to various and miscellaneous sphinx statuary. He was particular and emphatic about positioning her and getting the shots he wanted, with a view to capturing the decisive image. She, for her part, indulged him and was ambitious in her preparedness to play and be part of his game; she leaned forward provocatively, keen to arch her back and emphasis the line of her bottom, like every other member of the sphinx kingdom around her. She acted, wore grimaces and adopted facial expressions as dynamic and convincing as any beast within the surrounding menagerie. She was intoxicating and sexual, a sphinx herself. Periodically she ran around parodying an exquisite lunacy, lifting herself into the air with the presumption that she too might fly like them. She was both cat and bird at the same time. Ponting had his breath taken away by her unbounded, exhilarating sense of energy and her joy in each passing moment. These two had become bewitched children, delighting in their proximity~ lost to the cause of love~ or so it seemed to him. But more than this, they exuded a natural innocence and energy together. Perfectly defined, in no way could it have been simpler or purer. The sky above opened up to let in more light just for them.

They finally succumbed to the day, as the afternoon turned slightly misty. Maybe it was a kind of fog produced by the day's excessive heat, a haze that had grown out of the lingering moisture from the previous night, a blanket that was wont to return as everything moved towards evening once more. The lovers, at last, went for tea in the summer pavilion. It was placed at the highest point in the park, overlooking the emperor's summer palace, which could be seen at least a mile away in the distance below. The open vista allowed for impressive views across the landscape. It was here that the tired throng of visitors that day assembled to show off their staunch humanity and sweet hubris. Mothers cradled sleepy offspring as fathers perched little ones on their knees amidst a sea of pushchairs, prams, discarded coats, jumpers, and exhausted, crumpled carrier bags. Tea was supped and cigarettes smoked. The lovers sat arm in arm looking out onto and into the world. Everywhere they looked they only saw themselves, strangely detached; they were lost in a soft place and delighted. Waiters glided effortlessly past with cakes and confectionery, delivering teas and squash~ everything might have been a dream. There was an enchantment all around that was infectious. Ponting remembered his own life and felt some loss, with eyes that glistened and an unfamiliar lump in his throat.

Ponting recalled the day as though it had been his own, equally participating in the sweet passage of time~ its occasions slowed and made relaxed. He had not only seen but also felt and experienced wonderful moments, having eavesdropped on the joy of two lovers for an entire afternoon. Maybe there was a salutatory message to himself in here somewhere~ maybe he too needed to 'get a life'. Ponting began to wonder why he had been given this assignment, indeed why had he accepted it, allowing himself to ever get involved. This strange brief should not have been his. It was becoming more difficult to undertake than those jobs in which there were real dangers to accommodate, where lives might be lost and people could be killed. Unusually, he felt demoralised, apathetic and right now, in territory he did not recognise. Nothing seemed right to him. What was going on? Where was the inferred criminality he had been told of, that was about to turn the political world upside down? This was supposedly, after all, a case one priority assignment~ he had been told this and yet there seemed to be nothing of importance to worry about. It contained no apparent espionage, nobody dying, nothing changing hands, no money laundering. Where was the nut that he was to crack? He was spending his days observing domestic bliss, tailing lovers, having to guess the secrets of magicians; none of this made sense at all. Surely this was not the kind of thing a nation state needed to be spending its taxpayer's money on. Ponting was confused, he was a highly trained spy, after all~ *and a killer, if needs be~ with the license to prove it and the highest-level security clearances.* What was going on? Had this world turned mad? He concluded that there must be a subtlety that had been lost on him. The greater meaning, he decided, must be in the detail~ a detail he had without doubt missed!

'Maybe being confused is a necessary prerequisite to getting close to knowing what might actually be going on,' he thought to himself, as if attempting to pinpoint what he had learned/discovered/found out.

He dare not write up the report of what he had spent his afternoon doing, no more than he might declare how, in truth, he found himself indulging in and actually enjoying the experience. Nor, in particular, could he allow himself to note the three miscellaneous occurrences that happened which he could in no way explain.

1. The stone did not land; this was baffling to him, but apparently not unexpected to Mannikin. It was a peculiarity that perplexed Ponting more than it perhaps ought; he kept returning to his remembrance of the moment, most notably whilst he had been in the greenhouse, where he had imagined its belated and unexpected reappearance through the glass roof.

2. He saw Mannikin go into the greenhouse on his own, but curiously has two memories of him and the woman coming out. One as they left and he was watching from inside the building, and a second in which he saw them come out whilst he was standing against a plinth on which a monumental sphinx preened itself. He, in his imagination, is convinced he saw both views.

3. Whilst seeing the two exit the greenhouse, *in the scenario where he saw himself watching from outside*, a person~ a woman, caught him

unawares. She appeared in front of him, walked up to him and apparently into him, passing through his body and disappearing into the monument immediately behind. There was no other explanation; his back was against the stone. He turned to see how, or if, the thing had indeed passed through solid matter! He was profoundly confused in the moment and shook his head to release the spell and astonishment that overwhelmed him. On noticing the ground in front of his feet, he saw that his pistol, a German Walther PPK 7.65mm automatic was laying there, the clip removed, the shells emptied and the silencer unscrewed! He quickly scrambled after the parts and reassembled them before anyone might see or discover his disarray.

Surely he could not declare any of these things without undermining his own perception in the eyes of his superiors.

'Maybe it is at last time to retire from the service,' he conjectured.

His thoughts return to the present. The opera is over. Tonight he had lost the man he was intending to tail. He was losing his touch. What could he do? Go back to his hotel, get back before the storm clouds finished gathering over the city. For once the thought of an early night didn't appeal to him. He was feeling lonely and isolated; he would stop on the way and buy cigarettes, maybe a bottle of cognac too. Maybe he needed to wander the streets; maybe he needed some company. Where might he find a beautiful piece of the orient on a night like this? Maybe there was something else he should be looking for!

The look of a being with the face of an angel enters his subconscious. Where had he seen this remote physiognomy before? A flock of sphinxes rises into the air; their cry is a primordial scream. The noise transmutes into the sound of a police siren passing along the street at speed. Wheels skid as a driver badly misjudges a corner, causing his vehicle to collide awkwardly with the kerb, which it mounts, slamming into a fire hydrant before coming to rest. The vehicle is badly damaged, steam rises from the radiator. In the next moment, a fountain of water under extreme pressure bursts forth from the hydrant~ to stand indomitable in the night air, hissing like a snake. Luckily no one is hurt. Ponting watches the action for a moment and then moves on, walking deeper into the shadows.

The sky darkens, the world is evolving, transmuting, becoming different by tiny degrees and it has always been so~ as ever, hardly anyone at all is noticing the minutiae. For the first time, Ponting has caught a glimpse of its passing~ and attached to this is perhaps a thing he needs to know. He has become aware of his own consciousness in a heightened manner. There is 'knowing' in him.

What can he do with its substance~ is he enabled in this moment, or cast further adrift?

★ ★ ☆ ★

64.

Making the insightful moment speak, causing it to make an utterance that can be identified, quantified, captured, weighed down, in order that it might take on a role or function within reality that has purpose, that assists in the definition of existence, that explains a universal dilemma~ it all requires a bit of work.

There is a short, wooden ladder leaning against the flagpole. Xavier is naked but for loose fitting underpants. The man stands precariously on the top rung, his back to the flagpole, facing outwards with hands placed behind him, so that he can hold on for support. His position looks hazardous, although there is little danger of him falling and if he were to, it would only be as far as the flat roof of the old factory building~ although in truth this remains a substantive distance. The night is well advanced; it is already quite dark. From this curious and temporary vantage point, he experiences magnificent views across Warcapest. Xavier has a desire, a compulsion to be as high as possible, in order to see over, to see further, to assess distances, to correlate information and tonight, *not for the first time*, this is his way of doing it. Furthermore, he understands something of the particular cause of his bizarre need. He has identified an aspiration, maybe a desperation, to be like the statue in act three of the opera~ *as well as a subconscious need to explore the possibility of throwing himself from a great height.*

The envelope of air that lies over the district remains heavy from the day's heat; a build up of moisture readies itself for a torrential downpour. Massive, black clouds scud across the sky's canopy; they travel towards and over Warcapest from a far off distance, an impossibly supposed place elsewhere. Seeing and experiencing all this resonates at a deep and significant level within Xavier's consciousness. The atmosphere in the uppermost regions of the sky is cold. Thunder can be distantly heard rumbling; there is immediate and imminent threat that the heavens are about to open up, releasing their massive, pent up energy.

It strikes Xavier that he is on stark scaffolding, like a hanging gallows, or a gibbet. He feels conspicuous, vulnerable. Moisture in the air and perspiration has made his skin slippery to the touch. Breathing has become difficult. He looks up, intently pressing his gaze directly overhead, anticipating the impending storm just about to burst all around, imagining the prospect of tying himself to the flagpole to see out the uproarious squall, whilst trapped in its midst. Might he allow himself to be blown by the winds that are about to be unleashed and become soaked by the tempestuous rain and its accompanying deluge? That would be part of a hero's life surely, like the famed English painter of light, Joseph Mallord William Turner who, it is said, allowed himself to be lashed to the mast of a sailing ship, that he might experience the full barrage of a mighty and violent storm whilst at sea, without fear of being swept away and lost forever. The painter's need to experience the world around him was so great as to necessitate such dramatic action.

The pressure in the air intensifies. An extra weight of cloud, like an eiderdown of immeasurable size, is thrown over the top of the upper atmosphere. The compression builds, the sound of thunder moves closer and in consequence of the resultant stress, lightning streaks silently across the sky.

Xavier deliberates about coming down, but decides to tarry longer; there is emotional sanctuary in remaining where he is. The heat of the intense, summer sun had been, without remission, draining energy from his body all day long. He is wilted and desperate to cool. The first drops of rain arrive and hit his skin; they seem to be unusually wet and as cold as anticipated~ icy indeed and possibly from some other juxtaposed world, a different place to the one he finds himself in. The rainfall is moving him from one state of being into another. In haste, two frontiers touch; in this way two worlds collide. He is at that interface where he can look forward and back in the same moment. This is the place where magic occurs.

Such experiences and sensations are uppermost in his mind~ his flesh tingles and tightens in response to the dynamic and tempestuous night unfolding around him. Simultaneously, subterranean thoughts indulge in memories of Sara Phielnx. He is full of joy, suddenly inexplicably euphoric. Emotions and remembered impulses concerning their night at the opera return to him, and then of their time at the greenhouse and in the old factory. He collects and holds on to her. Past images journey back to him, surrounding him; he sees her travelling back to their hideout. This is where she will always find him.

Her electricity flows into him and through him; she is his muse, an inky angel. These things are so obvious. He is incredulous that a person might be as much as she. Her secrecy, her dynamic sense of self, her energy and her wild, uncontrollable sexuality sucking the life out of him, all point to her awareness of the greater truths contained within reality. She is a superior being, living in the very midst of the ordinary and commonplace, he thinks. She is rarified, exclusive, remote and enigmatic. So much seems to be a deception~ but he feels her to be real. Might this be a clever charade on her part, or is he confusing himself, willing her to be 'other' out of personal need~ perhaps a lifetime in her company would make her commonplace? Or maybe all things simply conspire to make the illusion seem momentarily tangible. The ecstasy, in any event, is worth it. The accompanying rapture opens up horizons in his mind.

The cold rain is falling faster, taking the heat out of the air as the heavens continue to roll onward. A strong wind is blowing in from the west. The downpour lashes his face and body, making his underpants wet and transparent, the fabric stuck closely to his skin, outlining his sex, and vulnerability. The storm is directly overhead, the air full of moisture and loud rumbling~ accompanied by multiple forks of lightning. A building in the distance receives a direct hit, a revolving red star is displaced and falls from its roof completely, crashing and disintegrating into pieces as it tumbles to the ground below. Xavier experiences insurmountable energy in every direction, deriving and demanding extravagant pleasure from it, whilst realising, at last, that he is frozen to the core and desperately cold. It would be safer to climb down and go inside. He had hoped to stay on the roof long enough to be seen on his gibbet, anticipating that Sara might find him there, but that possibility seemed to be vanishing. It seemed that tonight of all nights she might end up being late for their rendezvous. He was surprised and disappointed, but would move on. He had begun to shiver and his teeth were chattering.

He lowers himself carefully from his impromptu vantage point, sliding slowly off the flagpole, his cold, square feet inarticulate at the ends of his legs, the muscles prominent and stiff. There is trepidation in his actions, more appropriate to a circumspect older man. He is descending the ladder the wrong way, facing outwards, prior to obtaining the safety of the rooftop. Xavier is curiously preoccupied, unaccountably aware that~ something has in fact gone terribly wrong. His universe has shifted. It flashes up in his consciousness, first as a kind of horror, before subsiding and leaving him with a perception of vast emptiness; he involuntarily begins to weep for no apparent reason, sobbing out loud into the wind and making a brief wail, before sinking to the rooftop on his knees, taking up a fetal position. The world in this moment has emptied of significance; a thing has become vanished and been lost. A terrible tremor passes over him.

There he lays amid the storm, under stars hidden from view, the heavy rain striking the rooftop, forming deep puddles all around.

Before long he shifts, acknowledging that time has passed and aware that he remains perilously, and dangerously cold. The electric storm is vicious and unusual. Xavier picks himself up, *as best he can,* and walks stiffly, slowly, semi-upright, suddenly ancient~ heading for the rooftop door leading to the floor below. Once through, he moves hesitantly down the flight of stairs into the room. He flops onto the bed, rolls into the top blanket without attempting to dry his cold, wet body. Here, he is to lie for an hour, sleeping deeply and dreaming of the void that has opened up before him.

On waking, Xavier continues to feel disorientated and very lost. The storm has relaxed, but still persists; wind-blown rain taps gently, like invisible but benign fingers against the windows of his room, perhaps sustaining the echo of an idea once remembered. He has warmed and decides it is time to seriously question the whereabouts of Sara. Where might she be? What has happened? Never before has there been an occurrence in which their plans have been so corrupted or remained unfulfilled. They had never, ever been late for one another! Such an eventuality, he realises, has never been discussed within their shared organisation or vocabulary.

Xavier stands and crosses the room to heat water on the stove. Cats purr nearby as they follow his movements with interest. He wanders into Sara's work area to see if there are clues to reveal where she might have gone or currently be~ his eyes scour the organisation on her desk, hoping for a sign. There are scattered prototypes of curious, wooden boxes haphazardly placed, including maquette designs for the one he had seen her carefully painting. It was a slim container decorated with green and black lines in repetitive stripes constructed from a discarded cigar box. She wanted to wear it around her neck as a kind of satchel when cycling. It was to contain something special~ he had wondered whether it was to be a birthday present for him. There was no way of knowing and he wouldn't presume to understand or attempt to interfere with her creative processes. Her inner world was extremely precious. It was enough for him that she was magic~ he didn't need to know how she did it.

He wanders back into the kitchen area and makes tea. Soon, he holds the warm cup in both hands, drinks from it slowly, playing for time, all the while hoping for, or imagining, the sound of the outside door far below, or her footsteps distantly echoing in the main staircase. The storm outside continues to rage with an intensity equal to the one in his heart. He cannot explain how it is that she has become a memory; what was here has gone. He insists his mind is playing tricks, worrying where there is no need. He decides to dress, with the intention of going to the gatehouse and checking with Ryman, to see if anyone has tried to enter the grounds. He will ask him if he has seen her. He might break down and ask him what has gone wrong. Would if be an overreaction if he did?

The anxiety filling his mind has expanded by the time he is ready~ if needs be, the man will travel out into the wild night in search of his soul mate, his beloved. He puts on an oiled waterproof coat and cap, walks out of his flat and down the stairs to the unlit floors below. He takes a torch, kept for the purpose, to light the way, knowing that there is another at the base of the stairway, four flights below, as is the established method used in these parts to make one's way through the unlit stair well at night. The sound of the storm outside wails larger in the empty, resonant space.

Having reached the floor below, he turns to descend the next wide, stone flight of steps, then stops in his tracks, imagining he hears a faint, unfamiliar sound from beyond the double door leading onto the factory floor. What did he hear? Something fell~ a noise was made by a trapped animal, perhaps a bird or a little deer~ could it be something dangerous? His sense of reality is too seriously disturbed for him to rationalise the situation.

In any case, he has a need to check out what is going on, and with a sense of precipitous anticipation, pushes against the heavy, battered, door leading onto the barren factory floor. The un-oiled, dry hinges groan against his weight and will not close once open. In the gloom, lit only by his torchlight, Xavier makes out the expansive space stretching before him. Strange outlines greet him across the dreary vista, making it difficult to see what barriers are solid or maybe illusory. The effect is further compounded by shimmering light entering through windows from outside; the diminished glow from the streetlamp passing through trees that dance and shift in the wind, causing unnatural shadows to flicker and move across the interior. There are ropes, cables and curious fittings hanging from ceilings; they sway ever so slightly. The space is partitioned in a few areas but apart from this, the floor is vacant and empty. Pushing forward into the gloom, he discovers there is danger underfoot. Parts of floor, where light machinery and mechanical devices had once stood, reveal places where missing concrete and gaping holes open to the level below. His anxiety and temperature soars as he puts a misplaced foot into a hole that could, so easily have resulted in a fall into a darker void. He continues moving with trepidation, flashing the light, checking his footing and the murky blackness ahead of him. The sound of dripping water can be heard and the flapping of wings; a bird somewhere has become trapped and is in distress. The intensity of sound increases as Xavier moves towards it. The clamour seems to suggest something might be pulling itself apart in the anxiety of the moment.

The noise is coming from behind a partitioned area a little further ahead. Xavier moves towards it and turns a corner to confront the cause....

...to be met by an unprecedented and unexpected horror.

He discovers a lost image; it might be a ghost of a hiding, crumpled and pathetic Sara Phielnx. Where has this come from? In no way is this real~ he refuses to believe it. The whimpering thing looks up at him pleadingly, irradiated from within by some soft, simpering light~ it might be about to extinguish itself completely.
'This is my only chance...' she says in a tiny voice that is so delicate and frail, but undoubtedly her.
'I have to leave. I cannot exist anymore. I am being taken away from you~ I don't know why, maybe it is because our relationship is too extreme and full of strangeness; it cannot be sustained or resolved. I, like you, have been made into a person who is unable to exist in real space. We will not be here for each other anymore. We have become too dangerous for the world and for one another~ although I long for the unknown territory we inhabit, I can no longer understand it, and am now damaged and destroyed by it. There is no future now for me. I can only see death before me. There is nothing more I can offer you or give and so there is no point, since it has, by necessity, become impossible for us to complete or finish our adventure. I have come to fear precisely this~ there is no point. Before long, it was to be over anyway. None of this can last and even memory is lost too soon; we will all forget what it is we do. I have to leave, to continue is impossible and would only court destruction. To disappear is our only choice possible. What has happened is terrible.'

'I have left it too late and now you can never find me,' she says.

'But STAY, oh please, *please*! Nothing can be worse than losing you. Without you there is...'

Some minutes pass. Xavier at last moves, confused, bewildered it would appear, seemingly out of his mind and prone to muttering or talking to himself. The aberrance of the preceding event had caught him unaware and, in this new moment, made no sense at all. This episode was inexplicable and seemed impossibly joined to all that had gone before by the briefest and flimsiest of threads.

Elsewhere, in this large, open, defunct factory floor, breath reveals itself. It can scarcely be seen and only faintly appears as a remote, warm haze escaping from within a protecting blanket of black shadow; this is some way off and away from where Xavier stands. The hidden Ponting remains motionless. He had not seen Mannikin in this state before and was pleased with his stealth, which had allowed him to follow and observe his prey so closely and right onto this expansive factory floor. The detective was particularly satisfied to have discovered the hideout and was now convinced of Mannikin's secretive nature. Ponting's cunning had finally paid off and a circuitous, fortuitousness of circumstances had allowed him to get very close, whilst remaining cleverly hidden in the gloom. From a safe distance, he had been able to observe Mannikin's form, strangely illuminated by some curious glow or light from behind the partition he was facing into.

He waits for Mannikin to leave, which he soon does, once the curious glow before him turns off or diminishes. His grim, somewhat pathetic figure moves carefully, apparently shaking, slowly inching its way past where Ponting is hiding. Mannikin is painstakingly picking his way over the hazardous floor, avoiding the gaps and holes and the obstacles that hang down from the ceiling. The far door, against expectation, groans and closes behind the exiting figure, the man's frame somehow made curiously small by the events just witnessed, or experienced.

Ponting, without doubt, recognises he is onto something. The factory hideout explains every gap in their inventory of Mannikin's movements. Moreover, he understands that this is where the girl and Mannikin meet to spend time together. The convenient arrangement with the man in the gatehouse ensures that no one else might pass this way. Ponting had gone to some lengths to breach the perimeter of the factory site, having found a raw edge where damage to the fencing afforded an entry point that would remain inconspicuous to the gatekeeper.

What had Mannikin been taking so much interest in? Indeed what was he looking at in those brief moments? Ponting waits, listening for his quarry to pass down the stairway to the very bottom of the building. He hears the distant bang of a door and breathes a sigh of relief. Mannikin was probably on his way to meet the woman now. The spy hoped his sleuthing partner, waiting in the street outside, had the sense to follow Mannikin as he exited the premises. Ponting was aware that he had been left in the factory on his own and might now, without interruption, explore the general layout of the building and more especially, expose the secret hideout and meeting place of Mannikin and the woman.

Ponting was at last onto her trail too; it had been discovered where she worked and his team were tailing her right around the clock. He had taken the rash decision to dedicate a team of four agents to ensuring she could not be lost, so that her life and story might be fully discovered and documented. His suspicion was that it was she who carried the Egyptian key, possibly around her neck in a strange, occult-looking box of eccentric-striped design, or perhaps somewhere else on her person. Ponting had instructed his team to be more vigorous in acquiring the artefact, if they thought she might have it. Indeed, if they could get away with making it look like daylight robbery, all well and good. He had sanctioned this as an extreme tactic to use, if necessary, since time was beginning to become an issue.

Things were heating up~ and a good job too! Ponting was getting anxious about his lack of success in such a straightforward case; he needed hard facts to put before his superiors. This investigation was testing his patience and his credulity concerning strange things that he could not explain. He had inadvertently become involved and was no longer as impartial as he wished to be~ *about such things he continued to tell no one.*

Ponting begins to move carefully forward from out of his hiding place; he needs to see what Mannikin had been looking at so carefully. His pencil torch, held high, helps plot his way through obstacles and debris. Soon, he arrives at the floor-to-ceiling partition. It might have been part of a glass-fronted office for a shift foreman; it was, in any event, an overused, grubby little space of some kind. He turns the corner to look in; the area is clear, apart from a couple of faded, oil-stained playing cards stuck to the floor next to remnants of a discarded calendar, out of date by a decade. There is nothing particularly to see, no evidence of a light source or anything that might usurp a person's interest at all. Ponting is perplexed. A wind picks up; he feels a breeze pass across his face. A draught has invaded the interior of the building from somewhere. What had Mannikin been looking at or talking to? Had he been hallucinating; was he out of his mind?

Confused, and none the wiser, he decides it is time to move on. Ponting begins to trace a route through the building to the door. In that moment, he feels something eerie occur. Something has walked through him, as it had that day in the park. He turns to see a ghostly, illuminated figure standing immediately behind him. It is the very banshee he saw in the public gardens, the strange sphinx-like woman who walked through him then; she had found him again. She smiles and walks into him once more and there remains in his space, her light irradiating his insides, digging into him, discovering his soul, excavating him. He can feel her presence in every aspect of him. She is sifting through his very being, exploring every characteristic of what he is. Powerless to escape, he begins to feel himself lifted and pulled into the air, rising into the eaves of the roof and then through the ceiling into the sky beyond. The world becomes smaller and vanishes below at great speed, as he becomes lost, even to himself.

★ ★ ☆ ★

65.

An incredible sense of emptiness fills Xavier as he descends the stairway in the old factory. Where has all this despair come from and why? He is bereft~ life has suddenly emptied. Is this a passing convulsion or an indicator of a sea change in the fabric of existence? He exits the building and quickly leaves the factory site, using a side gate, whose catch can be released from the inside. He moves alone and lonely, feeling abandoned, cast adrift. The street shrinks away in every direction. A sensation looms up~ unusually large, making him anxious; it is like a tidal surge. He feels the arteries in his neck press against his windpipe, making him want to retch. His heart is racing, his pulse is beating across his entire body, his hands move of their own volition, pounding in time to the blood coursing through his veins. Time and splendour have... just gone! Everything he thought he had... has simply evaporated. Existence has dropped out of the picture completely for him. What he feels is like death, is death~ death as he might own it. Is this as it has been for every creature that has known life; that has once lived and thereafter departed henceforth into that timeless and dreadful oblivion, that dark about which we know nothing? How can time become so lost, so quickly?

The ever present, in its immediate decline, falls into an instant past, slipping away~ like quicksilver. It is too willingly, swiftly forgot, mislaid even, amidst the clamour for the next, new, prevailing or anticipated moment~ *one, that in truth, we should never dare to expect, for it will not always be so, as Mannikin too knows in this instant.* He has, with haste, unaware of his own response, as an involuntary action, pressed an iron foot against some imaginary door. He is already holding back a tide of time; he needs to temporarily suspend the advance of all futures, stop them in this very moment~ he must take stock. Ideally, he would go back if he could. His stance is to press forward whilst his head eagerly looks behind, ready to dive back into the recent time pool he has just left, or is it that he waits for slow moving objects to catch up with him? He is missing something that has left him incomplete, vulnerable~ without which he cannot sustain the next moments he might need to confront.

He cannot explain what has happened. Perhaps, during some recent streak of lightning, he has become altered and been transformed. Or has the world changed around him? Options have been removed; important elements that were keys to his existence have seemingly vanished.

His reminiscences of 'her' flood into his conscious mind, seeking to supply an answer to the sudden unexplained mystery. Multiple images of her are standing before him, or can be seen running alongside the road with him, their differing complexions and numerous viewpoints distracting him as he walks. Each projection vies for his full attention with each mighty stride. He sees them all with clarity and yet, seemingly for the first time, he recognises how imprecise and imperfect these memories are. In addition, they are insistent that lost time cannot be reclaimed. As he looks, he can see that which has already been forgotten~ detail is missing. Without a living experience of Sara Phielnx on which to feed, his imagination will no longer deliver a credible image of her within his memory. She has become detached, even in this short time, from the present. He can, try as he will, see no future with her in it. His mind is desperately attempting to make up contorted and strange stories of their imminent and imagined reunion, and when he runs them in his mind's eye, she is wooden and static, like a doll. She smiles at him as once she did, but not as she might. The image is cardboard and flat. What has changed? How dare the change be so resolute and unbending! Might it not allow for some discrepancy in its assumed permanence? Where would be the offence in that? Why is there no route back? Why might he not enter some underworld to collect her?

How a space in time can disappear, fade beyond redemption from our memory of 'before', or 'once there was'. With it, those ingenious, glowing, abundant thoughts that were manufactured within the light of the moment, become detached, perhaps stranded, alienated from the continuity we had always intended to afford them~ our heartfelt wish to allow them to travel into the future with us is forever denied. Such memories once knew their anchor, *they were illuminated by their prime player and source*, they shared a space in time with their heroine and without the prompt for that remembered point; we see how quickly they become grey, dead, partial and incomplete. The loss of an iconic marker detaches the memory from its story. The irreplaceable, irredeemable memory exists on its own, lost, solitary within a bleak place in which it desperately tries to continue to shine. It can no longer be nourished by its fountainhead, the umbilical link broken forever~ and then, like a fallen leaf, the memory petrifies, slowly losing all colour, drying, in process of becoming the skeleton of what *once* it was. Only in the yet living can a memory of what once was, paint a dry, crisp image back into life, but this too often is no better than rouge or make up on a corpse; the residue of an experience is all that remains~ the jigsaw becomes permanently imperfect, the piece, as it dries, shrinks, will no longer fit precisely; it cannot be remembered accurately~ and yet curiously this unknown, lost emptiness, within some bigger picture, becomes more relevant than the still known space all around; more important than reality itself, an enigma that stops time.

Some hours have passed and as we look we see Xavier Mannikin standing on the roof again, this time wondering about his height from the ground. It is raining, still. An angel stands behind him, *as in the roof scene that took place in the opera, under the watchful gaze of a petrified statue.* There she is nudging him, willing him to empty himself into the universe. Mannikin is thinking for Xavier, is thinking hard and wondering what they can do to atone for, or replace what has happened.

Is he serious~ will he jump?

★ ★ ☆ ★

66.

A phone rings and is answered.

'Harry, I doubt I am going to be in work this week; something has cropped up. I need some time to sort my affairs.'

'Okay...' a dead silence at the other end of the phone indicates that Harry Towers is all ears and listening carefully. The tone and measured stance of Mannikin's voice indicates to him that, far from being a normal request for time off work by an employee, something has struck the young man to the quick.

'...Are you okay, can I be of use, can I help?'

'No it's fine... I just need...' his voice falters.

'Does your father know of this?'

'No Harry, this is the point. No one knows, and I really need to keep it this way. I want you to cover my absence, if you can. I would like you to do this for me. I need a week. It's nothing illegal or anything that might compromise you or anyone, its just personal stuff.'

'Okay... I can do this. Let me know if you need anything else, I'm your man, I can be discreet.'

'Thanks Harry, you're one in a million, you always have been.'

The phone goes down.

Early morning daylight has returned. Mannikin has phoned from his bachelor flat.

After leaving the factory the previous evening, Xavier had spent the night walking over the face and body of Warcapest. He was used to walking at night and had traipsed the rain-soaked streets. The summer rain at last felt warm, even when it soaked him through to the skin, bathing him in its nocturnal splendour, recognising him as a son and trying to sooth his turmoil~ it had been persistent in its down-pouring. Lightning intermittently cracked across the sky, forking amazingly, but without sound. He walked in a state of delirium, trying to get a grip on what was happening, desperately wondering what was going on, unable to think and feeling desolate and abandoned.

After some hours, he had, unexpectedly, perhaps accidentally, found himself back at the factory. He recognised himself to be seriously disturbed; somewhere deep inside he needed to check whether Sara had finally shown up. Mannikin was quite prepared to mock his despair and deeply felt turmoil if it could be proved she had arrived. 'Sara might finally be here,' he thought. The real Sara, not that strange, crumpled, imagined vision, which against his will he kept reimagining; that gross thing had arrived from some other place outside of reality, wherever that was. The gates, as expected, were locked. He proceeded, against his better judgment, to awaken Ryman. An ashen, bedraggled, blood-shot eyed Mannikin, soon asked if Sara had shown up. The man in pyjamas shook his head slowly. She had not been seen. Ryman was emphatic and concerned; he could see that things were amiss; something had happened. He was insistent and keen to help. However, the younger man revealed nothing more, other than to thank the gatekeeper for his concern. Ryman volunteered to wait up a bit, until Mannikin had a chance to check the flat at the top of the building again. Xavier laboriously revisited their secret room for the second time that night~ he lifted cold, empty sheets and let them fall, before going up onto the roof yet again. It was then that he had looked over the edge and saw into an eternal abyss.

Mannikin returned within fifteen minutes. Ryman's poor, crumpled daughter appeared behind her father in grey vest and knickers, half hidden in the shadow of the hallway beyond the front door. She too had woken, tired and confused at the nocturnal disturbance. The girl inexplicably reminded Xavier of the gently twisted vision of Sara seen earlier. With tears in his eye, he apologised for the disturbance and told them they should both go back to bed, promising not to disturb them anymore that night. He left Ryman, thanking him for his concern and forbearance~ and in this way Xavier wandered off again, allowing himself to become absorbed into the black shroud of the shadowy city, moving slowly, with indeterminate effort, traversing miles in the general direction of his apartment. He became lost and indistinct within the body of the sleeping metropolis, as much alike any brick or paving stone; as dumb and as distant as any streetlamp, or cold memorial or bronze statue~ he walked without any sense of memory or meaning.

The architectural mouldings and statues, the dancing semi-clad figures, the nymphs, the angels, the beautiful carved mortals blazing in their depiction of ecstasy and youth adorning the streets and buildings~ and the very opera house itself, *as he passed*, were vibrant in their petrified life, in comparison to him.

★ ★ ☆ ★

Things had changed in a fundamental way. Every page of his story up to this point, without consultation or agreement, had altered. Everything, of a sudden, is affected by this new subtlety. And if the narrative were to be reread from its inception, it will be seen to have rewritten itself due to this seminal incident~ in anticipation of which, every moment from this point on will likewise become altered too. The world might appear to be the same to others in their lives, but it was not so for Xavier Mannikin~ of this he was certain.

By morning, Mannikin had tired his body and was exhausted. In desperation, whilst dragging his feet one after the other, a kind of half-baked plan had formed. Not a very good one, but such was his state of mind that doing something was going to be better than accepting that a major part of his life had evaporated without explanation~ indeed vanished without trace.

He would wait a day or so, three days at most, and if there were no word, he would begin a search. Strictly speaking, he continued to feel that the rules of their secret relationship made it difficult for him to seek her out. He had been banned from ever trying to follow her; she had said it would be the end of them for sure if he ever dared to find out more. She was emphatic about this, to the point of hysteria. *'We can only ever meet by agreement; that is the nature of our bond,'* she had said.

★ ★ ☆ ★

67.

Time has passed. Days have gone by; there are still no signs. Sara has indeed vanished~ maybe she never existed. Xavier is bereft and more confused than ever. What could be the cause of such a catastrophe? His world had emptied, his house of cards was in disarray, nothing remained and horizons in every direction had become bare and featureless. He grieved and mourned for her. Wherever she might be, he intrinsically knew she did not want him to follow or find her, nor would she allow it. He hoped it was out of love for him and to protect him~ although he understood it might be for reasons of her own. Was this how it was meant to be all along? Was this where the strangeness in their relationship was always supposed to lead? How could he know? Feeling helpless and in the petrifying absence of her, he had to do something to fill the void and, against his better judgment, began the process of stalking a shadow, *at least this much,* to find a soul that could not be seen, to discover that which had become invisible, chasing an idea about a thing that he had once owned and which seemed real, but had evaporated. She must still exist, because.... he felt it but realised it might be in the way that an amputee remembers a limb that has been removed.

Mannikin didn't mean to, he didn't want to, he tried not to, but he had, in utter desperation gone to her place of work to ask after her.

People came to help, but no one in the building knew her by any of the names the sad and tearful young man had for the woman. He did his best to describe her without breaking down and sobbing. They soon recognised her as another person who had not turned up for work for the previous fortnight. They told him that despite their best attempts to get in touch, the address and telephone details they had for the employee were dead ends. There was no way to contact her detailed next of kin~ they could not be traced. All the recorded addresses they had for the woman had never existed in the city, and the names of her supposed relatives appeared to be non-existent too. Mannikin asked, in despair, whether the woman had any colleagues or friends in the office or within the department. He was referred to a fellow worker, who told of her lovely personality and great intellect. She had documented and assisted in the compiling of magnificent exhibitions and catalogue notes over the years. She was fun to be with, but always rationed time and never fraternised with colleagues out of work or even at lunch times.

With manic compulsion, Mannikin collected bus and tram timetables in the forlorn hope of reconstructing and remembering the course through the city he had once taken when he had secretly tried to follow her. The remembered route was eccentric and haphazard; it wasn't a straight line to anywhere. He tried, at least, to anticipate the direction she may have circuitously been moving towards, thinking hard about the districts she could realistically afford to live in, or ones that might suit her sense of self. But none of this got him anywhere.

He frantically checked newspapers for recent stories in the city, but nothing struck him as significant. The central police station, not known for their particular wish to help in the cases of missing persons in a country where communism had left a stigma concerning vanished individuals, waved him on in a perfunctory kind of way. There seemed to be little he could do. In any event, he was convinced of her secretive nature; she was somewhere and determined not to be found, least of all by the authorities.

He stalked a shadow during these weeks, frequently imagining her out of the corner of his eye or in the reflection of a window. He found himself looking at other women, trying to make them become her, testing them for their similarities, suspecting they might be her in disguise, as some covert misrepresentation that he was not supposed to see through~ he was exhausting himself with his insatiable need for her and his grief. He sat on trams peering out of their windows for hours, travelling to terminuses, before returning, gazing out at the city as the opposite sides of streets passed by. He travelled the circle metro line remembering place names they had shared, analysing inventories of words they had used together, desperately looking for clues. He searched his mind to remember locations that she knew of and had shown affection for, or demonstrated an interest in. He visited bookshops and boulevards which sold clothes she liked, although strangely, avoided all the venues they had been to together, thinking that in order to hide from him, she would not go back to any of these places. In any event, he did not want to remember them afresh without her presence. The apparent irrationality and psychology of his thinking was becoming a contortion unto itself. How might he know she had ever existed? He looked to the city to understand what it might tell him, convinced it was trying to help him find her. There were signs and symbols that might give him the answer he needed; they were all around and they were everywhere.

Late night city wandering becomes a regular routine, an obsessive habit, a convenient diversion from having to face the reality of great loss and the quandary of his unknown bereavement. Mannikin, partially shaven, scruffy and unkempt, *in process of growing a moustache like Zapik's, it would appear,* is walking streets, stepping through dark shadows and moving anonymously. He wears a long coat, unwittingly emboldening his silhouette amongst the so many others on the street. A thin, emaciated, sidewalk performer catches his eye on a well-lit boulevard some way off. There is a small crowd around the entertainer. He watches from a quiet distance. The insipid, slight man appears to be walking forwards whilst moving backwards. The illusion is humorous, but magnificent.

In spite of the glory of the showman's feat, an involuntary look of wretchedness falls into place across Mannikin's brow. He inhales and lets out a large sigh as he turns to journey onward. He lifts his head to look around; the jaundiced, yellow glow, emitted from within a stationary tram, pulls at his vision, capturing his gaze. More especially, his attention is drawn to the outline of a woman sitting with her back to him; the occurrence causes him to draw breath~ it could be her, or a sign at least. Immersed in his torment he runs to the tram, as it begins to move on. By the skin of his teeth, he jumps aboard and penetrates into the vehicle's interior light as the doors close. Breathless and panting, he moves through the carriage, finally seating himself in an opposite aisle, one row behind the woman in whom he has taken an interest. She turns, offering an opportunistic glimpsed profile, allowing him to see that she is not the person he seeks~ in no way is she the same. Slipping his hand into his pocket, he pulls out a blister pack of tablets. This is medication to calm him; this is new, meant to help, but after a couple of weeks, the prescription was beginning to make his stomach sore and his head ache. He takes a tablet and has difficulty swallowing it. The same prescribing doctor had made an appointment for him to see a psychiatrist. He had that to look forward to.

The sad man feels an enormous pull in his chest; his heart is screaming, telling him it would like to rest or is about to burst, or cry out with an indescribable ache. Might Xavier cry to ease the tension in his face and the pressure in his head? He knows he cannot. The gate that might open to allow his excess of emotion to escape is firmly shut and he is trapped behind it, slowly drowning. He watches people as they get on and off the tram, investigating them, wanting to see, gazing into the souls of each light that shines within them. The sound of the tram bell punctuates the air.

Three men enter the carriage and display official badges, causing the driver to waive them past without interest or ceremony. Mannikin looks to see if the Chinese man, the one met at the opera, is amongst them, *which he isn't.* The unknown men seat themselves, two at the front of the tram whilst the third moves through the coach to sit at the rear. The strangers smile cordially, sympathetically~ perhaps they know something. They look away to talk, by turns returning their gaze, watching him as he apparently dreams inwardly.

Looking into and beyond the finger-streaked, wet pane of the tram window, Xavier imagines the effect of light from the tram's interior passing through and over the darkened face of Warcapest. He is pleased with himself in a sad way~ knowing that no one else is likely to be having the same, insignificant thought. Why should they? What could be the point? The reverie flourishes into an ambient moment, reminding him of similar trips, whilst a boy, when travelling with his governess, or more especially on less frequent occasions, with his heroic father. The men who are watching him would shrink away if his father were here now, for sure. Ding ding! The sound of the bell resounds, muffled and less shrill. The tram is passing by the street that contains the little antiquarian shop; he remembers the little winged statue he purchased there. An inadvertent glance past the 'men in long coats' causes him to notice the vacant seat where the lady had been sitting earlier. Xavier becomes transfixed. The woman had left one of her leather gloves~ by mistake no doubt. The glove blossoms as he looks~ it becomes lovely, like wings on a little statue; it becomes a winged glove. Exquisite wings beat in his imagination; the thought overpowers him, filling him, taking him over. He touches the stubbly growth beneath his nose, aware that he too is becoming a winged thing~ in possession of a moustache. It becomes the badge describing who he needs to be. Somewhere in his head, he is with Sara, jumping from a high roof amidst a rainstorm. He is in an opera, can hear music playing, but can't remember the tune~ *the singing is silent.* The crescendo in the moment is too great and all of his focus is taken by the plunging descent. It occurs in slow motion, the whole world moving past in a dream as the ground insistently rushes up to meet them; he is with her, but detached and watching separately as they plummet through the air. *He is saving himself by remembering that he knows how to walk backwards whilst falling.* In the instant the ground is met, she empties of glory, becoming hideously broken, crushed, punctured, twisted, made ugly and so shockingly wasted. He picks himself up, unharmed, and stands to look down at the shell of the person he still loves, *despite her instant and incomprehensible absence.* In his reverie, on broadening his gaze to look around, he discovers that they have come to rest in a cobbled street, having just missed a deaf-blind girl who hula-hoops, oblivious of the horror that has landed so near. Tears fill his eyes, but he is laughing as he cries. Ding ding!

It is some moments before he moves; it may be that he has fallen asleep just for a minute or two. He rouses himself, remembering where he is.

A woman with her elderly mother enters at the next stop. They move to sit in the seats where the glove lays. Mannikin quickly reaches forward and pockets the lost property before they can discover it.

He becomes anxious, anticipating that his theft might have been noticed and glances guiltily in the direction of the officials, but it appears the men have left, maybe at an earlier stop. There were no long-coated men left on the tram. Were the men ever really there? How could he know? He should have been keener to keep them in his sights. It crosses his mind that they might have become invisible. He responds to the ridiculous thought~ briefly believing it to be real.

He tenses, waits... and then just as the tram begins to move off, dashes to the door and leaps off the vehicle. Mannikin jumps into the air as high as he can, projecting himself clear of the tram and into the road, intent on reaching the pavement if at all possible, hoping that in some way the winged glove in his hand may help him in his flight. He achieves his goal but lands awkwardly on the ball of one foot, whilst twisting the ankle of the other and falls ignobly back into the street. Cars behind screech to a halt, vehicles swerve and horns sound. Mannikin quickly hobbles to his feet and tries to run with shaking legs that do not want to bear his weight or move with fleet efficiency. Slowly, awkwardly, they respond and he begins an ungainly run, lurching down the late night, congested street, avoiding collisions with passing pedestrians and nocturnal revellers. He dare not look behind, feeling the need to make the most of any advantage his hurried departure might have afforded. Only when a hundred metres down the street, does he turn to check whether his escape has been clean. However, he is not alone, there are different men in long coats everywhere, heavily in pursuit from all directions. He has become like Bluto running across a curtained stage.

Does each pursuer have a look on his face? He sees that they are all the same Chinese man, duplicates following him, constantly turning to face him, like machines homing in on a target. There is, he decides, no more that can be done. Mannikin stops, comes to a standstill, out of breath and suddenly tired. Let these avatars, these mere impressions of people that chase him, that seek him out, catch up with him. Let them do their damned worst! Mannikin wants them to get him; he might as well give himself up to whatever it is that pursues him. He is, at last, out-manoeuvered by the confusion and the pressures that leave him standing with nowhere to run... the lonely man waits, a lost individual in the centre of his own storm.... just about to be swallowed!

Gradually, without realising, he sinks to the street and finally collapses in a heap on the pavement. In the nick of time, whilst a semblance of consciousness remains in his poor brain, he hears voices around him.

'Don't worry, it's fine. I know this young man, officer. I will vouch for him. I can sort this out. Help me get him to my car and the problem is over.'

Mannikin is aware of being dragged along by two men~ a police officer and a heavily sweating, fat man.

'Mannikin my boy, I am so pleased I found you. You'll be okay now.'

'Harry is that you? Oh, it is so good to hear your voice.'

'Harry Towers to the rescue, you lucky fellow.'

Mannikin opens his eyes briefly. He sees, *or imagines he sees,* young girls hula-hooping in the street, shouting and giggling. The night, like a black crow, descends.

68.

'I want you to relax; everything is going to be fine. How do you feel today, Xavier?'

'I am okay, Dr. Hellmoth. What do you propose we do this morning? I am already a lost cause, I warn you now. I have always been so.'

'Nonsense, I am really looking forward to talking to you again. You are a fascinating young man.'

Mannikin is being somewhat disingenuous in his exchanges, having already decided he has little interest or intention in letting a psychiatrist diagnose his situation. Despite his professional expertise, Xavier is certain the learned doctor will have no understanding of his particular dilemma. The esteemed Dr. Hellmoth had been recommended; he was the best and continued the line of great names from the golden age of Viennese practitioners. To Mannikin, this said it all. Indeed, the consultation room confirmed all his prejudices; it was a cliché. It might have been the film set for Hitchcock's 'Spellbound'. He could predict the types of responses it was meant to elicit from clients the moment they entered the space. He was not going to play this game. There was an ingrained cultural pattern in play; it struck him immediately. The placing of chairs and couches made Mannikin want to laugh out loud, although he managed to be discreet and only secretly smiled inwardly. The psychiatrist, Dr. Hellmoth, had spent time in the preceding session subtly establishing his credentials in the mind of his client. The charade had been undertaken with weighty solemnity. Only when complete, had the worthy doctor shown any serious concern in turning attention to his patient. During their attempts to know who or what they were dealing with, Mannikin detected that the esteemed Dr. Hellmoth was possibly more anxious about meeting 'Master Xavier Mannikin' than the other way round. The diminutive doctor struck him as a delicate man. He had a precise and closely trimmed goatee and moustache, a slight tremor and a mild speech impediment. In truth, it seemed that both men were stalking each other. Certainly Hellmoth could smell Xavier's resistance to psychoanalysis.

Today, Mannikin appears to be ambivalent and detached, although at a deeper level, he was watching every move or potential direction the learned practitioner might want to nonchalantly establish. Since Mannikin was already intent on giving nothing away, the man would have to work hard or so he assumed. Would the esteemed Dr. Hellmoth be looking for textbook patterns and behaviours that he recognised? Was he expecting to make a diagnosis that confirmed his own predilections and prejudice about his own science or could he indeed miraculously see Mannikin's specific dilemma? How could a man, whom he had only just met for a second time, make any judgment call about his consciousness? How could the psychiatrist, in the short time available to him, see anything of the full complexion of Xavier Mannikin? That people might be so similar or predictable to the point where a psychiatrist could use 'psycho-analysis' to reveal their complexity, offended Mannikin's sensibility and belief.

In the silence and impasse of the moment, poor Dr. Hellmoth's tremor visibly increases. Mannikin takes pity and capitulates at last, wondering if he has fallen for a tactic.

'How did our first session go, Dr Hellmoth? What remarkable insight did you glean? What do you see as the problem?'

'Ah, you want to ask me the questions? That is good. Thank you very much sir! You are very kind. I am not so sure I see any problems. Why not sit, please; make yourself comfortable. I will sit too, if I may; my advanced age has weakened me. How do you feel? Can I get you anything?'

Dr. Hellmoth, with a gesture, invites Mannikin to take the low-lying chaise longue; to sit in it comfortably, he has to lean back. The room is warm, perhaps too warm, the lighting appropriately subdued for the man's profession and Dr. Hellmoth sits, without notes, detached, remote and sleepy.

'Are you going to hypnotise me today?'

'Today?' Dr. Hellmoth seems to awaken, seemingly surprised. 'No, maybe some other time; today, I do not think we need that.'

He reduces his movements and appears to shrink into his own skin; his green, tweed suit seems too large for him. It is not easy for Mannikin to see him properly and soon he stops trying. He lies back to face into the space.

An elegant, mahogany desk stands at the far end of the room. From this distance it seems to be carefully laid out and immaculately organised. Its surface displays a clutter of little statues and ancient figurines~ there are small pieces of Greek statuary, sculpted or cast in metal~ of warriors, soldiers with spears, men with sheep around their necks, naked women carrying amphora or combing their hair. Amongst these are miniature marble heads in poor repair, of Byzantine and Roman origin. All are regimentally laid out like disparate chess pieces without a board beneath them.

'Like real life,' thinks Mannikin to himself.

More especially, they strike Xavier as talismans representing humanity's auspicious development over millennia. They signal and celebrate the weight of a species; or are they simply comforters/pacifiers for the man who occupies this office? No doubt Dr. Hellmoth is a sophisticated and intelligent man. Mannikin had begun to wonder how deep his schemata might be and how flexible his thinking. The patient looks further around the room. Dr. Hellmoth has extensive bookshelves that reach to the ceiling, neatly organised into a leather-bound library of hardback tomes and published papers, all describing the mysteries and histories of his discipline, no doubt. These will be scientific tracts describing all manner of mumbo-jumbo.

'Xavier, would you describe yourself as happy?' says Hellmoth.

'Here we go,' thinks Mannikin.

'I am not sure the question is relevant to anything. I am fine, since you ask. I don't mean to be impolite, but it's not a question I would pose myself or want to answer. I experience the world for sure and that is interesting in itself. I take an interest in the things around me and monitor their progress and my own. Is that good? Happiness doesn't feature. I am~ and what I am fluctuates; all positions are equal. Is this an answer to your enquiry?'

A pause ensues. Mannikin has given a response and purposively replied in such a way as to finish with a question of his own, with no intention of adding more. He recognises the doctor's resistance to answering him. Hellmoth is waiting in the hope that the silence will appear awkward and that Mannikin will feel the need to start talking again. After a moment's uncomfortable quietude, Hellmoth speaks.

'What do your observations reveal to you, Xavier, concerning these things in which you take an interest?'

Xavier fails to answer and in the hiatus, Dr. Hellmoth has to speak again.

'For example, you have again spent much time looking around this room and noticing as much as possible. What do your observations tell you?'

'I am just looking to see where I am, and trying to make sense of things.'

'Yes…and….'

'Yes what!'

'You were keen to look out of the window when you first enter this room. You did so on the first occasion we met and you did the same again today. Tell me more.'

'I don't want to sit down. I think you need to let me walk around.'

'By all means, feel free.'

Mannikin ambles across the room with hands in pockets, head down, to avoid any awareness of the room orientating itself around his shape. He moves to the desk and picks up an ancient cast form in the shape of a Trojan warrior. It is simply modelled, depicting a man about to throw a spear, although the spear is lost and missing or perhaps it has already been thrown, or is in process of travelling still. He looks at it closely then turns to speak, brandishing the little character as though the thing were a weapon with which to beat the psychiatrist.

'How can you or anyone possibly purport to understand the complexity of a human being? You may be trained in this area and quite likely you are cleverer and more intelligent than I, but that doesn't give you answers. You can only guess like the rest of us. Human beings are amazing, diverse and their motivations obscure, even to themselves. We are endlessly creative and deceptive. The life of a person is no open secret. We have so many systems for operating, many of which can be switched or alternated mid-flow depending on whom or what we feel might be watching us, including ourselves. Are we analytical or intuitive, spiritual or spiritless, selfish or altruistic, social or anti-social in our teeming complexity and underlying biological functioning? How can it be known? Where do our insights come from? The likelihood is that we are all of these things. The miasma of being and what we find we have to be, in order to satiate our needs and diverse drives, is complex. Any analysis is like catching the wind in the hope of seeing the invisible. None of this is good enough is it? Furthermore, we systematically blinker our thinking by living the prejudices of our age and lack the motivation to think beyond their constantly shifting boundaries. Consciousness exists in a moving bubble that can rarely see beyond itself. How can we know so much more, whilst making rules that demand we understand less? I sometimes wonder whether there may be thoughts, notions and aspects of consciousness we have lost from those times before we learned our place amongst the stars in the heavens. We imagine we can see the proximity of one idea or reality to another, but no longer see the spaces in which these 'everythings' exist, as we once did. In order to truly understand wouldn't one have to become godlike, so conscious as to have the ability to exist outside of humanity and our selves too, most probably? How else could a person know more and be aware of how perceived phenomena fit together and the ramifications of everything? Simply knowing how understanding works and fits together or knowing the patterns that make a recognised attribute work, *or enable it to have existence,* doesn't necessarily help us in the least. No doubt you have studied psychiatry and the behaviour of animals, but by being of the same mould, where making sense of life is based on your own independent subjective experience of thinking, you must know you can ultimately do little more than make an intuitive analysis of what thinking appears to be and why it causes the outcomes that can be observed. None of us are machine enough to make sense of an event and understand it without our emotions coming into play. As soon as that happens, the truth is changed. Were there ever impartial truths, they would be lost as soon as the idea became conscious. Therefore, you cannot know me; you might only intuit more of yourself through me~ that is all! I have met scientists whose chief interest, if they did but know, was their own conundrum. They deceive themselves into thinking they understand the very thing they understand least about themselves. Too often, this is the sum total of the human condition.'

'And yet you, Xavier, appear to know me by all accounts. You have measured and quantified me in your little speech, very nicely indeed, if I might dare say.'

'No I haven't, I have simply defined the role you allow yourself to play. I have gone some way to quantifying the manner in which society has contrived to give you a speaking role, but of you yourself, I have said nothing. You have an existence within yourself that you keep well hidden too.'

'You know of such things? How can you be sure?'

'Touché, Dr. Hellmoth. Well done.'

'I am as amazed at the way we live our lives as you, Xavier. I too am a collector of the meanings we have about the universe and ourselves. Why else would I honestly want to be a psychiatrist? I doubt we are that different. I can see you think deeply about important things for which, I agree, there is much conjecture. Consciousness is a constantly moving line as you intimate, and as it moves realities and truths shimmer in curious ways.'

Hellmoth had stood and walked across to Mannikin, carefully retrieving the Trojan warrior from his hands and replacing it back on the table in the 'right' place.

'Now, I suspect, is the time. I have decided. We are lucky. Come and sit down. Let us make ourselves calm and relaxed. I want you to lie on the couch. Please do this for me. There, that's excellent.'

The venerable doctor slides his chair nearer. Hellmoth clicks his fingers to attract the patient's attention and begins to move his index finger slowly from side to side in front of Xavier's watchful gaze, imperceptibly lowering his hand on each passing sweep, causing the younger man's eyelids to droop a little each time.

'Think of how relaxed you feel, Xavier~ think of how comfortable you feel. Close your eyes at the point they become so heavy you can no longer keep them open~ you have to give in~ don't you Xavier. That's it~ eyes closed ~ and SLEEP!'

Xavier finds the moment irresistible. A space into which he gladly enters opens before him. Hellmoth's voice is soothing, confident and alluring; it becomes the key to a new place.

'You are slowly falling~ deeper and deeper~ into a soft place where no harm can come to you. As I count down from five to zero, you will find yourself going deeper and deeper still. Let the new space open for you. Move gently~ float smoothly~ tread lightly.'

Dr. Hellmoth's voice becomes distant, somehow further away, despite Xavier sensing the man remains close. He feels safe and warm, curiously lighter. He had unwittingly collapsed his antipathy to the shrink and had stopped resisting him. The doctor's voice had become beguiling and mesmerisingly hypnotic.

Xavier did not mind what was happening to him. He was prepared to give in. He could hear Dr. Hellmoth in the background somewhere else, exerting control, explaining that from now on, whenever he touched Xavier on the shoulder and counted backwards, he would be pleased to resume the trance automatically and that it was only he, Dr. Hellmoth who could do this. This was a curious idea to Xavier, for whilst he was hearing Dr. Hellmoth's voice, he could see that the man talking was Count Zapik, whose frantic gesticulations were intent on keeping the Egyptian key well hidden. Xavier scribbles on a sudden piece of paper that appears out of nowhere~ the Count looks over his shoulder as he writes *'It is not a problem, no one will know.'* The spectral figure of the Count seems satisfied and fades into the background.

Xavier turns in the ethereal space and is surprised to see that *elsewhere* he is engaged in conversation with his dream brother. He wonders why he has only just discovered this, since these two remote spectral avatars appear before him in mid-conversation~ *they seem to have been at it for a while, without him knowing.* They are phantoms, mirror images sporting sad masks that insist he look at them~ one has a moustache. *He cannot decide which one them is him!* A recalcitrant echo begins to be heard, the sound distantly arriving into his ears from some far off place, filling his mind and expanding like a wailing, mournful siren. The cry is one of anguish and despair~ a remotely felt self, screaming to be heard. Consternation fills the air. There is a thing become tangible that is misplaced~ he looks down as he stands before the plagiarised apparitions. The problem doesn't emanate from him or them~ it isn't their fault. The impediment is out there somewhere in the world beyond, *and past their reflections~* that is where the discrepancy lies. There are quizzical looks on the sad faces before him; they lower their arms in the act of supplication or surrender. How can they discover the source of this hindrance in order to understand their own sense of perpetual dilemma? He mouths silent words to his other selves, suggesting he has an idea, a potential key to explain the dilemma. He is conversing without using words. All around, it begins to snow. A strange, balloon-like version of a belly-laughing Harry Towers enters onto the scene, appearing from some other place. He floats between the spectral Xavier Mannikins, slowly rotating and turning in their midst, whilst guffawing and messing uncomfortably with his uncontrollable hairline, trying to make it lie flat~ but it keeps standing up, blown by the invisible wind that carries the snow within its grasp. In a fit of desperation, to help the poor man, the replicated Xavier Mannikins step forward and hold him still, while they part his hair on the other side~ *low and behold,* the noise ceases, everything brightens and all becomes perfect. The snow fades away, the inane laughing stops. A quiet buzzing in his ears, which he hadn't noticed before, has gone. The moment is revelatory. Acid in his stomach turns to alkali. The surface of a turbulent ocean on the edges of his perception turns to glass. The imitative Mannikins begin to mouth words repeatedly to the now quiet Harry.

'Everything can be seen from two sides, Harry; everything can be seen from two sides, man. Don't you know that?'

The scene disintegrates as everything is blown away. The night in Xavier's solitary, primeval world darkens further; he is outside. Within the expanse of the impenetrable pitch-black, he becomes aware that he is dreaming or maybe hallucinating for, despite an impression of wind and apparent cold, he can feel none of it. In the sky, through a cloud clearing, the distant figure of Dr. Hellmoth peers down from the lit room above, as though looking down a well or through a microscope. The man sees an insect moving in the bottom of a damp, poorly lit world it has been forced to inhabit. Everything is nebulous, slithery, moulded and green with algae. A gate that Mannikin recognises materialises; it leads into the old factory. Ryman and the girl are opening it to invite him into a mysterious place. He senses he is about to achieve some kind of salvation and prepares himself to move through....
'5- 4- 3- 2- 1- 0 and back~ eyes open and wide-awake. How are you feeling, Xavier? You did well to come back. I felt I was just about to lose you.'

There would only be a couple of short sessions after this. Most recently, Dr. Hellmoth had said little and seemed detached. Mannikin suspected he had let go of the case, either through disinterest or because he really didn't want to engage in the effort required to see it all through. There were to be no more sessions on the couch.

'I think you might take a nice long rest; it would be good for you.' Hellmoth had said as he sat behind his desk; the man might have been a chess player about to make a move, his pieces lined up perfectly before him, his calm dignity and authority on display. The room was bright and light flooded in through the window.

'I suggest you go away for a while and take in some new air and fresh surroundings. We have prepared a place for you at our mountain sanatorium at Chauchat in the high Alps. I have gifted colleagues there who are keen to help your recuperation. They will be able to look after you. This will be a perfect cure. You have become mentally disturbed and are distressed~ that's very apparent. You've lost an appetite for living too~ that might be a fair assessment. You demonstrate signs that indicate you have suffered a breakdown. You have stabilised remarkably well, I might suggest, but I fear you are still weak. If you are in agreement, I feel we have a way forward and I won't need to see you for a while, maybe a couple of months. In the meantime you can take things easy, be relaxed and learn to enjoy life again. You should continue with the prescribed medication. I ask you to seriously consider the importance of your health; you are too young a man to be suffering these kinds of malaises.'

Within that same week, Mannikin made the prescribed trip and, in no time at all, was laid out on the roofed balcony of the high altitude clinic, wrapped in thick, warm blankets and healthily exposed to invigorating mountain air. Here, during the following days and weeks, his time was to be spent lying recumbent, alongside numerous other patients who were similarly cocooned. A bevy of warped, detached minds were spread out evenly along the suspended veranda, their supine bodies supported on wooden, reclining chairs with footrests. Each pale, weakened constitution looked out with a dull, vacant expression, allowing its watery gaze to travel across the impressive and awe-inspiring range of snow-covered peaks and mountains. Xavier soon fell in with the monotonous routine and made himself into a pleasant and compliant prisoner, an unresponsive inmate, and did whatever was required of him. He became deliberately reclusive and avoided other patients as far as possible, choosing to keep to his room when not taking the air or being examined by numerous doctors. The convalescent seldom talked to fellow sufferers at dinner and never attended the communal rest rooms or community evening events. Instead, he would idly think of this and that, of his life, experiences, happiness and regrets, often contemplating Sarah Phielnx and wondering why everything had become so different, without a reason. Xavier considered Dr. Hellmoth's diagnosis of his situation during this time, recognising that, as he had predicted, the learned doctor knew very little that could really help. Nevertheless, there were things Dr. Hellmoth had said that he dwelt on and kept coming back to~ they were alarming suggestions! The psychiatrist had said that there seemed to be no proof whatsoever that Sara Phielnx ever existed and that Xavier may need to embrace the possibility that he had been fantasising her for many years past, and may need to take medication for the rest of his life for his apparent schizophrenic tendencies, should they continue.

Xavier tries to think hard about Sara Phielnx. She is vanishing by degrees from his memory. He struggles to remember her with lucidity. She begins to shimmer and change in his thoughts, transmuting before him, shrinking, becoming an icon of her former self, a fixed emotion, a remembered entity embodying so much of import, a fantasy of what he wants her to be. Recollection and clarity is reduced, less precise, muddied. His memory of her~ he cannot help it~ is in danger of becoming stylised, rationalised and deified. She appears before him like an angel, more of a fixation than a person. He embraces the possibility that he made her up and, if he did, decides that is good, because in that case he has the power to reinvent her. Surely, if she was a figment, she can be brought back. It was his destiny to try to find her *and everything she had come to represent.* If he fails, only then, as a last resort, will he learn to live with her in his heart, keeping her with him at all times, as one keeps the memory of a dead person alive. However, he is determined to put the work in to convince himself that Sara is no figment or abstracted memory of a thing that no longer existed. He finds himself loath to accept such a reality and could have given proofs when Hellmoth confronted him about the mysterious woman's actuality, but he chose not to. He had not revealed all of what he knew or felt to the awfully nice Dr. Hellmoth. He had played at drawing lines across white surfaces using a fork, during one consultation. Hellmoth had ignored the impertinence. What should Xavier care if others thought him mad, or indeed if they knew he was not?

His particular angst attached to living could not be mitigated by therapies or even the impressive medication prescribed for him. The unease continued~ but only as it always had. It remained the condition within which he operated. Nevertheless, Xavier felt at home within his new environment and was curiously 'most content'. He quickly acclimatised to, and enjoyed life as an invalid~ although he felt a charlatan in the role, not really ill at all. The glorious idleness allowed time to reflect on all manner of things. He discovered himself to be unusually tranquil.

To his mind, to his way of thinking, there was indeed therapy to be had from lying for hours on end, looking out over snow-topped mountains, feeling warm, secure and removed from the world. He liked it. The staff at the clinic did everything for him and the other patients. His room, although austere, was clean and bright, just like the mountain air. He hadn't had to organise himself for weeks. Being away from his usual world made him remote from his own dilemmas and the full extent of the disquiet he experienced. He had, in fact, come to rely nicely on his medication and looked forward to it. The remoteness he felt and the lack of anxiety was like a holiday. He didn't really feel like doing anything, nor did he feel anxious to go home. Was this Ulysses blissfully immersed on the sweet Isle of Ogygia?

He shifts his position on the wooden-slatted recliner. His legs are supported; he is lying face up with his torso lifted from the horizontal by about thirty degrees. He embraces a hot water bottle beneath the thick blanket that covers him from head to foot. The top edge of the coarse material has been pulled up to cover his nose, only his eyes peep out across the vast, open vista that is the snow-topped Alps. The freshness in the chill air made for a perfect constitutional, made glorious by being outside. Xavier is as cosy as toast and decidedly mummified within his swaddling~ a chrysalis no less. He grips his vital parts and delights in their warmth and vitality. The distant valleys disappear below the line of the balcony, beyond which, the majestic, rugged peaks appear, towering in their magnificence across the awe-inspiring panorama. He moves his head to free his face from the blanket, revealing the broad wings of a wide handlebar moustache, newly grown and now complete, its tips moving to graceful points. In addition, an expanse of Van Dyck beard can be seen on his chin. The caterpillar becomes a butterfly *at last~* or perhaps a moth in danger of being drawn to a flame. The enigma of Moustachio is revealed.

His sojourn in the clinic amongst the high mountains, where spectacular peaks invade the great sky's dominion, would prove to be vitally important to Mannikin's next development. Within his first few, short weeks in the sanatorium it could be seen that the change of air had benefitted his sense of well-being~ the detachment from his usual world had undoubtedly altered his perspective and calmed him. Indeed, he at last understood aspects of the wisdom of Hellmoth's prescription; he needed to devote time to rebalancing himself~ it was true. The venerable Dr. Hellmoth had been correct in this regard. And so, whilst incarcerated in the sanatorium's milky bosom, he began to formulate ideas with the intention of improving his situation and moving forward. There was a plan materialising. He developed a new agenda, which he decided was best kept to himself for fear of being thought a madman. These things were beneficial, if only because he regained a sense of control. Then, quite out of the blue, a spectacular revelation came over him, one that he had enormous difficulty explaining. The discovery confused him at first and, for a short period of time, caused him to most legitimately question his sanity, even to himself.

The insight had grown, *by accretion or perhaps incrementally*, as if he was talked to in a quiet whisper, as if somebody was speaking to him with a voice that was so gentle and veiled as to go unnoticed, unless he turned all attention to it and concentrated very hard. It dawned on him that he had time to see things deeply and listen to his surroundings carefully. There was less background noise disturbing his thoughts. By centering himself and learning to listen, he began to hear the quiet, indistinct voice with clarity; it told him of things he should never have missed. Soon after, came the first portent. It arrived whilst he lay in his reclined convalescent chair watching the mountain ranges ahead of him, wrapped, as he so frequently was, in embryonic splendour. The grand, granite rock edifices all around him, the grandiloquent lusty mountain ranges, the Herculean monsters that everyday elicited a sense of awe and wonder, allowed him to see his own small part in the scheme of things. Furthermore, he became obsessed by the recognition that they could be viewed and imagined from more than one position, *from everywhere concurrently*, and that by so doing, each time their magnificence would be reinvented anew/afresh. The beauty of the concept flourished and blossomed exponentially in his mind. It occurred to him that he was only ever seeing one side, which, he realised, he foolishly thought or imagined to be the front. He began to wonder about the infinite other aspects to these giants and the alternative viewpoints they presented. The mental endeavour of such imaging and conjecture had a profound effect. It seemed so obvious but in identifying these things, the dilemma of reflections/orientation/alternative realities took on a new meaning. He wanted the scale of such cogitation to be made enormous, to more easily grasp the potency and potential of the thing that seemed curious to him and which held him spellbound. He moved his attention up a notch and began to think of the constellations in the same way, *as if they too had many faces*. He knew the stars were fixed in relationship to one another when the heavens were observed from earth, they could only be viewed from the same tiny spot, merely a two-dimensional dot, or point, in the boundless equation. The prospect and observation of all else on terra firma could be persuaded to alter its viewpoint, change scale and shimmer in light, by virtue of time and man's changing proximity to his surroundings, *enabled by his ability to navigate within and through their range.* For him, there seemed a relevance and fascination in such conjecture. He had unwittingly posited a notion that prepared and led him by an unreasonable route to his apparent revelation. Significantly, preposterously, he looked up into the dark canopy overhead one evening and realised for the first time that his view of the stars was misplaced~ more than this~ it was diametrically wrong! He was bewildered in extremis, wanted to fall to the ground, felt a need to vomit; his recurrent nausea filled him entirely. Why had it taken so long for him to see this? The last time he looked, the constellations were the other way around. They were the reverse of how he expected them to be. Where was the discrepancy that had allowed this lie to creep in undetected? How might this be? How can constellations be seen from two opposing sides? He was perplexed, caught off guard, disorientated, cast adrift. He held the thought for some time. Days passed, and during their span he looked carefully at every aspect of reality he could think of. He questioned the fundamental truth of everything that constituted both him and his perception of existence. Mannikin had a sudden, overwhelming and powerful reason that at last proved to him that something was terribly wrong, either with this world he inhabited, or maybe it was just him who was misplaced. The viewing machine that he thought himself to be was perhaps wrongly calibrated. It was confirmation of the alienation he had felt deep down for some time, indeed for years past. At last, he had discovered a proof that might account for his anxiety, a validation to explain all the pressure in his head. Might it even justify his sense of loneliness and loss? The stars he saw in the sky at night were, to him, displaced, misplaced, at variance to the laws of harmony. The pattern was incorrect. Mannikin just could not bring himself to mention this to others. He had further established and consolidated the error in the fabric of his reality some weeks later when, quite coincidentally, he had witnessed another celestial occurrence. He, along with a number of other patients, had been persuaded to watch the transit of Venus. They had stood together on the balcony, having been primed for the event by a doctor, whose intention was to add interest to the patient's moribund morning by marshalling them to see the event. He was an amateur astronomer, by all accounts. The doctor had obtained small sheets of dark, surgical glass to enable the group to view the sun at a much-reduced brightness. Everyone took interest in the event. There was increased patient participation at the point where Xavier demonstrated how to use pinprick holes in white paper to cast an image of the sun's disc onto a second white surface, in essence using the science of the pinhole camera. The images were difficult to see at so small a scale, but it did work and he was shocked to discover that the incredibly small dot of the planet Venus passed across the face of the sun from right to left and not left to right, as he assumed.

Mannikin had later checked astrolabes and star maps to confirm his deductions. He had the long suffering Harry Towers and Alyesha bring encyclopedias and books of constellations to him on their occasional visits. He was certain of it; he had noticed something tangible he knew to be erroneous, without doubt. What did this mean? He wondered when the anomaly began. He was so convinced of his facts and sure he was not mad.

69.

The transit of Venus, as it passes over the sun's glowing disc, is poetry in motion~ the revelation of its movement across such an intense inferno, whilst retaining and maintaining its own deep mystery, is quintessential and beautiful. Such occurrences are rare; they are brief moments in time that resonate within our precious consciousness. A thought might materialise, arising like a light out of a space where there is none at all, where light is devoid and not apparent. Like the full wonder of absolute consciousness, it exists beyond and outside the manner in which we poor things think, most often~ is there more than that which we see, do we tie ourselves too readily to words and numbers to the exclusion of greater bounties and beauties? It may be that there exist elusive places in which the dance is yet mightier. Within these imagined realms may lay an Olympian tango of the heavens, rarely found, visited hardly ever, possibly never experienced. Of what do we talk so idly in our chatter?

In a picturesque sense, these apparently silent, distant worlds, like immense gods, could be gliding past one another all the time, forever kissing, without knowing or ever touching, like immense ideas that can never or perhaps rarely connect. The absence of sound in the vacuum hypnotises our sensibilities into a kind of romanticism concerning the heavens. Below, it's just another noisy day on the Earth planet that we have made stunningly explicable, logical and habitual. Where we live has become unused to the intense mystery of things beyond our self-imposed realities~ although nothing has really vanished. It might seem that difficult mysteries, beyond our easy comprehension, have become hidden, but only as if behind curtains. Out of sight, out of mind and therefore made manageable to our narrowly defined perceptions~ all things conveniently systematised and made neat by the prettiest and most logical of patterns that appear before us and make sense, as far as we allow them to go. The child sees its reflection in a mirror and wonders who it might be. It looks behind the mirror, as if behind a curtain, and finds its presence is not apparent; indeed nothing is! Such absence of self makes it believe that it is not there and yet it is. The view behind this curtain, where nothing appears, is in truth where its real self is. What is the explanation? The language of words, numbers and logic, so important to how we have learned to think so far and make sense of a complex universe, has run its course. The precise parameters no longer reveal as much as once they did. Indeed, their restrictions blind us to what may be beyond. Our true ability may yet be in seeing the invisible; we waste precious time by perpetually quantifying all that is already here.

There is a potential development waiting in the wings. Mannikin feels it and becomes increasingly desperate to move. There is a thing that needs to be brought into existence, as an adjunct to him for the understanding of all else. A new tool lies on the other side of the curtain, within reach but invisible. Where is it to be found, where in space might he detect it? It may not exist in his space and this may explain why he cannot find a way forward. And yet, why so? For curiously, seeing the imperceptible is what he seems primed to do best! Mannikin is convinced. There is much that exists outside the realm of that inquisitive biped that thinks itself to be large-brained. He watches in the mirror of his room as he talks to himself of such things.

'Were we able to see beyond our overly well defined meanings and the senseless logics we profess, there may be that chance to see further than we have hitherto. We voluble beings, of which I, *Mannikin*, am an unfortunate part, so annoyingly loquacious, may have internalised more of the external universe than we realise. Does this thing lurk within our ancient depths, in those spaces that once flourished and may still exist in a dormant state? Were there things that were nearer the surface then, in those primordial times before language and semantic elaboration learned to say so much whilst meaning so little? Maybe we should ask the little birds; perhaps some of them can remember better than we.'

For Xavier, a new awareness of such a vast, elemental force fills his spirit. In its contemplation, he takes solace. The description of such energy, as it exists across the firmament, is a clarion call. A long forgotten trumpet sounds within him and an ancient yearning is brought into play. Some invisible power begins to move towards him from unknown places hidden across the universe~ a description of the invisible begins…

70.

After his time of recuperation at the world famous mountain sanatorium, Xavier Mannikin returned to Warcapest, having checked out of the clinic prematurely and against all advice. He had spent a total of six weeks away from the city and came back restored, appearing to have enjoyed a thoroughly peaceful vacation~ *his 'revelation' remained a secret.* On his return, he stayed at his father's house where he relaxed, read and played the part of a recent invalid, having no qualms about enjoying the advantages that appearing delicate conferred. He was well attended by Mrs. Scripture who fussed and comforted him as a compassionate auntie might. Harry and Alyesha visited, but stayed only for short periods. His father was pleased to have his son so close and there were times in the afternoons when the two Mannikins met~ to take tea, sherry and homemade cake, and talk of the old world they had passed through, as was Leopold's wont. Xavier, in truth, found these times as comforting as his father. His recent breakdown or impasse, as he chose to see it himself, allied with a decline in Leopold's health, brought both men closer to a questioning of their sadness and transient place in the realm of things. Dear ancient Izziara Sphinx seemed to be older and sadder than both of them. He took less interest in the proceedings than either the father or the son. The clever bird looked on with gummy eyes and failing eyesight, appearing to muse or perhaps invoke an ancient acceptance of the inevitability of all that was passing before him, and them.

Towards the end of the second week, Mannikin began to make efforts to move events forward. His regular short walks in a nearby park had proved beneficial and made him feel stronger. Seeing the daily activity of other lives as he sauntered through Warcapest's streets impressed on him that his had stopped; he felt an imperative to get back on track~ to make things normal again. He was ready to build a new life, since Sara Phielnx could no longer be a living part of the one he had once cherished. It was time to find out what he had missed at the company and, more importantly, to return to his bolthole at the old factory. His hand, in this regard, was forced by the news that an industrial estate agency had found two potential buyers for the property. The interested parties were keen to purchase the land and were pressing to act quickly. He decided he should go back soon~ and felt no anxiety at the prospect of returning.

If Mannikin was saddened and disappointed at all, it was because so much of his life seemed to have been taken away from him. He was goaded and forced to accept a new future, whether he wanted it or not. He had no choice. If he was to thrive, he had to make himself stronger, get a grip; he needed to move on, find a way forward, he needed to adapt to the newly materialising environment.

His decision to travel out and opportunity to get back to the factory came the following week. The season was moving on; there were signs that summer was giving way to autumn. Winter was approaching. Warcapest was reinventing itself, being redefined, reinvigorating itself with an endlessly renewable splendour; maybe he should join in and make himself part of it too.

Mannikin paid the driver through the window of the cab and thanked the man. The taxi drove off, wheels rumbling over the dilapidated cobbled street. He watched the vehicle grow smaller before it finally turned a corner and disappeared from view. Mannikin stood staring at the empty spot long after it had gone, listening to the diminishing engine sounds passing along unseen streets. When the sound became indistinct and had all but faded~ like a lost memory, barely clinging on~ he made ready and walked the remaining half-kilometre to the old, derelict factory entrance, passing over broken flagstones en route. He knew and recognised the unevenness of the paving underfoot, and enjoyed the green of the moss and lichens that had opportunistically summered in the cracks. Mannikin stopped to watch a young factory cat preening itself on a wall. Deep in reverie, he moved on, savouring the passing moments~ or did he not want time to move too quickly? The once noble, still elegant edifice came into view as he turned a corner and thereafter Xavier looked towards the top of the building, intent on catching glimpses of the turret, which housed his space. The room seemed so high up, so aloof, distant and alluringly secretive. He was charmed by the decadence and faded splendour of what he saw, including the plant life that had invaded the uppermost gutters~ and realised he was getting older and the act of seeing was transforming without his consent. He was genuinely saddened and moved to a kind of remorse, recognising that aspects of his life and experience were about to vanish for all time. Memories of particular places~ the factory~ his father's house~ Warcapest itself, had punctuated so many of the key moments in his life. Tears welled up inside as he inwardly tried to deny what was happening~ *he was especially in denial over the loss of his SPx.* He attempted to blame the cold breeze that blew directly into his face, for causing his eyes to water.

When he got to the factory, the main gates were closed and locked as expected. Mannikin noticed the rusting, barbed wire along the top edge and became conscious of how infrequently he saw the place in daylight. He approached the side entrance and rang the bell four times, using the shared code that had long been agreed. The door to the house opened and the gatekeeper's daughter appeared, moving forward in a series of jerky movements, aided by sticks, in order to pass keys to Mannikin. She greeted him with a smile that suggested she no longer cared about or even remembered her affliction. He smiled back and mouthed words to thank her as he gained entrance, then replaced the padlock and returned the keys. Mannikin walked past the girl as she manoeuvred awkwardly back into the house. A cool, fresh wind was blowing around the factory; summer weed and rogue growth was dying back, opportunistic vegetation, fast growing vines and buddleia had flourished during the season. Virginia creeper appeared high on a sunlit face of the building, its riotous growth out of control. The site, through neglect, had allowed nature to return. Bounteous nature had found opportunity to secure its own abundance. Xavier remembered that the last time he was here, the path had been saturated in black shadow and darkness. Everything looked so different now. The place was overgrown, dilapidated and sleeping.

He walked up the side path, not daring to imagine that Sara might have been back during his long absence, totally resigned to the unlikelihood and impossibility of such a thing ever happening again. On passing through the classical archway he saw Ryman a little further on, sweeping up shattered glass after blocking up a window that had broken, or been vandalised.

They met, shook hands; neither man made reference to recent events. Mannikin took an envelope from his inner breast pocket and handed it to the caretaker before hugging him in an embrace. Ryman looked into the younger man's eyes and saw the factory vanishing for them both. Mannikin explained that the caretaker would soon hear from the company and would, in due course be offered alternative employment in the new factory. The gatehouse would have to be vacated of course; indeed the whole factory site was to be knocked down in order that redevelopment might take place. Mannikin looked away and then walked on, as the reflective Ryman watched.

The side entrance to the building was compliant and responded as intended when Xavier's shoulder pushed hard against it. The hinges made a little shriek, as though greeting him/remembering him. Would this be the last time he breached the threshold that held exterior and interior spaces apart? He climbed the staircase to the very top of the building, his feet treading heavily, more than he had ever previously been aware, making this his saddest visit.

On arrival, the room seemed darker, colder and smaller. It seemed remote and alien, he sensed it was no longer a living part of him. In some way, it had separated from his reality; it appeared to be used up and depleted like an empty wine bottle. He was struck by the smell, possibly caused by summer damp, although briefly wondered if something were rotting. Ryman had been in to tidy the place. There had been empty milk bottles and fruit in a bowl that had been cleared away. Sara's workspace remained untouched, as far as he could tell, her clothes were in evidence~ she had been there; he had no doubt of that. However, the accommodation had become petrified and was lost to him.

The sharp sound of the rope on a flagpole snapped in the breeze, calling Xavier back, beckoning him once more to the top of the building. He ascended the short staircase and entered the high, open vantage point that was so beautiful to him, evocative of sanctuary and yet more than this. The lofty height was his roof on the world, close to where angels might fly and soar, a place they might indeed visit. Birds flew off from the parapet as he entered into the space, their wings flapping confusion in his mind as his eyes adjusted to the brightness in the sky. The view across Warcapest was like seeing the face of a loved one. His gaze was met by an unexpected new wind that, without warning, blew into his face, like violent kisses, pushing his hair back, suddenly causing it to blow wildly, forcing him to stand his ground in order not to be pushed back. Sara Phielnx was gone forever and in this moment he finally confirmed it to himself.

'Forever and forever.'

He mouthed the words into the wind, as alike an epitaph to be precisely that~ the chamber of his mouth echoing with a sudden gust that enters into him.

When at last he returns to his room below, he finds that Ryman had been in to deliver fresh milk, water, bread, cheese, as well as a bottle of wine. Xavier begins to wander, losing time without realising it. He gazes out the window for what seems an age~ for what in fact is the entire day~ and only as night begins to fall does he notice that time has passed. He lights the stove, determined to spend another night on the planet in the one bed that he knows to be his own, the nest he had shared with a person he felt to be a fellow traveller.

The damp duvet is pulled closely around him; gradually the room begins to heat and he with it. The residual atmospheres of times past start to filter back into the space; perhaps they had become temporarily trapped in the walls. They escape to pervade into the aerie nest once more, filling it like a drug, causing Xavier to become irretrievably lost to a deep, intoxicating sleep.

The transit of Venus begins again for him. He sees it. Only now, he can also hear the intense noise of the event; the heavens are not tranquil, he realises, nor have they ever been. The intensity of sound in a vacuum is deafening, its energy is seamless vibration so unbearable as to seem like a tumult of silence.

Across the space, a figure approaches. Might this be Sara Phielnx? But it is not. There is some reality missing in this being. The floating spirit is itself passing across a sun as if in transit and yet 'concurrently' it appears in this room, in his very space, as if a visitation. Its lean finger points upwards, parodying the cartoon by da Vinci. It smiles with the same enigma, but without smiling~ it seems concerned with and convinced of a fact. The known movements of the heavens are somehow very familiar to this entity. Its strange, beguiling, beautifully feminine form looks in both directions at the very same time. And then, it points both upward and downwards in a single gesture, within the same action, in a single moment. It smiles and grimaces with the integrity of an angel and a devil, simultaneously. Xavier Mannikin sees that the figure is translucent, except for the contents of a sealed box it holds in its other hand. He sees that there is a key in the box that floats through it, towards him somehow, revealing itself, whilst remaining hidden within the container. Something has enabled him to know it exists in there. It appears to be the very receptacle he had been persuaded to store for safekeeping, by Count Zapik the magician, some weeks earlier. The spectre and Xavier look at one another and, in a moment, both their intentions coalesce.

There are stars that have become painted points of light throughout the room; they hang in the air beneath the domed ceiling. Pinpoint pricks of delicate brilliance spread in depth and distance across a firmament of miniature similitude. With a sweep of the spectral figure's arm, they reverse, becoming mirrored versions of themselves, as the mysterious form illustrates the dual nature of the cosmos and the opposing viewpoints that exist at the edges of infinity. The figure of EriKhe, in performing these operations, reveals herself more fully than before. She allows her shape to be seen, her sex glowing like an ancient mystery. She tantalises the sleeping Xavier with her deep enigma, little of which he can possibly fully understand. Nevertheless, he has such faculty as to be charmed and amazed at the story she unfolds, the web she weaves, the matrix she describes, the magic she deconstructs. He recognises he will never understand the things that momentarily seem crystal clear in this brief space. They are all about to be lost. For an enchanted moment, he is invited into the whole of everything.

Having slept the entire night through, he wakes, surprised at the intensity and vividness of his dreaming. Xavier opens each eye, one at a time, before rolling over to the edge of the mattress. On first standing, he finds it difficult to balance and is disorientated, lightheaded and confused. The experience is, thankfully, short-lived. There had been a catharsis in the night, the recognition of an idea~ the seed of a strategy that, bizarre as it seemed, really struck him as a way forward.

He glimpses his reflection in the glass of the window as he crosses the room and moves towards it, before looking out. Somewhere in his mind there is a deep-seated impression~ it tells him he needs to move through a mirror in order to find a way to be, in some other parallel and opposite place. It is simple~ the notion is potent and he feels the inclination to move out of himself to meet the new need. Had such vision been given to him by a sublime being, a strange person~ might it have even been a benign messenger from his own angel, Sara Phielnx?

71.

Sleep became an increasingly important feature in Xavier Mannikin's life. He threw himself into it, pitching himself headlong into trances and dream-like states, in order to seek out their impossible moments. It was preparation for what was to pass, training for the thing that was about to devour him. This was the desperate strategy that might allow him to locate and unlock the unseen door that concealed and hid the invisible Sara Phielnx.

During this period, *at his own insistence,* he went back to work, on the strict understanding that his initial return involved light duties only. His doctor begrudgingly signed him off and pronounced him fit, but warned that he should take it easy.

It was the first morning back. Feeling alien and unattached, his lean figure walked into the office with an air of decided apprehension, intrinsically and acutely aware of how remote and distant the world had become. Whatever it was that he might be, had become a stranger in its own territory. Was everything in the office where some former *other* self had once left it? There seemed to be few options open to him, other than to check details, make some attempt to remember past routines, whilst surveying and wandering the room. His presence in the space paced like an animal in a cage~ a cage that the vanquished beast only 'seemed' to remember. There were subtle changes. He observed streaks on the window, water stains on top of a desk, dust on surfaces, fruit flies upturned on a windowsill~ obsessively and meticulously tracing events back using consciousness and memory to determine when particular things might have happened or had occurred, wondering whether, in truth, the things imagined had been seen before, but not consciously noticed, or had become forgotten~ or might they have been invented?

'You have after all been very ill.'

A voice, only distantly recognised, sounded in his ears, as if in need of imparting information to an interested third party. A part of the 'him' being addressed wondered if he had been ill at all. Yet another part of his unique complexity wondered what all this 'talking' was about.

An indecisive moment materialised; the gaunt man in the midst of the room found himself standing very still, inwardly identifying a pressing need to check a non-apparent drawer in the desk that dominated the room. The necessary physical action to achieve the goal was hesitant, slow to materialise, and only undertaken with a degree of uncertainty~ the encouragement to do so eventually coming through the aid of a ridiculous convincer.

'The proof that Sara was once real would be the silver box in the hiding place', a quiet, barely audible voice speaking under its breath is heard to say. With overwhelming trepidation the man reached behind the desk to seek out the sacrosanct space; he felt a tremble in his hands and noticed that they shook more than he was aware.

With a sense of relief, after some strenuous, convoluted exertion, a box was retrieved from within the hidden depths of the table, the esoteric contents of the secret compartment had, at last, been *'openly'* revealed.

A heavy sigh went unnoticed, as his eyes observed the silver box. Surely this was proof of so many things~ that Sara was real and had existed alongside the person he had been. She was no merely imagined angel, as the clumsy psychiatrist had ominously suggested, with too little sense of doubt in his voice. All the men in long coats had been real as well. They too existed~ he knew this in the same moment, although they had not been clever enough to claim the key prize that they were probably looking for. The events leading to his breakdown did have some explanation after all. And yes, he had been suffering from a mental strain. He should at last acknowledge these things. It was right to do so, in order to attempt to properly recalibrate. He could face up to the facts; he had been a bit mad, but less mad than people around him suspected... he hoped.

He inexplicably recognised, without the shadow of a doubt, that the box contained a key. How was this possible? He even knew what the hidden object looked like! Furthermore, for some unaccountable reason, he understood precisely how to open the complex and puzzling container. Where had this information come from? Had it indeed been passed to him secretly during the angelic visitation? The angular, thin, young man handled the box dextrously, performing complex manoeuvres that required the deft application of manual skills and, to the sound of an audible click, the box opened before him, revealing its secrets. Within, wrapped in cloth and then in tissue, he discovered the very thing he had never seen before, but curiously could recollect from the abstract visualisations that only existed in his mind.

The key, the full weight of which was felt for the first time, struck him as a strange and dense article of ancient origin~ *the experience allowed him to recognise in these moments the difference between the abstract knowing of an idea and the actual seeing and experience of the phenomenon itself~ the two were in no way the same, outside of the abstract coding used to constrain their notional existence or reality.* The object whistled quietly in the air; it hummed, as if attempting to reach out into the space that surrounded it. The young man quickly realised the need to seal the key back into the box in order to hide it from the world that both he and it were in. Something deep within his unconscious spirit acknowledged this.

Once the key was safely concealed and hidden in the silver puzzle box, as before, it seemed appropriate to test the package in various suit pockets about his person, it was soon discovered to most conveniently fit into the one used to house his precious camera. It sat in the top pocket rather comfortably. The displaced camera soon lay cast aside and discarded on the table, its position usurped by the Egyptian key~ soon destined to become this distant, alienated man's gateway to a new world.

From now on, it would be best to keep it on his person at all times he decided. It would provide access to his next new future, probably when least expected.

The distracted and disinterested employee did no work that day, but simply wandered aimlessly, without conviction, along corridors, looking, peering and wondering. He might have seemed disorientated or conceivably been mistaken for a temporary visitor in a new place for the first time, seeing familiar things perhaps, but in ways that made the outsider question what they thought they understood or knew. The man observed a curious world in miniature, from which he felt decidedly detached; regular commonplace activity seemed bizarre, nonsensical and pointless, as he drifted passing through the office spaces of the Mannikin Playing Card Company. The firm's employees were, he half suspected, aware that the marketing manager had become strangely withdrawn and introspective. Walking past a row of offices, he caught a familiar glimpse of Harry Towers talking to a subordinate. His presence on the corridor was briefly noticed, and acknowledged, but there was no interest on his part in returning the darting look offered and his slight, familiar form walked on, outside of the moment, floating, aloof, cast adrift, detached in a way that signalled how deaf his consciousness had become to its surroundings. All the while a rush of noise filled his ears, intimating the proximity of illusive beating wings. A pulsating, flickering light entered in at the corners of his eyes, appearing like little flashes of lightning. What was causing his immaculate electricity to spark in such a curious manner? Had some other thing, something else, an alternative reality taken him over perhaps?

The man left work early, walking slowly through streets, treading a path that unrolled like a soft carpet beneath his feet. As he progressed, moving curiously, hardly experiencing the blank, faceless city that extended beyond the person that he only seemed to be, everything appeared to be reminiscent of a dream/*fantasy* before him. His perambulation through Warcapest led him, without effort or apparent consciousness, back to his apartment, a place he could not remember having visited for some time. On arrival, *some hours after his initial departure,* he discovered the front door to be resistant to entry; post had collected on the wooden floor beneath the letterbox and formed a wedge in the space between the bottom of the door and the floor, impairing its ability to open. Nonchalantly and with little concern he crossed the threshold, squeezing sideways through the half open gap, ignoring the proliferation of mail. He saw himself reflected in the benign mirror as he pushed hard to close the door, noticing the bulge in his pocket during the process. Yes, the key was still there, safely on his person. More especially, much to his surprise, he discovered himself to be holding a bag of groceries, not remembering having procured the goods at all. So, he had shopped, that was suddenly perfectly evident~ following his adopted tradition, no doubt. He tried to think back, imagining that he remembered traipsing through the streets in the manner that he did and assumes that he had. Why had he so little awareness? Was he making everything up? Probably not, since there was this tangible proof in his arms. Things escaped him, but not on such a scale surely, or at least he had always fought the loss of such moments and the abrogation of consciousness previously. He had, it would seem, stopped testing the world, suspecting there was no longer a need to retain control or understanding. He had given in, choosing instead to avoid ownership of the incidents that involved him, recognising that the reality he perceived was going to run its own course in spite of him. It would be whatever it chose for itself, whilst continuing to shimmer beguilingly before him as a continuing, inveterate confusion within the miasma of his being. Had he changed the rules? He presumed he had. Somewhere within him, he had a new vision of what was going on. He had a key although, as yet, little idea of how to use it. He was pale and wan, with a slight nosebleed. The man moved steadily forward, without control~ although a self-determining target was just in sight.

Once back on familiar territory, it was the balcony that beckoned. He walked out into the glorious aerial space and found himself disorientated to discover it was not the roof of the old factory. He slipped the groceries onto the patio table and moved to look over the edge of the glass railing. The city hummed in the distance, a strange tune, but not as strange as the one in his head. The combination of the two sensations syncopated within him like some hypnotic incantation struggling to find a common metre, looking for a way to coexist in this moment. The man was aware that at some deep level he was still resisting his future, despite his apparent resignation. He needed to abandon himself further to the remarkable inner temptation that was coursing through his veins.

He took the silver box from his pocket, deftly opening it again, despite the complexity of the actions needed, releasing the Egyptian key from its sealed space once more~ from the prison that had kept it captive; this device might be a genie in a green bottle. As he looked, he imagined it to be darkly glowing, as if it were the densest of materials possible, absorbing light rather than reflecting anything within its vicinity. Immediately, he began to feel the world amplified in its presence, he was surrounded by dynamic energies responding to the appearance of the key. These unknown powers and their forces tugged at his soul, nipped his spirit, tried to lift him, were attempting to carry essential parts of him away. He felt like a rod of iron, imprisoned and trapped in massive rock, whilst some external and irresistible magnetic force dragged at him, but without visible consequence, other than that which he felt in this moment as an abstract sensation. He wanted to move, but felt restricted and unable to do so, unable to respond to an ancient need that desperately reminded him of its forgotten presence.

The evening was cool, but fresh. The man was aware that he might be standing somewhere else, but knew that he wasn't. And yet... He was standing on an ancient shore line for the last time, looking out across a vast expanse of ocean, wondering if he might never see the world from this shore again~ about to embark on a long voyage to a new world. Already he felt homesick at the loss he had not yet let go of, and indeed had no need to part from, if he chose not to. To stay would not be so bad, would it? A colossal sense of Weltschmerz and ensuing ennui engulfed him; his world-weariness reminded him that to stand still was no different to dying. He needed to continue the journey that had begun, not because of himself~ but in spite of himself. He closed the box.

By the time he was ready to leave the balcony there was a distinct chill in the air; the atmosphere bristled with small, suspended droplets of water, like light fog, as far as the eye could see. Moisture had attached itself to the fine, downy hair across his face and the hair on his trimmed beard and moustache, without ever touching the skin; he sensed its close proximity. The man had turned noticeably grey over the last months. He stood motionless for some considerable time. There was no way of him knowing how long he had been there. He checked, but once again his watch seemed to indicate a time earlier to the one he had previously noted.

At last he turned to move on, collecting the groceries en route, first depositing the alien package in the kitchen before proceeding to make tea. Moving without passion or excitement, a grey utility accompanying his actions, he did whatever was needed to make the task occur, pushing events forward in the direction they needed to go~ to make tea happen. These things he could do; such actions responded to his goading but other important things seemed as elusive as ever. Where was the magic he craved, the world where everything he quested for... might become possible?

★ ★ ☆ ★

72.

Tiredness and the need for sleep exert their habitual drag once more. The man is exhausted and unusually so; exposure to the key has drained him, weakened him. He stumbles into the bedroom, tapping the wall repeatedly, unsuccessfully attempting to locate the light switch then proceeds to draw the curtains before standing still in the unlit, isolated space. In due course, maybe a short time, maybe a long time, in the semi-dark, he removes the silver puzzle box from his pocket. In some mysterious way, it immediately discovers what little light remains in the room and shines. He opens it as a blind man might, looking away as he does so, imagining his actions without monitoring the detail. He finally releases the key, throwing it onto the bed, before placing the empty box on his desk. In a stupor, intoxicated by his own fatigue, he undresses, stepping out of his raiment in the dark, allowing the discarded garments to fall to the floor where they will~ then flops onto the bed and in an effort almost beyond his strength, pulls the duvet partially over his naked form.

He lies in a room bereft of light and quickly becomes lost into a deep, high space that opens up around him and within him.

He is sinking, whilst simultaneously being raised up; there is no point or relevance in knowing what might be up or down. An awareness of being absorbed into something, or somewhere, provides a remote appreciation that an unaccountable transition is in progress. He does not move, consumed by the whispered sensations that demand his attention, like the gentle stroking of fingers on soft skin.

Awareness prompts him to open his eyes; he is struck by what can now be seen. He is above himself, floating in the air, whilst the shell of his heavy body remains lifeless on the bed, in the dark, lost and forgotten in shadow~ he senses its presence, although he cannot see it clearly. He has become light and spirit-like, suspended at some mid-point within the room. He looks down at his newly formed, unaccountable, alternative self. The chest, he sees, is broad and inflated, capturing what little light enters the room from the gap at the top of the curtains~ his torso fades away thereafter into shadow, his dark sex lost to view, his long limbs dangling above the bed. He observes the curious avatar, which appears and feels like him. A distant drone infiltrates his consciousness, interspersed with another, more immediate sound~ redolent of short sticks being whipped through the air at speed. The man listens carefully, his concentration usurped by a need to quantify the characteristics of the perplexing noises. The background murmur is suggestive of distant birds and yet, on inspection, there are no birds at all. Might this tintinnabulation, instead, be the ringing of many bells, intense precise pings, accompanied by an acoustic half-life of sound that radiates out from the first moment, creating a magnificent, dying splendour? The sound repeats itself and might continue over a vast expanse of time, reminiscent of the delicate, bronze bells revered by Buddhist monks. He directs his attention, lost to thought, transfixed by the experience, wondering and attempting to define what it is that has him in its thrall. And then, without explanation, he is outside of the building, having risen and passed through the apartment block, which, without registering the fact, he has left. Looking down, the huge, rectangular structure is seen visibly diminishing as his semi-transparent form rises yet higher into the air. An aerial view of Warcapest at night becomes increasingly laid out beneath his elevated gaze. He looks out to see the city he knows so well, recognising its features and parts with ease~ quickly identifying the opera house at its centre and the Ringstrasse beyond. He attempts to turn in the air, in the hope of glimpsing District 13 and locating that part of the map where the old factory lies, but it is too far away and he cannot turn to face that direction easily. The ascent continues. His trajectory is up, but his route slides somewhat, allowing him to wander laterally across the face of Warcapest~ he shivers and wonders if he is seeing all this for the last time. The scene begins to alter; it is as if thin, diaphanous curtains are drawn, obscuring the view. The panorama fades as light mists turn to transparent cloud, which interrupt and cloak the vista further. Soon, the glowing lights are no more than vague patterns peeking through from far below, delineating the roadways, the moving traffic, the buildings etcetera.

'The lights of Warcapest, when viewed at night from above, shimmer and glow~ like candles on a festive tree celebrating an event, or are they signposts along a journey, or windows leading to other places or...'

Xavier's ascent begins to accelerate and in a breathless moment his prospect modifies considerably, causing him to stare incredulously at the transforming and diminishing perspective. The known world is left behind and made enormously remote. As he watches, the sphere of an Earth-like planet and its accompanying satellite, like India rubber bouncing balls, are cast away through the heavens at speed. The massive objects rapidly or slowly diminish to become lost, despite the absence of a horizon beyond which to see them vanish~ and yet, in an inkling, they do.

In their absence, the absolute bleakness of the dark solar system becomes all-powerful, all-encompassing. Black silence~ but for the distant twinkling of faded stars. Even their long diminished magnitude is hard to detect; they too are soon lost, becoming invisible memories to that glimmer that briefly filled a once moment. Everything appears to have been passed through, travelled across and over. Xavier suspects he is arriving or has arrived at the end of time. Is this the edge, the final frontier of consciousness? Could this be the extremity or periphery to that moving dimension that has enforced the allegiance of consciousness since its discovery of self? Amongst this uncomfortable, unaccountable lacuna, impossible to fathom, the vast quietude of an expanse containing very little is encountered. The space, existing without memory, is met for the first time, causing a new moment of little consequence and no meaning. Like a footprint into newly laid snow, its line is recorded, but lost. White on white~ black on black.

Xavier is enraptured by these events, these imaginings, this perceived reality, this impossible fantasy. Is this what he had been shown by the angel with the dark, empty eyes that contained pin-points of fire at their edges, in their extremities? He had been given the route through to an opposite end of the known universe, where all was a mirror image of what he had been before and what he thought he knew. He had travelled to that place in the firmament where the stars might be seen from the other side, where another world in harmony with the one he had left began, and thereafter existed, perhaps coexisted. In such a place, he would be who he currently is, but reversed. This was the point where one space met another space, each divided from the other by the sheerest of materials, a curtain to hide the beyond. If these things are indeed so, then in the new reality he is to move into, he will be right-handed at last. There would have to be such a debit for each and every new gain, but moreover, might every perceivable loss have to be replaced or reimbursed too? In the new space he might become allowed to find another 'SerapHielnx', to replace the one he has lost. There she might be, rising out of the ashes of the old, the phoenix always reinventing itself. Dare he move into the next square, out of the box that confines him now, beyond the present frontier that has only ever barely managed to contain him? He remains suspended within the very mirror itself, deeply entrenched in immaculate thought. It seems so clear now. The moment is poignant. There is a sense of remorse at what he is losing and a hope that the next world will be perfect.

He is to journey into the mirror of where he has been.

As he thinks these things he blankly views the emptiness before him. In the distant vacuum within reach of where he can detect light, there begins to be a new glow of some significance, a faint speck whose power to create luminescence is increasing. The glow is brightening as the light enlarges and, distantly, the image of a trailing meteor comes into view. In the glow, as he looks, he sees his naked self reappearing out of the void, reflecting in the brightness of the meteor. For the universe is black without light~ irrespective of whether there is a being to be conscious of it or not.

His journey needs to continue, his course is to be the shortest distance between two points. Is there a precise mark on his route, he wonders, where he might pass through the mirror to the other side? Will it be a point that can be noticed, might it be like passing through a curtain, or seeing the tail on a coin being turned in the hand to reveal the hidden head? Where does that, which is seen from below, become that which is seen from above?

In a state of limbo he begins to appreciate, for the first time, that this dilemma, his dilemma, is no more than the result of his consciousness. It is always this separation from everything else that exists, which antagonises him, causing the anxiety he feels and the existential angst that torments him. This is the thing that has brought him to this point. Were he to dare to relinquish his consciousness, surely all would be well. Were he to return to the larger whole, that mass of unloving, impartial, uncaring substance within the universe, then surely all would resolve itself. Whatever he might be then would only have to occur as a mute, dumb remnant of self, trapped within a cold rock, forever tumbling unconsciously through the self-unaware universe. Or equally, might his substance become a lump of unknown, undeclared matter amidst a vast bed of clay? Whatever he was then would be safe and part of something else at last, empty of being, devoid of spark, able to sleep quietly. The thought resonates as a kind of beauty within him. Is 'death' a name for splendour not in use? This is justification to embrace his demise and end. He opens his mouth to shout into the dumb, unconscious universe, but no words form as he mouths…

'… but the heart cannot forget its loneliness.'

The meteor is drifting closer~ either he to it, or it to him. It begins to fill space with light; he sees it floating brightly, silently, across the pitch-black universe, its distance from him diminishing. Such an immense presence begins to occupy Xavier, mesmerising him~ it fills his mind as convincingly as it fills the surrounding cosmos. The head of the beast, the fiery demon, burns with terrifying energy. This is white, nuclear heat that melts vision and turns images black when they try to penetrate its interior. The extraordinary, irradiated light is super-saturated with effervescence and explosive energy. The tail behind grows longer, glowing intensely, but less fiercely in comparison to the alpha star and colossus that it follows; there are detonations within its sweep that travel backwards at speed within the prodigious slipstream.

The meteor is sensational. In these heavens, it slices through the dull monotony of the expansive everything that surrounds it. Xavier sees it from afar and deliberates the possibility of moving closer in order to see or experience it with more clarity, to test the warmth of such an incredible beacon amidst the void that surrounds it and him. He becomes the moth to a flame. Remarkably, he finds he has jurisdiction over his movements and can will himself to venture closer. The vast spotlight begins to fill his vision; it occupies his attention, providing an outstanding diversion to his journey towards the mirrored destination.

The head of the snake now looms larger; the light in its eye is too brilliant, too vast and intense to look at. It is a sun that would blind those that dare to look on its form. The tail sails by behind, streaming to one side as if blown by cosmic wind, as if swimming against the current of its own direction; as a lost sperm might journey through a vast womb.

Xavier is intoxicated and fascinated by the phenomenon and involuntarily begins to move back and away from the mass of steaming, hissing chemistry in order to avoid collision, so as not to be eaten, to ensure his safety in this cosmic dream in which he is a player. A separate part of him has resurrected his consciousness of, and proximity to, his goal. He must achieve the realm beyond the mirror. Xavier realises that the opportunity to move across the line is now very close. And the opportunity must not be thwarted.

Despite seeing the illumination before him, there is a complete absence of sensation. Xavier cannot feel any temperature at all. The meteor must be further away than he thinks. It must be bigger than anticipated.

In the next moment however, he is made uncomfortably aware of the overbearing heat within the meteor and indeed within the void of which he is part. An intense, thermal wall crashes into the space around him. Sound, too, reaches him. The meteor begins to wail and moan; he can hear its hiss and splutter. It is filling his ears with a tempestuous cry and scream, a deep, ancient howl filling the vacuum. It had approached stealthily, unannounced and in silence until such time as it decided it had arrived.

A secret and invisible advance slipstream begins to exert its macabre influence. Likewise, a toxic pull emanating from the tail of the meteor becomes apparent, an unexpected sting that licks and cracks with the force of a whip. An unseen, gravitational energy applies its authority, and increasingly so. This current has a dark intention to drag all before it, to usurp everything within its devious ambition~ including poor Xavier. It will drown him in its suffocating heat, burn him alive and waste him. Such force will undoubtedly empty his frame of genius.

Xavier identifies the danger and is fearful. To be dragged into the tail of the meteor will be fatal. Having completed his journey so far, to end this way would be a travesty. His life's endeavour~ capable of bringing him to these impossible edges *and away from what he had once been,* would have been in vain. How could this happen when he is so close to his goal? How can he be left so alone in this time of need? The opportunity to continue his journey to a safe place would become lost. Is this some kind of cruel fate? Has this been planned? Is the meteor some kind of single, moustachioed gatekeeper that patrols the perimeter fence of the heavens, this side of an invisible and unknown line? Where is the angel that might in this moment save him? Where have all the angels gone? There is no escape.

Xavier Mannikin begins, through necessity, to embrace his death, for it has now become obvious that he is to lose his life. His brief, weightless form, a speck of dust across the face of the firmament, is by easy degrees being consumed, subsumed by the might of a meteor bigger than he had ever imagined it to be a moment ago. It is gigantic and seems at last to fill the whole of space around him in the same way it now fills and consumes his mind. He begins to burn, begins to hurt massively, in spite of the unreality of where he had half-suspected he was only thinking he was. He is dying a unique death in a space where hitherto there had never been conscious life, until now.

Xavier Mannikin is dragged into the slipstream, sucked into the tail of the meteor as it continues its path, impervious, unknowing, without any need or reason to explain. It passes onwards~ yonder, gradually diminishing, disappearing, losing that remarkable intensity of light with which it was briefly made notorious to a sentient being~ it is now disappearing by degrees back into the void. And yet…

…his eyes open once more. Darling Mannikin had closed them when he had shrunk back into his deepest recesses, in order to hide from his own anticipated demise. His eyes had been forcibly and painfully opened for him during the horror, but only briefly, as his skin and eyelids burnt away and melted. It was then that the suffering and terror of the experience had been most unbearable and greatest. After this, he had lost consciousness. And yet, by some curious twist of fate, some perceived need deep within the very fabric of nature, he had been spared. For some strange, inexplicable reason, he had managed to come through. He is still in existence, still here. He is incredulous. He has not been obliterated. He has not joined the dead, nor has he been allowed to pass into the mute, solid substance of the cosmos.

He looks out beyond himself and into the distance. That force of nature, the meteor, might be waving to him in this moment, but it cannot be so, although the irrational thought briefly crosses his mind.

He attempts to breath a sigh of relief, prompting an uncommon sensation. Only now does he look down at himself.

In the afterglow of the meteor's passing, he discovers with a sense of dread, consternation and overwhelming remorse that he has gone. His body is not there at all. He has become no more than the eyes with which he sees.

★ ★ ☆ ★

73.

Through the streets, a dark figure walks. It can only be viewed from the outside, there is no inside left. The shell of what once was, passes through the experience that is Warcapest, although this too has been emptied of meaning. How can the city be taken seriously when the place is in doubt, maybe non-existent, maybe of variable perception, of shifting consciousness? The notion that nothing here is real comes as a shock. And, within the lives of the inhabitants, the realisation that they each view their worlds using their own individual subjective experience of thinking, amidst the confusing miasma of being, makes the vast sands of time even more inconsequential. What actually is and is not, but thinking makes it so. There are no realities outside of arbitrary consciousness. There are few realities that can be tested within.

The empty mannequin walks... lurking in the shadow is a figure, hidden beneath a long coat. The lighting of a cigarette momentarily illuminates Ponting's face. As if aware he has just become conspicuous again, he looks out~ to see who we might be.

★ ★ ☆ ★

F I N e.★

The **M***OUSTACHI***O** Quartet.

★ ★ ☆ ★

By *Clive* WILKINS.

A series of four books designed to be read in any order, *as an intentional exploration of memory,* in which the action and involvements of the main characters infiltrate and overlap one another~ the main theme exploring the subjective experience of thinking, amidst the miasma of being.

We vicariously experience the unfolding journeys of four protagonists who reveal underlying secrets held deep and invisibly within a strange world. The mythical city of Warcapest is the heart and focus for action that only slowly becomes apparent. The work has been described as a book of thinks~ a thriller without the thrill, as if to suggest the plot is less important to an understanding of the action than a recognition of the clues, subtexts and symbols that infiltrate so many episodes within the scenario. The book is a complex investigation of consciousness. Four men and their associates, all of whom are at least partially known to one another, pass over and through the city of Warcapest. They are unwittingly observed and seen by notable others~ in this respect the reader is also a protagonist within the action. Their stories combine a sense of unconscious reality held

within a deeply rooted desire for there to be something more, a fundamental need for an extension to self, and the dawning realisation that anxiety can only be negated by nihilism.
The books are richly beautiful and poignant to the point of opulence in their recognition of the glory of wonder~ and the futility of tears.

Caruso Maelstrom

The dawning awareness of self and ideas emanating from childhood form so much of what Caruso is, despite a desperate attempt to acclimatise to the world the way it appears. He is ultimately forced to revert to type and ends up back where he started, becoming once again the person he was always intended to be. He cannot evade the blueprint of who he will become. Set amidst the streets of Prague and on a remote island in a northern landscape, Caruso explores memory and occurrences that define an inexplicable reality that he recognises he will never understand.

Count Zapik

The search for knowledge that explains the inner working of a vast, seemingly impenetrable universe has become the quest that occupies the entertainer known as Count Zapik, the magician. He travels the world's capitals with his assistant, the beautiful Nadja, performing uncanny effects that capture the imaginations of his audiences wherever he goes. Zapik is in possession of skills and knowledge that defy easy category. Furthermore, the extraordinary nature of his abilities has been noticed. He is followed and observed by a series of dark forces intent on ultimately taking his gifts away from him.

Xavier Mannikin

Mannikin has a problem with time, space and consciousness. It moves for him in strange and unconventional ways. This is both disadvantageous and advantageous in equal measure, providing insights into the nature of reality that are missed by others. He moves into and out of himself on a whim and experiences the opportunities afforded by living and seeing more than one world unfolding simultaneously. He has the ability to pose profound questions without understanding what they mean at all, or where they may lead. He moves like some abandoned leaf, swept along a fast-flowing stream after a storm, living a story that reveals a darkly hidden aspect to existence.

Eissenstrom

The life of a painter has passions and complexities that rarely make sense. It would be impossible to be close to the source of 'what is' were it to be any other way. Franz Felix Eissenstrom paints with a spirit and intensity that draws back a curtain, revealing a secret contained within human consciousness~ a living reality that is rarely seen, recognised or shared. Felix's resultant angst and dilemma is a dynamic burden only understood by his concubine, who sees what he is and has become. She subsequently has to suffer alarmingly for attempting to define the thing that should never be allowed to have a name.

A Hidden Planet Production

In association with

WIND on the WIRE